HER PAINED BLUE SILENCE

A.J. DOWNEY

BOOK FIVE

COPYRIGHT

ISBN: 978-1-950222-14-8

Editing by Barbara J. Bailey

Book design by Maggie Kern

Cover art and Indigo Knights logo by Dar Albert at Wicked Smart Designs

Photo by FuriousFotog

Model Dylan Horsch

Dedication

A big thank you to all my readers. For making the Indigo Knights as successful as the SHMC. I'm happy to keep writing as long as you're reading.

PROLOGUE

$\mathcal{E}$verleigh...

He was crazy, I didn't know what he was talking about. I *couldn't* talk. At least, not really. I mean, I only talked to him, when it was quiet, when we were alone, when I was calm and felt safe… and since he had started using, I hadn't felt safe in a very long time.

"You fucked up, Silence," he said, leaning against his bike, lighting his blunt. He looked at me over the glowing red coal and sucked the smoke deep into his lungs, holding it and saying, his voice strained with the effort, "You fucked up big-time."

I felt my eyes go wide, pleading silently my innocence, but it didn't matter; King believed wholeheartedly that I'd done something and I was filled with dread over what he might do.

"Boys," he intoned soullessly, and I was seized by either arm. I cried out wordlessly, and looked frantically from Joker to Rebel as they dragged me, unresisting at first, towards the trees. It took a second for my fight reflex to kick in, but it wasn't any use anyway as I writhed and twisted between them trying to get free. Even if I did, it wouldn't do any good. There were six of them and only one of me, and I don't think I would have been able to outrun them, no matter how hard I tried.

They forced me to my knees and slipped a loop of cord over each of my wrists and lashed me between two trees that were close together. I struggled against the bonds, the slipknots catching and tightening, the cords strangling my wrists and cutting off my circulation. I stopped, panting, and begged King with my eyes to please, *please* not do this.

"Silence, Silence, Silence," he chanted, using the road name he'd given me. He sighed and dropped the last of the blunt to the forest floor, grinding it out carefully under his heavy boot. "You didn't think I'd figure out it was you?" he asked.

I wept. I hadn't done anything! I didn't know what he was talking about! I couldn't speak. It was not that I didn't want to, I *couldn't*. What did he want from me?

"Never trust a bitch," King said. "Thought you were perfect. Pretty, hot, can't speak? Gotta love that. Almost perfect for a guy like me, but you lied to me, didn't you?"

I shook my head back and forth. He shook his, too, and called out, "Whiskey, you wanna patch in?"

The prospect perked up and looked over. "You know I do, King."

"Prove it. Show Si here what happens to traitors to the Knights of Crescentia."

Terrified, I struggled against my bonds anew as King dug into one of his saddlebags. He came up with a hammer and two long, wicked-looking nails.

He held them out to Whiskey, who marginally relaxed. I wasn't relaxed. I wasn't relaxed at all. I prayed, I wept, and I hoped against hope that any second, King would start laughing. That he would say 'Just kidding,' but I knew that look in his eyes, the cruelty in them. I shuddered and sweat dripped down my back between my shoulder blades.

Whiskey spit on the ground and plucked the hammer and nails from King's hands. When Whiskey had first shown up, I had thought he was handsome, cleaner than the rest of the guys, even King. Now I was forced to face him as he stalked with assurance in my direction, the hammer in one hand, nails in the other, his tread dull against the earth, each hollow thump of his footsteps ominous. My heart raced, the blood rushing in my ears, as I pleaded with my eyes and wept, my tears slicking hot down my face tightening my skin.

I clenched my fists and keened wordlessly from behind my gritted teeth when all I wanted were the words, *Don't! Please stop! I didn't do whatever it is you think I did!* I would give anything to speak them, but that's not how it worked. I couldn't. Just trying left me feeling like I was choking on my own tongue.

Whiskey stuck the nails in his back pockets and dropped to his knees by my left hand. I hyperventilated as he forced my fingers to uncurl and flattened the back of my hand against the rough bark. I shook my head back and forth, back and forth, begging with my gaze for him not to do this, and I swear I saw it reflected back in his eyes, the sorrow that he had to.

I swallowed hard and tried to prepare myself, but there was no preparing for it.

The pain was sharp and immediate, and I screamed, long, loud, and wordless. Each strike of the hammer reverberated through my palm and out through my fingers. I felt sick, nausea sweeping over and through me, and it was only made worse when I looked at my mangled hand, bleeding, the nail through the palm and into the tree.

I looked up at him, agonized, the expression on my face hopefully telegraphing *Why?*

He looked grim, his mouth set in a hard line behind his beard, his gaze hooded as he unfurled my other hand against the opposite tree.

I shook my head weakly and sobbed, damning my inability to speak in front of people. The overwhelming fear and anxiety all but paralyzed my vocal cords, my tongue failed to cooperate. I couldn't speak, but I was aware that, even if I could, it wouldn't matter.

I screamed again as the second nail bit into my flesh and Whiskey pounded it home. I choked on my own sobs. I dry-heaved, but, mercifully, didn't throw up, as the guys stood around laughing and chatting like they would if we were simply out here for them to shoot, which was the impression I'd been under when we'd left that morning.

I raised my head and looked at King, who stalked up to me and grabbed me by the back of the hair. He jerked my head all the way back and stared down at me coldly, indifferent to my suffering.

"Think I'm gonna put that mouth of yours to good use one last time. For old time's sake, what do you say?" he asked, a cruel smile flickering to life at the corners of his mouth as he worked at his belt.

"Might not want to do that, King," Whiskey called out. The rest of the guys looked a mix of uncomfortable and eager. I cast a grateful look at Whiskey for this small mercy but my hopes in a softer side in him were dashed when he continued, "You plan on leavin' her here to die, you don't want to leave any DNA behind."

"Good point," King replied. "Any of you fuckers got a condom?"

I guess I was finally fortunate to some degree. Heads shook and there were negative sounding grunts and 'No's sweeping through the men standing around watching our little tableau.

"Guess I'm out of luck, then," he said, tucking himself away. He let go of my head and I sagged with relief.

"You got a few hours to think about what you done, before either the animals come and get you or the cold does overnight. Personally," he sniffed, "I hope it's the latter."

I looked up and a new terror seized me.

"See you around, Silence. Probably in Hell," King declared, throwing his leg over his bike. He turned back to Whiskey and said, "Welcome to the Knights of Crescentia, Whiskey." He looked past Whiskey and said, "Rebel, give him his colors."

They left me there after that. They left me there alone, and terrified.

I didn't want to die.

1

*N*arcos...

I had a knot in my gut the whole ride back to what the Knights of Crescentia called 'The Lair'. It was their clubhouse, but that wasn't saying much. They didn't keep anything there. There were no quarters for sleeping and King would have your ass beat if he caught you crashing there. It wasn't how King rolled. He was careful, cunning, almost always one step ahead of the law – which was why I was here.

It'd taken me a year and some change to get this far with them, and I felt fuckin' sick at what'd it had taken to earn my colors, at the way Silence, King's ol' lady, had looked up at me, pleading with those startling green eyes of hers under the tangled mop of her long auburn hair. I felt a guilt like no other, had no idea how or why King thought it'd been her that'd narced out the last exchange when it'd been all me.

I needed to get a hold of Driller and I needed to find out what the actual fuck. That bust should have never gone down when it did. If they'd only fuckin' waited...

I couldn't think about it right now. I had to take my fuckin' orders even

7

with the fresh set of colors on my back, and get that shit handled, so I could get out there and prevent Silence's dyin'.

I was sure I was the last man she wanted to see, but I had no way of telling anyone where she was. It was one of those 'I would know the route if I took it, if I could see it' places, but those woods were a ways out along old forestry roads, and tough navigating even by bike, which was the only way I could retrieve her. If I took a truck, I'd be stopped by the barriers across the old road; bikes could go around them.

It was an ideal location to pop off rounds with their cache of illegal firearms, mostly fully-automatic shit, some of it, military-grade. The weapons would be just a bonus. I was after their drug trade. Of course, murder trumps all, and I was sure there were some dead bodies with the Knights of Crescentia's logo stamped on them.

I was also sure that King had just given me a shortcut getting to them.

I don't know a woman alive that wouldn't be willing to speak out against an old boyfriend who'd just had her nailed to a tree. Even a woman who didn't speak.

Of course, on the flip side, I didn't know a woman alive who would speak to the man who'd done the actual nailing, but here was hoping that saving her life might buy me some currency to bargain with in that exchange.

There were a lot of 'if's and a whole lot of hope riding on some useless prayers here, but sometimes all you could do was live on a prayer. I was just prayin' she would still be alive when I got to her.

I did what King wanted. I 'got rid' of her shit, wiping out any evidence of her ever being in his small house in the poorer section at the edge of the city. I took it to a safe place, a storage unit in the heart of the city, and actually rode past Poe at one point. He didn't even acknowledge me, which is as it should be. Never fuckin' knew who was watching. On the street, there were eyes and ears everywhere.

When I was sure I was good and there was nothing else that King wanted, I had to wait for nightfall.

My heart was all jammed up with apprehension, the whole ride back out to where we'd been that morning. I carefully guided the bike around the barrier and worked my way up the track of old, cracked blacktop, blanketed in dirt and pine needles mixed with decaying leaf litter.

I was half-afraid I would come up on one of the other Knights, the sovereign motherfuckers, King having put the idea into their heads that rape was on the menu. Silence was a fine-looking piece of ass according to every one of the men in the Knights of Crescentia, and they weren't lying.

She was a slight and fine-boned bohemian hippy-chick, younger than most of us, but ageless at the same time. I knew she had to be in her twenties, but she sometimes looked like a barely-legal teen, depending on the day and how much makeup she had on, which really depended on King's mood, from what I gathered.

My headlight swept the trees she was between and my heart damn near seized in my chest. She was still there, but it didn't look good. Her head was bowed, her long hair hiding her face. I turned off the bike and swung a leg over, grabbing the nail-puller I'd brought out of the inside pocket of my jacket.

Just when I thought I was too late, she dragged her head up weakly, the beam of my headlamp, weaker with the bike shut off, illuminating her pale face, which was rendered paler, my guess, from pain and loss of blood. Truth be told, I was more concerned about the latter than anything; the tree bark below her hands was glittering dark and wet.

"This is gonna hurt, hang in there for me," I told her, focused on getting her free. I braced the nail-puller against her palm, making sure that the head of the nail was secure in the notch, and torqued it free. She screamed and immediately tried to drag her hand to her chest; the paracord they'd bound her with stopped her.

"Wait!" I hissed and flicked open my knife. "Don't take it off your wrist," I told her and cut the line.

"Hang on," I said over the keening sobs escaping her throat, and I pulled a bandana from my pocket and wrapped it around her hand, tying it securely in on itself. She let me, but it was a little bit of a battle.

I got her other hand free and bandaged, and she knelt, clutching her ruined hands to her chest, bent forward until her forehead nearly touched the earth.

Her weeping was heartrending, but I didn't have time for that now. I had to get her to Trinity Gen, where she would be safe. I had to get in touch with Driller and get her into his custody. Then, I had to pray I hadn't somehow blown my cover during all of this mess, which I just had a gut feeling…

"Come on, Si, you've gotta ride with me. I gotta get you to the hospital." She cringed back from me and I understood it, even though it killed me.

"I'm the only ride you're gonna get out of here. Come on," I said, and it came out harsh with my frustration.

She flinched, but struggled to her feet, and I reached out to steady her. She sucked in a sharp breath and stumbled back, but I caught her elbow and kept her from going over.

"Easy," I said and tried to make it come out soothing, but I'm afraid I'm kind of shit at things like that.

I helped her over to the bike and got on. She got on with me and sucked in a breath when she saw my back. I wasn't wearing Knights of Crescentia colors. For this, I wore my true colors and I had headed out of the city on my bike, my *real* bike, with my face covered by one of the bandanas now wrapped around her bleeding hands.

"Hang onto me as best you can," I ordered and she did, miserably.

It was a rough ride to Trinity Gen's emergency room entrance, rougher on her by far than it was on me. I pulled up just shy of the bright lights and she got off. I looked her in her pale face, into those startling green eyes, the irises edged in an almost bronze or gold, and said, "Go on inside, get yourself taken care of. Some people will come to see you."

She frowned slightly and I nodded toward the sliding glass doors.

"Go on now," I said, my voice rough with emotion. The guilt over what I'd done to her rode me, likely a demon I would carry on my back for a while.

She turned and went, her feet shuffling across the too-white cement, patters and droplets of blood falling like tears in her wake. The doors whooshed open and she went through without so much as a backwards glance, and I pulled out my phone.

He picked up on the second ring.

"Yeah, Driller," I said before he could say anything. "Get your ass down to Trinity Gen ER, mute girl by the nickname of Silence. I don't know her by anything else. She's got puncture wounds to her hands. Bad ones. All the way through. You need to get her into protective custody."

"Slow the fuck down, Narcos, who is she?"

"She was Kingston Prentiss' ol' lady, until he had me nail her to a tree this morning."

Real silence on the other end of the line and finally, "Shit."

Yeah.

Shit.

2

*E*verleigh...

My hands hurt.

They were wrapped in swaths of clean white bandages and looked like mummy hands. I lay on my side in the hospital bed with them carefully cradled to my chest, where they ached sharply, but whatever they had going in the IV taped to my inner arm was working. The pain was much less. They had me on fluids, too, the doctor declaring I was dehydrated some. Not surprising, with how much I'd cried.

I was all out of tears now. If anything, I was uncomfortably numb. The shock had worn off, but the sorrow and pain was just beginning. I closed my eyes.

I jumped when, a short time later, the curtain was whisked aside on its track, revealing a man in black leather. I scrambled into a sitting position and back up against the head of the bed, but he pulled his hands from his pockets and held them out.

"Easy! Take it easy. I'm one of the good guys," he said, and I froze. I eyed him warily and he finally asked, "Are you Silence?"

I nodded cautiously, after a few more moments of sizing him up.

"I'm Detective Sam Stahl, with the Indigo City Police Department." He sighed, his eyes sweeping over me, a heavy weight seemingly settling on his shoulders.

"Mind if I sit down?" he asked, gently.

I weighed the pros and cons, and finally shook my head. *King was going to kill me for even remotely entertaining the cops...* But then again, hadn't he already? At least, as far as he knew, he had.

I waited for the cop to settle into the chair beside my bed, and then for him to say something. I mean, it wasn't exactly like I was a talker.

"I understand you're, uh, mute?" he asked.

I bit my lips together nervously and shook my head yes, anxiety jangling, more than I actually willingly nodded.

"Okay, I'll, uh, try to keep this to 'yes' and 'no'."

I stared at him, frozen in place, and waited him out.

"Do you know who did this to you?" he asked.

The hospital had been calling me 'Jane Doe in bed three' since they'd put me here. I had made a strangled noise when I tried to give them my real name, and immediately flustered and sealed my lips, embarrassed. The fact that he knew my nickname meant that he also knew who I was and that I knew who had done this to me. I nodded.

"Was it Kingston Prentiss?"

I stared at him and wouldn't nod or shake my head. I just stared at him, willing him to understand that I couldn't speak in any way about what had happened to me...

"Silence," he said gently, scooting closer, and I tensed. He stopped and let out a frustrated sigh. "Silence, he'll never touch you again. We won't let him."

I wanted to believe him, but –

"Detective?" The doctor stood at the door.

The cop stood up and gave me his back, and I gasped. He turned back to me at the sound and frowned slightly.

"You okay?" he asked.

I nodded without thinking, and he turned back to the doctor, where they conferred in hushed tones.

I let my eyes travel over the colors on the back of his cut. The light gray shield, the knight chess piece picked out on it in indigo thread. It was the same as Whiskey's when he'd brought me here hours and hours ago.

I knew it was a cop's club. I knew it meant Whiskey was a cop, and I knew how this man must have learned my nickname.

They were talking about me, about my name, adding it to my chart: 'Silence,' given name unknown, except it wasn't unknown, it was Tate, Everleigh Tate. As much as I wanted to tell them, I couldn't. I was tongue-tied and twisted, and finally, I decided that, ultimately, it didn't really matter. 'Silence' was good enough.

I settled down again and let the detective argue with the doctor, listening to them with keen interest. As far as the doctor was concerned, I was free to go. The detective, however, was practically begging the doctor to run more tests, to do anything he had to do to keep me at least one night, so he could get things set up with the department to take me into protective custody.

I closed my eyes and listened intently, as finally the detective managed to win his way, though I wasn't keen on staying here – or going with him when they let me go.

I was at a disadvantage when it came to my own agency with my inability to effectively communicate. With my inability to speak in any sort of social situation, I could conceivably communicate in other ways such as writing or even, potentially, with sign language if I had ever learned it, but not with my hands in such a state. I had holes clean through them about the third of a size of a dime.

They'd irrigated them and contemplated surgery on the one to repair whatever vein had been compromised to cause it to bleed so much, but then had dismissed it when the bleeding had begun to stop on its own. I'd been started on antibiotics and pain medicine, but they'd left the holes open to heal and close from the inside out.

I wanted to know why, had no way to ask, but had been lucky enough that the doctor seeing to my wounds had been educating some students of some sort – something about this being a teaching hospital. One of them had said it was because if anything had been left in the wounds, that stitching them closed could trap any potential infection and it could make things worse.

So, they'd bandaged me up, had given me a shot in my arm for tetanus, and had started me on some powerful antibiotics and IV fluids to ward off any infection and to help me recover from my slight dehydration.

I contemplated what would happen to me, and the answer was, I didn't know. I despaired, feeling lost and lonely, cut off from the world, trapped. My anxiety was spiraling, but I lay quietly. I couldn't fix any of it. I couldn't stop whatever was coming. I needed to be patient, to wait, to see what it was I was dealing with before I could deal with anything at all.

For now, all I could do was lay still, my heart and mind racing, until the next dose of pain medicine took me far away from all of it by finally plunging me into an exhausted sleep.

3

*N*arcos…

I shouldn't be here. I couldn't help myself, though. The guilt was driving me up a wall. I knew I could trust Driller when he said she was all right, but it was like I couldn't let myself believe it, not until I saw her myself. I wouldn't know where she was taken after this, so it was my last chance to see her before they took her to a safe, undisclosed location. I might not see her again for a couple of years, and that would be only if we managed to get enough to take King and the rest of his merry band of assholes to trial.

Nailing them for drug trafficking and distribution was my job, but that was just the tip of their dirty iceberg. Drugs, guns, murder and mayhem… these guys did it all. They were a bunch of sovereign militia types, the worst of the worst. Sovereigns didn't recognize the laws of today or the authority of the police and government as it stood now. It could be a pain in the ass for modern law enforcement.

None of that mattered right now, though, not with her lying there, looking fragile and wan in the hospital bed, her hands wrapped in thick white bandages, resting on top of the thin tan hospital blanket in her lap.

Pasquale grumbled behind me and I glanced back at him.

"I have *rounds*, you know. My own patients to see."

"Yeah, yeah, sorry. I'm good. I'll, uh, catch you later."

He gave me a look like he wasn't impressed and said, "Motherfucker, if you wake that sleeping beauty up and I get in trouble, I would like to kill you."

I shook my head and made a motion with my hand indicating he should quiet down himself and pump the brakes.

"I'm not going to wake her up, but you might!" I hissed.

He gave me another unimpressed look and rolled his eyes. He shifted on his feet and said, "Ten minutes and you had better be gone, before someone finds you here!"

"Copy that, Princess," I muttered.

He arched one of his overdone brows and turned like a model on the runway, fierce as shit, and went out the door of her room, out into the hallway, and disappeared. I turned back and her eyes were open, regarding me dully. I sank into the chair beside her bed and pressed my lips together, getting choked up.

"I am so sorry," I whispered.

Her expression gave me no quarter, and I got it. I did. *I* wouldn't forgive me, either.

"I couldn't blow my cover, and I know that's no excuse, I just… I just feel so awful, you don't even know."

I braced my elbows on my knees and pressed my fingertips into my forehead at the top of the bridge of my nose. I was perilously close to breaking over this, the desolate feeling of devastation rolling through me like angry storm clouds boiling across the sky. I brought my hands down and clasped them together, and her vivid green eyes searched my face, emotionless. Her expression was as stoic as I'd ever seen it; I was used to her wearing a semi-charmed Mona Lisa smile just about always.

She raised her hands feebly off her lap and set them back down carefully and I stared at them for a while. At the spot of rusty crimson on the back of one of the snowy-white wraps, my heart sank. My eyes flicked back to hers and I could swear I was drowning in the depth of her emotion, but I could only dream of interpreting it without help.

It switched from the nameless feeling she'd attempted to telegraph to sorrow and she sighed, her eyes closing. She opened them again, meeting my eyes, then very deliberately turned her head away from me to stare out the window, across the alley, to the empty brick façade across from it. When I stood, she flinched and I swallowed my guilt down hard.

"I'll make it up to you. I don't know how, but I will," I vowed.

She turned onto her side, carefully hunching forward and cradling her ruined hands against her chest.

"I'll put them away," I said. "You'll be safe."

She looked over her shoulder at me and frowned and the look said all it needed to. *I'll never be safe.*

"I'll fix it," I swore. "I promise."

She scoffed and turned her back on me again, only this time, I felt thoroughly dismissed. That was all right; that was okay. I had work to do.

I slipped out of her room and strode up the hallway, punching the down button for the elevator savagely with my fingertips, staring at the dark crescents of her dried blood still trapped under my fingernails. I closed my fist, and let those nails bite into my palm. Nausea at my actions rolled through me like a rogue wave, sucking me under and tumbling me dizzily like I'd been caught in a riptide.

It'd been hard not to notice Silence. She was a beautiful girl, in her mid- to late-twenties, with long auburn hair down past her butt and vivid green eyes, the likes to put that National Geographic photo to shame. She had creamy white skin and cute little freckles, and a body that was to die for under those hippy-chick skirts and peasant blouses she liked to wear. I always wondered where the hell King had picked her up, but he was a closed-mouthed bastard on the subject, and her? Well, she didn't speak at all.

King, the misogynistic chauvinist bastard that he was, thought that was great. "A gash that can't go spillin' secrets, can you believe my luck?" he'd always say, and I'd laugh right along with the lot of them like it was funny. The look on Silence's face said otherwise, deep hurt had been in her eyes, and for whatever reason, you could just tell that she had a real love for King despite all his bullshit.

He'd hurt her real bad with his betrayal, and I felt double the guilt for it. She hadn't sold him out at all. *I* had, but I'd never dreamed that it'd fall on her, or that I would do what I'd done to save my own skin. The poor woman.

Fuck! This elevator was taking forever. I bowed my head and heaved a heavy sigh. All I wanted to do was get on my bike and go for a long ride, by myself. No one to bother me. I knew it wasn't going to happen, but it's what I wanted with just about every fuckin' fiber of my being.

My cell buzzed in my pocket and I fished it out as the elevator pinged and the doors opened. I stepped on board and frowned at the screen. It was Joker. I let it go to voicemail. I didn't want the sounds of the hospital getting picked up and diming me out. I went back to my bike in the garage and as soon as I got back up onto the street, my phone started blowing up with notifications. I went a few blocks and pulled over and fished it out again.

Joker: Answer your fuckin' phone man.

Wraith: Where the fuck are you? Joker's trying to get you.

King: Bring your ass in. We have something to discuss.

Shit.

I pulled out my other phone and dialed up Driller.

"Yeah, man, what's up?" he answered.

"Dunno, but the Crescentia boys are hot to fuckin' trot and want my ass back like A.S.A.P."

"Probably to celebrate you patching in, yeah?"

Shit. I'd forgotten all about that, with everything else.

"Shit. Yeah. Didn't even think about that."

"Go party, make sure you got the right gear on."

I winced.

"Pasquale?" I asked.

"Drag Queen dimed your ass out, for sure, Brother. What the fuck are you even thinking, going to the hospital like that?"

"I dunno, man," I said honestly and sighed.

"Get your head back in the fuckin' game or you're gonna get yourself killed," he said, and he wasn't playin'. I knew he was right, but I don't think he knew how deeply this whole thing had affected me. Hell, *I* couldn't believe how shook I was over her.

"I'm good," I said, and I at least *sounded* convincing.

"You fuckin' better be, asshole."

"I said I was, now, I am," I said, the first thread of anger worming its way into my voice.

"Good. Report as soon as you can."

"Don't I always?"

"That you do," he said quietly.

I ended the call. I went back to my real apartment, got the mask off my face, traded my true colors for the farce that was the Knights of Crescentia's logo, and with a heavy sigh, went down to the garage to swap bikes and take the other exit out of the garage.

That was one of the reasons I'd chosen this building; there were three garage exits onto three different streets surrounding it.

When you were me, and into the shit I was into, you always needed to leave yourself multiple escape routes.

It wasn't paranoia when they really were out to get you.

At least, they would be, if they ever figured out I was a cop. I'd cut it real close tonight; there was honestly no tellin' if I'd given any of the boys a reason to suspect me as being anything other than one of them…

I guessed I was going to find out.

4

*E*verleigh…

The hotel I was kept in was so boring. It was me and Detective Stahl, for the most part. A male nurse, Pasquale, came daily to check on my hands and change the bandages. He was kind to me, and a bit of a fashionista who got me. He'd snuck me down into the basement of the hospital to go through big, giant laundry bins of clothing to find some things that suited me.

The clothing I'd arrived in were a mess of blood that would never come out of the white cotton, at least, not completely. Of course, I never saw those clothes again, anyway. Detective Stahl had taken them.

He sat at the little table in the hotel room on his phone and I eyed him from where I sat on the bed. He didn't look like a 'Detective Stahl' to me. He didn't even look like a 'Sam'. He looked like a 'Driller', the name on his cut. But, I didn't want to let myself get too familiar with him. He *was* a cop, after all. Not that I'd ever had anything against the cops. They'd never bothered me and I'd never bothered them.

The Knights of Crescentia, on the other hand? They were into so much illegal shit, it wasn't any wonder why they had a natural distaste for the cops.

In the beginning, my best friend Mariah and I had both been dying to get out of our small town in Indiana. Neither of us cared how, and when the Steel Wraiths rolled through town and stopped at her bar, going with them seemed like a good idea to her, and where she went, I went. Even though I knew it was, in all probability, a bad idea, anything was better than that town.

Sledge had been not my type – physically, at least. He *had* been, when it came to almost everything else: philosophy, reading, his views on what the world was and what it could be… There was only one problem. Monogamy wasn't exactly his thing, and it had hurt. So too had his cruel streak. Not physically, he'd never hit me, but he was mean when he was drunk and he was drunk nearly all the time. He didn't hesitate to make fun of my mutism to get a laugh out of the rest of the guys, and I hated that.

Mariah had stood up for me, and we'd been okay, but then… Then we'd met the Knights of Crescentia and King had swept me off my feet. She'd begged me to stay with her, to go home, but there was no home for me. I had no roots in that town, and I'd ridden away into the sunset and a new life and had relished the adventure of it – right up until the dream had become a nightmare.

King's drug use had begun to wear, to become more habit, more need than recreational. He'd been becoming increasingly paranoid, until the night he'd had me crucified to a tree. It broke my heart that he would think I would betray him. I would never betray him – any of them – but now that they had betrayed me, all bets were off. I would figure out how to testify, by god, and the secrets I could tell – I would ruin them *all* for this.

They said hell hath no fury like a woman scorned, and I think nailing a woman to a pair of trees *definitely* falls under the category of 'scorned'.

I stared at the white bandages wrapped around my hands. The right one had gotten infected, and I was taking strong antibiotics. It was painful irrigating the wound, so Pasquale was a godsend. He made sure to give me a painkiller when he arrived, and then waited, talking at me, for it to take effect, before we did the deed. It didn't help much, but it was better than nothing, and things were getting better… except for the extreme, unending boredom.

There was nothing on the hotel's TV, and if I had to watch another rerun of '*My 600 lb Life*,' I was going to scream long and loud and wordless into the void that was police custody.

"What're you thinking about so hard over there?" Driller – I mean, Detective Stahl – asked me. He was looking over at me, and I carefully picked at a stray thread on the thin hotel comforter.

I pointed at the TV and gave it the finger.

He choked on a laugh and said, "Jesus, tell me how you *really* feel."

I frowned at him and he smiled.

"Wish you would have said something earlier."

I glared at him.

"You're a smart cookie, you would have figured it out."

I scowled at him again and he just laughed, then he shook his head.

"I'd give you my tablet to watch Netflix, but until you're deposed and statements are on record, I'm not allowed."

I cocked my head.

"Why?"

I nodded.

"Because we don't want you contacting any of your friends who may be attached to the club."

My shoulders dropped, and I shook my head.

"Not sure what that means, darlin'. It could mean so many things."

I nodded. It wasn't like I could get any more detailed.

"You up to gripping a pen yet?"

I shook my head. Bending my hands stretched things, which hurt. A lot. So I didn't do it if I could avoid it. I sighed heavily, and he sighed too.

"Not sure how they're going to do that, either," he said, but that wasn't what I'd been thinking. Although, he had a point. I didn't know how they were going to do it. King had made a good choice in charming a mute into being his pussy. Of course, when the charm wore off, it was fear that'd gotten me to stay. Fear, and some semblance of love. As badly as he treated me, up until the night he'd ordered my crucifixion he'd *still* treated me better than I'd been treated back home.

"You've had a rough go of it, haven't you, Ms. Tate?" he asked softly and I startled.

"Surprised we figured out your last name?"

I nodded.

"Well, that was all Narcos."

I frowned and shook my head slightly.

"Whiskey."

My eyebrows shot up. His road name with the cop club was 'Narcos'? Seriously? What a crap road name.

"You prefer Everleigh or Silence?" he asked.

I shrugged one shoulder halfheartedly. I didn't suppose it really mattered.

"Was it always Silence?" he asked.

I shook my head.

"What was it before?"

I thought about it, and carefully drew my index finger back-and-forth across the top of my thumb.

He frowned and asked, "Violin?"

I rolled my eyes and shook my head, but had to smile. I tried again and willed him to get the answer, my mind screaming *Cricket! Come on! You can do it.*

He finally shook his head, laughing.

"Sorry, I suck at Charades."

I shrugged and heaved a frustrated sigh.

We didn't talk anymore, but I'd catch him looking at me like he wanted to say something. No, more like he wanted to *ask* something. The next time he looked my way, I met his eyes and cocked my head to the side.

He kind of laughed and said, "Boy, nothing gets by you, does it?"

I shook my head.

He raked his bottom lip between his teeth, and said, "He's real broken up about it," jerking his chin in the direction of my hands.

It wasn't what I was expecting. Like, at all. I let mouth drop open slightly to express my surprise.

"He went back and got you as fast as he could without drawing suspicion, which was hard as hell. I've never seen Narcos come that close to blowing his cover over anything before, but something about this… He could have called me, could have called it in, but he didn't." He looked me over, his eyes wandering over my face slowly, scrutinizing me, before he asked, "What makes *you* so special?"

I blinked at his question, taken aback, and shrugged. I had no idea; none, whatsoever. In my estimation, I was the furthest thing from 'special' as anyone could get, a neurotic mess on a good day – I couldn't tell this man why Whiskey had done what he'd done, but I could tell him, I had known there had been something about him. I should have suspected that what that 'something' was, was that he was a cop, but he was good at keeping secrets. I guess you had to be, in order to be undercover narcotics.

I settled back against the headboard with a sigh and just tried to stop thinking for a while. That was easier said than done when I had so much to think about and literally nothing to distract me from it.

5

*N*arcos…

Almost a full week had gone by and things were moving fast in the criminal underworld. At least, they were for me. It was a different world once you were patched-in to the Knights of Crescentia, and I had front row tickets to the main event. I was learning all sorts of shit, having given none of these motherfuckers a reason to question me or doubt me. It was a fine line to walk and one that was about to be blown all to hell when King called out, "Joker! Whiskey! Step into my office, boys."

I backed away from the bar and the random bitch I was talking to and took a swig of my beer. I looked over at Joker, who gave me a chin lift from by the jukebox. We moved down toward one of the last booths along the wall opposite the bar, and slid in across from King.

"What's up, oh fearless leader?" Joker asked, licking along the edge of a rolling paper. He didn't do cigarettes, but dude was way too into his fuckin' weed. They smoked like fuckin' chimneys in this bar; just one of the many laws these motherfuckers broke, but least among them.

The ceiling was yellowed with the tar from their cigarettes. I waved Joker off when he offered up the blunt to me first.

"Suit yourself, man." He stuck it between his lips and scooped up King's lighter off the table, putting flame to tip then clicking the Zippo closed.

"You done yet?" King demanded, and Joker grinned, holding in his lungful of the overpowering, earthy smoke. I didn't say anything, just took a drink of my beer and waited King out.

"You oughtta take a page outta Whiskey's playbook, here," King said decisively. He sighed heavy and said, "I got some disconcerting news."

I perked up a bit on the inside but played it close to the vest on the outside, keeping my expression neutral, waiting for King to spill it.

"That don't sound good," Joker said and finally exhaled. He laughed, and I hated this guy's laugh. He sounded like a hyena that had yet to finish fuckin' puberty.

King pressed his fingertips into his eye sockets and rubbed the bridge of his nose. I may not have liked the son of a bitch, but on this, I could sympathize with him. Joker was a fuckin' headache.

"Shut up and let the man talk," I said with a scowl, and Joker opened his mouth to snap something off at me but King interrupted him with, "Thank you." I gave a nod and smirked at Joker, who glowered at me.

"Word from inside the pigpen is my bitch ain't dead and is willin' to turn state's evidence. I need you two to go finish the job."

I felt my blood run cold. Word from *inside* the ICPD? What the fuck?

"Reliable intel?" I asked and King's eyes snapped to mine, his brow drawing down into a scowl.

"As reliable as it fuckin' gets." He slid a folded piece of paper in our direction. "Now, you wanna keep that patch, you go finish what you started."

I drew the paper toward me and frowned at it, squinting in the dimly-lit bar's interior to read it. It was where we housed witnesses, all right. The same hotel we'd kept Chrissy at. Their intel *was* good. Shit.

"On it," I declared.

"Should only be one guy with her. Cutbacks, don't you know?" King asked, sucking in air between his teeth. He tapped the blunt he'd taken from Joker against the heavy glass ashtray overflowing with butts. I stopped my slide out of the booth and gave a nod.

"We'll get it done," Joker said.

"Kill her, no fucking around."

"Awww…" Joker bounced on his feet and pouted.

"I mean it. She's still my fuckin' property regardless of if she's sold me out. That pussy is, and always will be, mine. Double-tap her and be done with it."

"You got it," I said.

My adrenaline was coursing hardcore. I had a wire on. I'd caught everything this motherfucker had said, but that wasn't why. It was because I didn't know how to warn Driller without tipping these assholes off and getting myself dead. That, and I was still reeling on the inside from King's bombshell.

They had intel on the inside of the force, but not enough intel to know I was a cop. Maybe it wasn't the force, then. Maybe it was the prosecutor's office? My mind was racing the whole way out to our bikes, Joker chattering away a mile a minute as he was apt to do, fuckin' meth-head.

"What's the matter with you?" he demanded, and I had to think fast.

I scowled and said, "You heard him, right? I wanna keep these colors, bitch needs to die."

I cut off any further conversation with him by starting up my bike, revving the engine to drown out his noise. I had no idea how I was going to fucking do this. We rode through night-blackened city streets, the pavement dry, but the air slick with heat and humidity. The summer was bearing down on Indigo City with a vengeance and I felt bad for the rest of my true brothers in blue. The temperature went up, and so did tempers, and along with them, the crime rate and incidences of domestics.

What I wouldn't honestly give to be walking a fucking beat right now.

I rode through a yellow that Joker had slowed for and took my fuckin' life into my hands to shoot off a text one-handed, then pulled off and waited for Joker's ass to catch up. We were blocks from the hotel and I was hoping that I'd given enough warning, that Driller was there and on duty, and that he could, at least, get Silence out of the line of fire. It was mandatory that Driller, or whoever it was who was with her, was wearing a vest, so at least there was that.

We got to the hotel, took the garage elevators up to the lobby, and took advantage of a blind spot for the front desk to skate into the stairwell. I made some mental notes to pass on to the higher-ups. This hotel was compromised six ways to Sunday and weren't no good for housing witnesses no more.

We took the stairwell up one floor and sauntered to the elevator like we belonged here. The elevator took no time at all whisking us to Silence's floor and I hoped I'd been able to tip off whoever was on the other side of that door that we were coming in time.

Too soon we were standing outside the room number listed on the piece of paper King had passed us and Joker was grinning at me like a fool. He nudged me with his elbow and said, "If the bitch is dead, ain't no one to tell King what we did."

I grimaced on the inside and scowled on the outside, playing the ever-loyal foot-soldier to the bitter end.

"King told us to kill her and be fuckin' done with it," I whispered harshly. "So that's what we're gonna do. You can get your dick wet back at the club."

Joker, a weasel-looking motherfucker, with eyes too close together and a nose for days, rolled his deep brown eyes at me so hard I was pretty sure he saw the back of his own skull.

"You're a fuckin' downer, Whiskey."

"I'm fuckin' loyal, you should fuckin' try it."

That earned me a glare and amped him up. He kicked the door to the hotel room, once, twice, until it gave way with the third well-placed kick. I had my gun out, and he went through the door, right into Driller's tazer, which he held with one hand, and his firearm, which he aimed with the other.

Joker jerked, went ramrod straight and flopped onto his back, the two electrodes protruding from the front of his Ozzy Osbourne tee shirt, adding a couple more holes to the already pretty threadbare material.

I shoved my gun into the back of my pants and rolled Joker onto his stomach. Driller put up his gun and lifted his handcuffs from the back of his belt and tossed them to me, smooth and efficient, like we were trained. I slapped the cuffs on Joker, who was moaning and groaning, trying to recover from having his synapses fried.

"You good?" I asked Driller.

"Yeah."

"Where is she?" I asked.

"Bathtub, in case bullets started to fly."

"You get my text?"

"Yeah, thanks for that."

"Yeah. Backup coming?"

"On their way, but your cover is fuckin' blown."

"Yeah, but it came with getting these sons of bitches dead-to-rights on attempted murder, and conspiracy to commit murder."

"You got it on tape?"

"Every bit of it."

"You're a fuckin' cop?" Joker screamed, his voice muffled by having his face mashed into the carpet.

"Surprise, motherfucker." I pushed off of him and went to the bathroom.

"City isn't safe," Driller called.

"I know."

"You thinkin' what I'm thinkin'?" he asked.

"Yeah, but not in front of the kids. Nothing out loud."

He grunted and nodded, and I went through the bathroom door.

6

_____

$\mathcal{E}$verleigh…

"Shit!" Detective Stahl exclaimed.

I jumped and looked over from the television to see him leap to his feet. He was coming towards me, all crackling energy, urgency radiating through him like lighting through a thunderhead. I flinched when he grabbed me by the arms and drew me to my feet.

"Gotta hustle, they're coming for you."

Fear lanced through me and I looked at him, stricken.

"Not now, baby doll. Just do what I say and everything's gonna be fine. In the bathroom and lay down in the tub."

I shook my head but he towed me through the open bathroom door and shut it behind me, my skirts swishing around my bare legs that I'd only just gotten to shave for the first time that day, my hands finally relenting enough in their deep and abiding aching, the wounds mostly sealed.

I swallowed hard and did as I was told; I got into the still-damp bathtub and lay down, my heart pounding, the blood swishing in my ears. My head throbbed in time with my heartbeat, my face was hot and tingling with fear and the tears threatened to spill from my eyes.

It was quiet, so terribly quiet, then I heard Detective Stahl's urgent voice, muffled by the door, barking out orders – presumably into a phone.

Quiet again, as silent as my namesake.

I breathed shallowly, as if they could hear me in here, fear doing funny things to my mind, when all of a sudden, **Boom! Boom! Crash!** Two swift kicks and the sound of splintering wood as the hotel room door gave way out there, in an explosion of shards.

I half-cried out, hunching down further into the tub, when a man gave a strangled yell, and then it was quiet again.

Too quiet.

A male voice said a few words, indistinguishable. Another grunted something in return. The bathroom door opened and I jumped, covering my face with my hands.

"Easy, Si. It's okay."

I lowered my hands and Whiskey was standing there, wearing his Knights of Crescentia cut. I cringed, and he put out his hands.

"We gotta go. Come on. It's not safe here anymore."

I shook my head but sat up. He reached for me and I cried out, shaking my head vehemently. He backed off and I carefully got up, struggling to do so without using my hands much, bracing my elbows against the edges of the tub.

"Shit, right, we ain't got time for this."

I yelped as he reached down and picked me up, hauling me to my feet by my underarms like I was a child. I scowled at him, but it was at his back. The large crescent picked out in the Maryland state flag, the sword behind it, sent creeping shivers over my skin.

I went out into the room, and jumped when Joker started spewing profanities at me from where he lay face down on the carpet, struggling against the shiny pair of handcuffs they had him in. I smirked at him, cruelly. I couldn't help myself.

"Gonna fucking kill you, bitch! Gonna fuckin' kill you!" he shouted.

"Shut the fuck up!" Driller yelled over him, but to his credit, he didn't hit him. He was a better human than me. I wished he would kick him in the face.

Driller was shoving my things that he'd brought to me into my big brown leather bag that was reminiscent of an old carpet bag. He thrust it into my arms, and fished out his keys, handing them to Whiskey.

"Take my bike, I'll bring yours later on."

Whiskey nodded and handed him his keys in exchange.

"Thanks, bro."

"Just go, before the cavalry arrives and tries to get you to stay."

"Yeah, yeah." Whiskey held out a hand to me. "Come on, Si, we gotta go."

I frowned, clutching my bag to my chest, and looked beseechingly at Detective Stahl.

"Believe me, I wouldn't say it was for the best if it wasn't. You gotta go, and Whiskey is the best person to keep you safe right now. He's in the same boat."

I shook my head and Detective Stahl gripped my shoulders and looked me in the eyes.

"No argument, not now. You've *got* to go. Trust me."

I bit my lips together and nodded begrudgingly. Joker's incessant screeching and hollering was setting me on edge. Whiskey stepped forward carefully. He took my bag from me and put a hand on my shoulder. I shrugged him off and he looked grim but nodded.

"Let's go."

I nodded and thrust my chin at the door, telling him to lead the way, and looked back reluctantly at Detective Stahl, who nodded his encouragement.

I didn't like it. I didn't like it one bit, however, I didn't know what was going on and I *did* like and trust Detective Stahl. If he said it was what I should do, then it was probably what I should do.

Whiskey took off the Knights of Crescentia cut and threw it on the floor. He gave a nod to his partner and stepped out the door, and I followed. He moved us up the hallway to the elevators and pressed the button to take us down. I tugged on his jacket sleeve and he looked at me.

"What?"

I stuck my bare foot out from beneath the hem of my skirt.

"Shit, where are your shoes?"

I shrugged and pointed at the bag. He rolled his eyes and hustled us onto the elevator.

"Figure it out in the garage," he muttered.

We slipped out of the elevator in the lobby and went for the garage elevators, the front desk clerk occupied with someone either checking in or out. Blue and red lights flashed outside, cars skidding to a stop as the elevator doors closed and whisked us down into the garage.

We went to the motorcycle parking and Whiskey – I guessed I should be calling him Narcos, now – dropped my bag to the floor beside one of the bikes. I sat on the seat while he riffled through it.

He said, "Ah ha!" and came up with one of my favorite pairs of knee-high fall boots, which were more than suitable for riding, with their thick brown leather and heavy soles. He unzipped them quickly and, kneeling in front of me, slipped them onto my feet and zipped the zippers along the inside of each leg to the top.

He stood up and shook his head, cramming my bag into one of the saddlebags on the bike.

"I know you like your dresses and skirts, but it really isn't good for you to ride in them. You need to dress for the slide, not for the ride, honey."

I rolled my eyes at him and rolled my hand over and over as if to say, *I thought we were in a hurry.*

He grunted and got on the bike, sticking in the key and starting it up. I got on behind him but barely held on. I wasn't thrilled to be riding with him, but I couldn't wait to go outside. I had been suffocating in the hotel. I had only been out once, to go to the prosecutor's office to write my statement. I hadn't been able to tell if they had been pleased with it or not. Considering I was still in protective custody, I had to imagine they were, indeed, happy with it.

He pulled out of the garage and I had never been so happy to be out with the sky above me in my life; I had felt like a prisoner locked away in that hotel. Of course, wherever we were headed to could be a lot worse. I guessed I would see when I got there. When you didn't have a voice, you got really good at just going with the flow and seeing what happened.

7

*M*arcos…

She let go with her hands and flung them wide when we hit the highway. I checked her in the side mirror, and with her head tipped back and her long hair streaming out behind her, she was the picture of biker-chick freedom. She was beautiful when she was that at peace, and I had been around her long enough to know she didn't get these moments of happy peace very often.

Driller and I owned an old fishing shack in the woods outside a small town. It sat on the edge of a river, the living quarters built on stilts, a shed and garage underneath. There wasn't a lot in it of any kind of worth, just an old Ford pickup and a bunch of junk. The place definitely had its pros and cons, and I would just have to see how she dealt with it when we got there. That would probably be around dawn, judging by the time we left the hotel and the ride ahead.

It was my intention to ride her through the little town three or four miles out from the cabin before anybody was up to see her. That plan got shot to shit when we arrived, the false light of pre-dawn just starting to paint the horizon through the trees. She tapped my shoulder

39

urgently and pointed at the town's little bakery and café, which was just starting to open for breakfast for the old timers.

"You hungry?" I called and she nodded emphatically. I knew there was nothing at the cabin, I'd have to hit the general store; so I pulled up to the curb in front of the little place and cut the engine. She got off the back of Driller's bike and pressed her hands to her lower back, stretching.

"Come on," I said, and it came out terser than I intended it to. She frowned at me slightly, but followed me up to the café's door. I dragged it open for her and she slipped inside with a gentle nod of thanks. I tried to smile at her, but it felt awkward on my face. I wasn't one to smile a whole lot.

"Mornin', folks!" the baker called from behind the old wooden bakery counter to the right. "Here for the baked goods or for breakfast?" He smiled affably and tossed a white dishtowel with a blue stripe over his shoulder. He had the whole getup: white tee shirt, white pants, and the long white apron covering his ample middle. He even had the paper hat on his balding head. As middle American as you can get, and straight outta the forties or fifties.

"Breakfast, for now," I answered.

"Well, go on and seat yourself. My wife Laurie will be right with you. I'm gonna get these muffins out of the oven, and I'll send a couple out hot. On the house!"

"Appreciate that," I said, "but I'm happy to pay for 'em." I caught Silence looking at me curiously when I turned. I took her by the elbow to steer her through the doorway on our left into the country dining room and as soon as we stepped through the archway, she lightly pulled her arm from my grip.

"Sorry," I muttered under my breath, just loud enough for her to hear. She cocked her head slightly and took a seat at one of the tables meant for two people.

I sat across from her, and two minutes later, the woman I presumed was Laurie came bustling over with two menus tucked between her elbow and her body, and a small plate with a steaming muffin in each hand.

"Good morning!" she greeted us, and set a muffin in front of Si and one in front of me. She slid the menus on the table next to each of us and asked, "Can I start y'all off with something to drink?"

"Uh, coffee for me, please. Black."

"And for you?" she asked Si. Silence picked up her menu and looked over the drink selection on the back and pointed to something. Laurie pulled her red-framed reading glasses down from the top of her head and peered through them.

"Orange juice?"

Silence nodded.

"Small or large?" she asked and Silence used her hands to indicate 'large'. Laurie smiled, a bit puzzled and said brightly, "Coming right up."

"You know what you want?" I asked when Silence stared at me a little too long to be comfortable.

She shook her head and went back to her menu, her clear green eyes skimming what was on offer. I skimmed mine, too, but my eyes kept wandering over the top of it to Silence's face. She looked like she was doing well. A little thinner, but that didn't surprise me. Worry ate at a person, and I was sure she was stressed.

"Alrighty, then. Here we go." Laurie set down our drinks and asked, "Need a little more time?"

Si shook her head and pointed at something on the menu. Laurie smiled and brought down her readers once again, and nodded.

"Okay, and how do you want your egg?" she asked.

"Scrambled," I answered automatically. "With a little cheese." That was the way she'd always gotten them when the Knights were out on a ride. At least, that was the way King had always ordered it for her. She'd always seemed happy enough with it, and when I looked at her to check, she nodded, looking at me curiously again.

"Sausage or bacon?"

Si held up one finger for the first option, and I answered, "Sausage."

I placed my order and folded my hands, propping my elbows on the edge of the table and settling them against my lips as she stared at me unabashed, her lovely green eyes roving over my rough face, the gears and wheels visibly turning in that pretty head of hers.

"You aren't stupid, but that doesn't stop people from treating you like you are, just because you can't talk for whatever reason, does it?"

She shook her head carefully.

"People don't tend to pay a whole lot of attention, do they?"

Again, she shook her head.

"I'm not most people," I said, and the light in her eyes dimmed slightly. I cursed myself out inside my head. I hadn't meant for it to sound like I was berating her, but I had the feeling she took it that way anyway.

We ate quietly. I didn't try to say much after that, but I didn't know if that made things better or worse. When the meal was through and both of us were sighing in satisfaction, I asked her, "You want to stop in at the bakery on the way out? I don't think the cabin has anything."

She perked up and nodded, and I got to my feet. I was weary, but I'd pushed myself harder than this before, and I likely would again. She followed me and we stopped at the bakery counter. She looked in the glass case to the left, then let her eyes drift over the loaves of bread on the shelves behind the counter. Each type was neatly labeled by a little chalkboard affixed beneath the line of loaves.

She pointed at a crusty-looking loaf of some kind of white bread, labeled 'Snowy Mountain Loaf', and I gave a nod.

"How about some of them blueberry muffins they served us?" I asked, and she smiled big and nodded.

"You going to be able to carry it on the bike? Saddlebags are kind of full."

She nodded and I placed the order with the baker, Ed. He loaded everything into paper bags, and then tucked them into two plastic grocery sacks he found somewhere, saying, "Sorry about that. We only do paper here in the bakery. It lends to the old-fashioned vibe, you know?"

Si smiled warmly and nodded, and I felt a faint smile hit my own lips.

I said, "Thanks for scaring these up. Much easier on the bike. I'll, uh, try to find some reusable ones for future trips."

"Snowy Mountain Loaf makes for some great rustic sandwiches. You should hit up the butcher two doors down. He's got a great selection of smoked and cured meats, and some cheeses from the creamery a county over. Best stuff you ever ate."

"Really?" It sounded good, actually.

"Of course, another good ol' standby is peanut butter. Toast the bread first, though. You want I should slice it for you?"

"Yeah, that would be great," I said and Si tugged my sleeve and held up two fingers. I nodded, thinking I caught her drift, and said, "Why don't you give us another loaf and just slice it."

She nodded and I had to smile that I'd indeed understood her just fine. Ed beamed at us and took one of the crusty, flour-dusted loaves in back.

He returned with it wrapped in a plastic bread bag, the end twisted and secured with one of those paper-wrapped wire ties.

"Thank you," I said, and we went out, to Ed calling out, "Y'all come back now and tell me what y' think!"

"Will do," I said, and Si waved gently as the door shut.

"What do you think?" I asked. "Check out that butcher?"

She nodded and looped the two bags over one wrist. We went down the block and slow-rolled past the butcher's shop, but it was still closed up tight.

"Well, shit. I'm going to have to come back into town later, anyhow. I'll see if he's open then." She nodded and we went on our way.

The fishing cabin on the Blackwater River sort of butted up against the hillside. There was parking up on the hill, and a walk across a narrow dock-like structure led to the cabin itself. It had a wrap-around porch and a set of stairs off the back left corner down to the garage underneath it. There was a switchback, steep drive down the side to get down there.

The truck that was locked up in the garage down there was so old, we didn't give a damn if the river flooded it. We'd been meaning to get rid of a bunch of shit that was left by the previous owner. I figured, being stuck here for god-knows-how-long, I could put my ass to work making some improvements to the place.

I cut the engine to Driller's bike and heeled down the kickstand. He'd likely ride mine out here, and we'd swap then.

We were best friends, so we already had keys to each other's place on our rings. I was hoping he'd have the presence of mind to pick me up some shit from my place. I wasn't sure how much I had here in the way of clothes. It'd been a while.

Si leapt off the bike as soon as she could, putting distance between us. I couldn't say I blamed her. I'd been the instrument of some pretty serious trauma. She didn't know the real me, only what she'd seen of me first hand. That was rough. It pained me more than anyone could know, but by the same token, that was the job…

"Come on," I said, my voice rougher with emotion than I'd like, as I pulled her leather bag of wispy hippy-chick clothing out of the saddlebag I'd locked it in. "This is home sweet home until further notice."

Her face was unreadable as her lovely eyes roved over the silvery, weathered wood-shake cabin. She nodded carefully as I marched across the walkway to its front door. It took some fishing to find the right key for the lock, which grated a bit from disuse as I turned it. Silence picked her way carefully across the walkway, dubious as to its stability, and I chuckled.

"It's newer than the cabin. Driller and I share this place. He's my best friend. We repaired all the structural defects before I transferred into Narcotics and went undercover."

She gave me a careful nod of understanding and preceded me through the door. It was dimmer inside; the windows in the back overlooking the river were in need of a wash, plus the porch was roofed in, shading the windows all the way around. There was a loft on the front side of the cabin, but it, like the garage, was full of junk.

The cabin down here was pretty much one big room except for a wall separating off the kitchen. The bed was down in the one big room. The bathroom door was on the left as you came in, a two-seater couch against the wall separating the kitchen from the rest of the room. From the bed, you could see it all, the front door to the left, the back door leading out to the porch, and the stairs down to the garage on the back side; all of them were visible.

I dropped the leather bag of hers by the bed and reached for the plastic ones of our bakery goods. She handed them over and I went around into the kitchen.

"You can take the bed, I'll take the couch," I called out, and jumped when I heard the sharp slap of leather against the worn floorboards. I dropped the bread on the counter and went back around. Her leather bag had been relocated to the end of the rough-upholstered loveseat and she was curled on it resolutely, her back to the room, huddled in her brown, tough suede coat with its hippy fringe.

I shook my head. "Suit yourself."

I went over to the bed, which was made, but dusty like the loveseat, and flopped down on my back. I grunted and dug my gun out of the small of my back and set it to the side within easy reach. I didn't tend to move around a lot in my sleep.

I was out inside two minutes.

8

*E*verleigh…

I slept harder than I could have imagined despite the oppressive heat of the cabin. I was finally jarred awake by the sound of an engine trying to turn over. It was disorienting at first, not knowing where the sound was coming from, but finally I realized it was *below* me.

I stood up and tossed my jacket down over the arm of the loveseat. I wanted to take my boots off so badly, but I didn't know what I would find by accident with bare feet around this place. It was a tetanus shot waiting to happen… I looked down at my hands, at the healing marks both front and back and thought to myself, *I'd already had one of those.* Still, I didn't want a matching set of holes through my feet, so the boots stayed on.

I went to the back door and opened it out onto the porch. I wished it was just a screen, but the porch itself, though it *should* be screened-in, was open-air. If it had been screened, it could be so much cooler in the cabin, but the windows didn't have screens and I wasn't a fan of bugs, as much as I loved nature.

There was another door at the back corner of the porch, just a screen, and I opened it to find a landing and square twist of stairs. I heard a bang, the clang of metal as a tool skittered across cement, and a curse.

I couldn't help but smile, but I quickly wiped it off my face as I quietly descended the stairs.

Most men didn't like it if you smiled or laughed at their expense. Bikers were even worse about it. I swear, it was some kind of complex the men I'd encountered had. I believe Margaret Atwood expressed it best when she said she'd asked a group of men what the worst thing a woman could do to them was. They'd answered 'Laugh at them.' When she posed the same question to women about men, their answer was stark. 'I'm afraid he will kill me.'

I found it best, with my background, to not provoke any man in any way that I could think of and I was always thinking about it. Of course, there were some things that couldn't be avoided… like things I hadn't done but got blamed for, anyway.

I stood at the bottom of the stairs and looked around. The barn-like doors of the garage under the stilted cabin were flung wide. Inside, an ancient pickup truck, more rust than faded tan paint, sat with its hood up, and Whiskey - I mean Narcos – half-hanging out from under it. I didn't know how to approach without startling him, so I stood back, and kind of just waited for him to notice me.

I didn't have to worry about it, though, because he glanced at me from under one arm and asked, "Don't suppose you know anything about cars, do you?"

I shook my head and he smiled and sighed.

"I think it's the starter; I'm not real sure. I guess I'm going to have to take the bike into town and have it tested."

I made a kicking motion with my foot, and he choked back a laugh.

"Have I tried kicking it?"

I nodded.

"Don't think that's how it works, honey."

I gave a shrug. That was about the extent of my expertise when it came to the subject.

"You're funny," he said, nodding approvingly. "You got jokes."

I smiled faintly and shrugged again, looking around. There was a lot of random junk in the garage behind and around the truck, same as I'd spied in the loft inside. This place needed a lot of work.

"You good if I head into town, do some shopping?" he asked.

I kind of frowned and looked around, giving a weak gesture with my hands, not sure how to express my question if it was all right if I were here on my own. He seemed to get it anyway, though.

"Just stay in the cabin or on the property. Don't go in the river past your feet, the current is strong and there ain't no one around to help you if you get dragged under."

He had straightened up and was wiping his grease-stained hands on an old red rag. He looked me over and said, "I think its best you stay out of town, but if there's anything you want, make a list. I'll grab it for you."

I chewed my bottom lip. There were some things I wanted, but nothing I was willing to ask for. I gave a weak shrug and his keen green eyes, so unlike my own, swept over me.

"You good?"

I nodded, a bit too quickly.

He said, "Power's out in the cabin; I need to get some fuses. Place is super old-school. That's why I was trying to get the truck running, so I could make a proper supply run. Nothing ever really goes as planned out here. Usually you gotta adapt and make do. That's half the fun of life out here."

I looked around and he smiled.

"Have a look around. I'll be back as soon as I can."

He left me standing there, taken aback that he trusted me not to run or disappear… Well, it was that, or he knew there was literally nowhere for me to go. I shivered despite the too-warm afternoon sunlight and ducked into the garage to look around. I hated not being busy, and if I was lucky, this place might provide me something to do.

As I suspected, the pile of junk in the back was a gold mine of home improvement things that just had yet to be utilized. *Including* a giant box with a mammoth roll of screen! There were other things back there too, things I could use to make things a little cozier upstairs, like pots for plants; there were plenty of things around the woods and river that were edible, I was sure of it…

I went upstairs to check the loft which was where I found, buried behind boxes and pots and pans, the true treasure – at least to me.

I smiled to myself. *I could do a lot with this place, a little at a time.* I mean, if I was allowed, but to be honest… I didn't exactly have the ability to ask permission. But, beg forgiveness? That, I could do. That, I was an old hand at. It all came down to how brave was I willing to be?

9

arcos…

Kch-thwack!

"Ah!"

She sounded like she had hurt herself. I didn't like that. I didn't like that, at all. I slid the armloads of groceries onto the dining room table and rushed out the back door to find Si shaking out one hand, the other one occupied by an industrial staple gun. I frowned, confused, and then the rest of the scene caught up with my brain and I chuckled.

"You know, the screen gets stapled to the outside of the porch."

She frowned slightly and shook her head, and I hung mine and lightly punched to door frame a couple times to keep from laughing at her. I didn't want to hurt her feelings.

"It's true, and I got some ladders down in the garage. I was planning on making some improvements around here. Starting there seems like a good bet."

She nodded and waved a hand at the open door, stepping down from the dining room chair she'd co-opted for her mission.

"Can't get the electric up and running until the day after tomorrow; fuses had to be ordered, so we're slumming it tonight. I grabbed some stuff that didn't need to be refrigerated."

She nodded and set down the staple gun on the porch railing, and I pushed the back door wider.

"Sorry, it's gonna be hot sleeping, again tonight."

She shrugged and went to the grocery bags and started to snoop. I watched her, my arms crossed, as she pulled oranges and then a jar of peanut butter out of the bag. It was getting dark out, but I realized she had thought of that already, setting the things she'd plucked from the bags down and lifting a tin of lamp fuel up from behind them.

"What am I supposed to do with that?" I asked.

She pointed to the kitchen counter. There was a lantern and a couple of hurricane lamps she'd found somewhere.

"You wanna make sandwiches while I light these up?"

She nodded and went to the sink and turned it on. Nothing came out, and she shrugged.

"Ah, yeah. Need electricity for the water, we're on a well out here."

Her shoulders drooped and she wrinkled her nose.

"Sorry. We'll get the screen up, I'll get the truck running, and maybe we can wash up down by the river. Best I can figure for now. There's a couple gallons of drinking water, at least."

She peeked into the bag she hadn't looked in yet and nodded, then turned, taking her spoils into the kitchen.

Well, all right, then. I guess we had our jobs to do.

She moved around the kitchen, quiet as a church mouse. I never really got that saying – I mean, what made mice living in churches quieter than any other mice? I filled the two hurricane lamps and the one old-fashioned copper lantern she'd scared up from somewhere and got them lit.

I divided them up around the living quarters. One above the kitchen sink, one on the dining room table, and one on the rickety bedside table, which, admittedly, was probably a bad idea. I needed to shim that damn thing up.

"Watch that side table, it's shaky as hell," I warned her and she nodded, giving me a look like *Thanks but, what would I be over there for?*

I'd never looked at her long enough to realize just how expressive she was. Of course, I'd been playing the part of a good little street-rat foot-soldier, and I wouldn't be caught dead lookin' at the president's ol' lady. Now, though? No more games. No more disguises. I was just me, and she was just her.

She paused and gently set a plate with a peeled orange and a peanut butter sandwich on the table. I went over and took a seat and she set another one down in front of her. She looked self-conscious as she took a seat near mine, and I said, gently, "You don't have to sit near me if you don't want to."

She startled and looked at me wide-eyed and innocent, but I could see right through it. It killed a part of me that she thought she had to do that with me, protect herself; try not to ruffle my feathers… I under-stood it, but it didn't kill me any less.

"I'm serious, you're not a prisoner here. You're a witness, and I'm a cop. I'm here to keep us both alive. Bonus points that I get to fix this place up. There anything else you want to do other than the screen?"

She chewed a bite of her sandwich slowly, carefully, her eyes searching my face, trying to decide. She finally nodded, slowly, carefully, and I cocked my head.

Too fast, I had moved too fast, because she jumped slightly.

"What else?" I asked.

She shook her head, and I didn't want to push it too much too fast, so I let it go for now.

"Okay, I'll just get that screen up for now. When I go back into town, I'll pick up some citronella candles."

She waved her hand in front of me and I looked up. She got up from the table and went out the back door and to the end of the porch, just around the corner. She came back toting an apple crate that looked almost too heavy for her and I raised an eyebrow. I got up and took it from her, and she closed the back door behind her. I set it on the dining table on the last free corner and scowled down into it.

"What is this stuff?"

She pulled out a bottle and I held it out, squinting in the dimming light. "Citronella oil."

She moves some things around to show me empty mason jars and a big ol' block of wax.

"You want to make your own?" I asked.

She nodded.

"Do you know how?"

She nodded again.

"Let me guess, you need electricity."

She waffled a hand back and forth and pointed down.

"There's stuff in the garage?"

She nodded.

"Knock yourself out," I told her. "Just grab my attention if you need any help or heavy lifting done."

She cocked her head, and I smiled at her, chuckling.

"Yeah, I'm sure."

She smiled then, and it was almost as if a truce had been declared. We sat back down to finish our meal and I said, "You were busy when I was gone, huh?"

She nodded and a secret little Mona Lisa smile painted her lips. I liked it. I was hoping I'd get to see it more.

"Good deal," I muttered. "Place could use a woman's touch."

She smiled a little bigger, but wouldn't look at me. I was hoping if I let her boss me around some, turned her loose to go a little buck-wild on the place, that maybe, just *maybe,* it would relax her some. I didn't deserve her trust, but I was hell-bent on trying to earn it.

There wasn't much left to do after dinner. She put things away around the kitchen; I got a trash bag out from under the sink and packed away the shopping bags and some odds and ends she didn't need that were in the bottom of the apple crate.

She was resourceful, I'd give her that. I'd also give anything to know her story. How she got with the likes of King in the first place.

I lay in bed that night, the soft glow of the lamp illuminating her back as she lay hunched and curled on the too-small couch. I'm telling you, it was a deep, satisfying pleasure just watching her shoulders rise and fall with her deep and even breathing. King had fucked up with his cruelty, and I couldn't be happier about it. He could have just as easily made it quick, and blown her head off, which would have given me plenty to send him up for life, but wouldn't have done anything for poor Si.

I still wrestled with my part in her suffering. I tried to justify it to my own mind, but I couldn't. There was no justifying what I'd done to her, in pounding the nails home through her delicate hands, but it was either that, or one of the other guys would have. The guilt was a constricting thing that'd like to choke me, keeping me awake long into the night, until I simply got up with the first blush of dawn.

She wanted the porch screened, I could do that for her. It needed to be done anyway. I quietly went out the back and down to the garage to set up what I would need, letting her sleep as long as possible.

I figured at least one of us could use the rest.

10

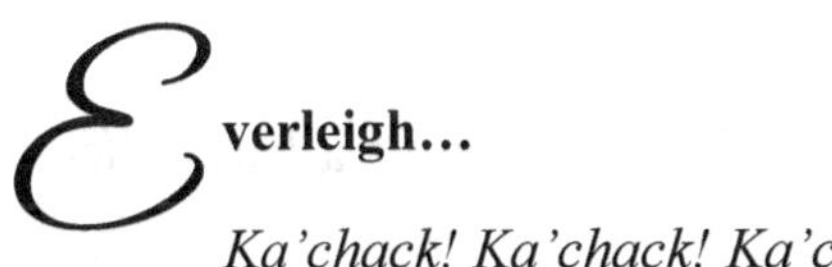

verleigh…

Ka'chack! Ka'chack! Ka'chack!

Each sound came in rapid succession. It wasn't exactly the sounds I'd expected to wake up to, but honestly, it could only be one thing. I got to my feet, and assured, the day before that the boards in the cabin and on the porch held no loose nails and were all worn to a satiny finish, padded barefoot to the back door. I stepped out into the morning sunlight streaming through the portals left between the roof supports on the porch to see Whi – Narcos on the other side, as if floating in midair, stapling screen to the very same supports.

Ka'chack! Ka'chack! Ka'chack!

"Morning," he grunted, and climbed down the ladder to move it over.

I leaned out one of the areas yet to be screened and waved down to him. He chuckled and moved the ladder, climbing back up. He reached for the roll of screen, which he'd rested inside the closed-off porch rail, and I helped as much as I could.

"Thanks, but I've got it."

57

I let go and stood back while he stapled it first along the support, then along the rail, then along the top and finally along the next support, closing the back portion of the wrap-around in.

I smiled. I was excited. With this done so swiftly, as soon as he went to town I could leap on phase two of my little master plan.

Ka'chack! Ka'chack! Ka'chack!

Ka'chack! Ka'chack! Ka'chack!

"Mind getting me one of those gallons of water?" he asked and I jumped a little, coming out of my daydream, and nodded rapidly. I went into the cabin and retrieved a big quart Mason jar from the cupboard above the sink. I poured it to the rim and took it out to him. He downed half of it in three or four large swallows and handed it back.

"Thanks, if you could hang on to that for me and give it back when I need it, that would be helpful."

I nodded, and just kind of stood around while he completed the last half of the back porch. He had me hand him the water at the corner and polished off the glass. I kind of shook it back and forth to ask if he needed a refill. He wiped the excess from his beard and mustache and shook his head.

"No, thanks, I'm almost to the bank here. I'll come around the front, here, and get the screen door from the garage and hang it at the end of the walkway. This went a lot faster and easier than I thought it would. I wish I'd done it a while ago."

I smiled and made a motion of eating and he nodded.

"Some of those muffins would be great."

I went around and back inside and fetched them and my own glass of water. We sat on the porch in the shade of some trees along the side of the little cabin. He put his back against the wood between the railing supports, and I put my back against the cabin itself, the jug of water and plate of muffins between us. I munched happily as he considered me, and finally he said, "All it took to make you happy was putting some screen up, like really, that was it. That's kind of amazing."

I shrugged. Not really, not if he hadn't wanted to do it. I think that's why a lot of relationships had a tendency to fall apart – couples not really listening to the intent or meaning behind little requests. Then again, we weren't a couple, and, frankly, never would be. I mean, how we could be, after he'd nailed me to a tree, was a little beyond me. Was he attractive? Sure, I'd always found him attractive but I'd also thought King was handsome and look at what he had done… he was supposed to love me and he had given the order.

I smoothed my hands over my skirt, my palms suddenly sweaty, the wounds in my hands aching, though I couldn't tell if it was from my train of thought encouraging them or if they were legitimately hurting at the moment.

"They hurt?" he asked, eyeing my hands.

I waffled one of them back and forth some and he caught my eye with his.

"May I?" He held out a hand, palm up, and I tucked my hands in my lap, shaking my head. He sighed, a heavy disappointed sound with the weight of the world in it, and nodded.

"I get it," he said shortly, and drained his water jar. He stood up and threw a leg over the railing, climbing back onto the ladder.

I didn't know why, but I felt… bad… for hurting his feelings. Which was crazy, considering he was the one who nailed me to a tree a little more than a week or so ago. Maybe two? I didn't know. The days had begun to blur together at the hotel, the walls closing in on me.

I liked it much better here.

Here I could breathe, there were trees and sunlight. The sound of the river was soothing, and the knowledge that nobody knew where I was or could find me was the most comforting thing of all.

I got up and cleared the dishes. I couldn't wait for a hot shower. He'd said 'tomorrow', but if I had to, I would clean myself up camping-style and rinse off the worst of the sweat and dirt in the cold river. It would be nice to at least have soap, but I don't think he'd bought any.

I figured I'd better start a list for when he went back into town. I couldn't expect him to think of everything, could I? Just the thought of writing anything down made me nervous, but I bucked up and made the list.

Just as I finished, I realized there was no more sound of the staple gun biting into the wood, and to be honest, I was glad it was staples and not hammer-and-nails. I shuddered at the thought.

"Hey."

I jumped.

"Sorry, didn't mean to scare you. I'm going to get to work on the truck, try not to wander too far, okay?"

I nodded and he ducked back out the back door, which I had left standing open since the porch was screened in. He went out the screen door at the end of the porch and clattered down the stairs and I felt my tense muscles ease with his absence.

I shook my head to clear it and picked up my apple crate with its candle fixings and went out onto the porch. I plucked up my courage and followed him down the stairs, setting it on the old metal desk full of tools, odds, and ends in the garage.

"Need help?" he asked.

I shook my head no, and picked up an old metal pail by its wire handle to go look for some plant life goodies nearby.

11

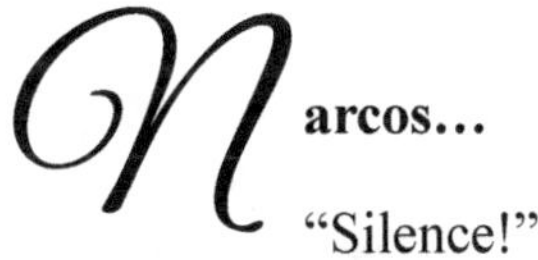arcos…

"Silence!"

I waited, the light breeze rustling the trees, the sound of the river water rushing over stones the only answer to my call. I frowned, worry gnawing at my gut, and I cupped my hands around my bearded mouth and called again.

"Silence!"

One of the shrubs at the edge of the clearing rustled and she came around it, dirt streaking the front of her white skirt, her long hair tangled and with at least one leaf in it. I watched as this wild woman picked her way gingerly across the bare earth in her equally bare feet, the bucket she'd taken brimming with dirt and bits of green.

"What have you got there?" I asked.

She held out the bucket, beaming and I looked inside.

"Are those leeks?" I asked.

She waffled her hand back and forth and I raised an eyebrow. She rolled her eyes at me and I had to laugh.

"Guess I'm going to have to trust you aren't going to poison me."

She nodded and it was as matter-of-fact as she could make it.

I shook my head and said, "I got the truck up and running. I'm headed into town. Did you make a list?"

She chewed her bottom lip and finally shook her head. I cocked mine and said, "I know we need more food, but what else?"

She set her bucket down and made like she was showering and I nodded.

"Soap, shampoo, probably some dish soap and laundry soap, too, huh?"

She nodded and made like she was brushing her teeth.

"Oh, believe me that is at the *top* of my list. You don't even know."

She giggled lightly and it was a good sound, like a babbling brook, laughing over stones.

I smiled and asked, "Anything else, Silence?"

She made a face and shook her head, waving her hand back and forth. It was a strong reaction to have to wanting to know what she wanted from the store, so that couldn't be it.

"What? 'Silence'? You don't want me to call you 'Silence'?"

She nodded emphatically and I had to smile.

"Well, what do you want me to call you, then?"

She frowned, then frowned harder. I chuckled and with a sigh said, "I'm sure you'll figure out how to tell me. You're crafty like that."

She cocked her head and nodded slowly.

"For now, it's all I've got."

She looked a little dejected, but nodded.

"Be back as soon as I can," I told her and she nodded again.

I climbed into the old truck and fired it up. It wasn't happy about it, but it started and it stayed running. I climbed the old switchback driveway up to the front of the cabin where she stood just outside the front porch and waved, her lips twisted in what looked like regret at my leaving.

I didn't want to get my hopes up that that was what it really was. I mean, shit, if I were her, I wouldn't be able to wait to see the back of me after what I'd done. I just wanted to get into town, get the shit I needed to pick up from the general store, get the fuck out, and get on with it.

Part of it was I shopped like just about every other guy, except Pasquale, but fuck he was some kind of mutant hybrid, I swore. Too good for the likes of us, for all that he kept hanging around. The other part was, I didn't like hanging around where I was seen and people got curious and started asking questions I'd have to lie to answer. The thing about lying is how much and how many lies were you going to have to keep straight down the line. That, and these were good, salt-of-the-earth kind of folk. They didn't deserve to be dragged into our melodrama, because, unlike television, ours was very real and got people really dead.

I pulled up at the auto parts place first to return the starter; it had turned out it was the battery and some really filthy sparkplugs. I got it running with the battery I picked up along with the starter here yesterday. I'd bought the battery; the parts guy had actually *loaned* me the starter and told me if that was the trouble I could just pay him for it today. If not bring it back; no harm, no foul.

Yeah. That's how Podunk small-town this place was.

"So, I see you got her runnin'!" he called jovially when I went through the front door.

"Yeah, yeah I did."

We chatted amicably, and I got the fuck out of there before the questions could start.

"She sure is a beaut, ever thought about fully restoring her?" he asked before I ducked out the door. I looked at the old, tired truck and shook my head.

"Naw, it was just there with the cabin when we bought it, title for it came with the deed to the place."

"Shame, she'd be worth the love and attention. Ain't many like her nowadays."

I nodded and said my final goodbye, and got over to the general store as quick as I could. I only had an hour or so until closing.

I was thinking about Si as I went up and down the narrow aisles with my basket. The final words of the parts guy echoing in my brain. There sure weren't many like Silence nowadays. You could tell she'd been through some shit, with her always jumping and flinching, always trying to please everyone around her. Yet, resiliently, she still managed to trust people who she honestly had no reason to trust. People like me.

She hadn't put up too much of a fight back at the hotel. Hadn't tried to run away, or bounce on me. Hadn't tried to back out of testifying – and I still didn't know how the fuck we were going to pull that off.

I stopped in the hair-care aisle and picked up the box of her red, that deep auburn she was so fond of that made her spectacular green eyes something out of this world. I remembered this one time, we were on a run with the Knights of Crescentia and stopped at this gas station-market hybrid store. More than a mini-mart, but less than a full-blown grocery or drug store, you know? King had sent Si in for road beers and smokes and she'd come back out with those items, but when he'd demanded the change, he'd nearly blown a gasket, until he got a hold of the receipt.

He'd laughed and said, "Leave it to a bitch. Send her in for smokes and beers, she comes out with that and a bag full of fuckin' hair dye."

She'd pulled the box from her bag and had pointed out the clearance stickers on it; at that price, if I were a chick, I would have scooped them up, too. I remembered the box, not for the smiling model, but for the pink flowers on it. I'd had the stray thought that those pink flowers belonged in a crown on Silence's head. How she'd be the perfect hippy chick, straight out of a Woodstock photo with her white hippy skirts and dresses.

I picked up two of the boxes. It'd been a while since she'd colored her hair, and with as much of it as she had, I couldn't imagine one box would do the trick.

I rushed through the rest of my shopping and got up to the cash wrap. Dick, the store owner gave me a nod and rang through my items by hand on the old-school register.

"Mitch over at the hardware store said he managed to scare up a couple of them fuses you was lookin' for after you left. Said if I seen you, I should send you over," he said as he bagged up my purchases.

"Oh, yeah? Thanks for letting me know, much obliged to you."

He gave me a solid smile and I dumped my change in his dusty little donation jar by the register.

"You have a good night, now, y'hear."

"You too, Dick."

I took myself to the hardware store just as Mitch was flipping the sign to 'closed.' I halted in my step and waved, backing off but he unlocked the door and opened up for me.

"Glad you got the message," he greeted me, and I nodded and said, "Yeah, Dick just told me about it, but I can come back tomorrow, it's no problem."

He chuckled and waved me in with one gnarled hand. "Naw, get in here. I haven't cashed out my register yet. You made it in the nick of time."

"Oh, man, you're saving my life right now, you don't even know."

"Ed over at the bakery said you come ridin' into town with your girl; I think I might have an idea."

Shit. I thought to myself. *Word travels fast in a small town. Thanks, Ed.*

I bought the fuses with a promise to pick up the others coming in the next day as spares. The sun was just starting to set when I got back to the truck. I made sure everything was secure and headed back to the old fishing cabin, suddenly nervous about what kind of project Si would have for me this time. Although, I was pretty sure I wasn't going to regret the screened-in porch tonight when I had all the windows flung wide and the cooler air moved through the cabin.

I felt weary all the way to the bone and was totally ready for a hot shower and some rest. Boy, was I in for a surprise when I got back to the cabin.

I got out of the truck down by the garage and took a load in each arm, to head up the outer stairs. Si appeared out of nowhere at the bottom as I turned from the truck, and I jumped, taking a faltering step back and just barely keeping myself from accidentally dumping the paper bags from the general store.

"Jesus Christ!" I gave a restrained cry. "You like to scare the shit out of me!"

She hunched her shoulders and wrinkled her nose in this adorable sheepish expression that screamed *'Sorry not sorry'* and I took a second to catch my breath.

"Jump-started my heart, that's for sure. Can you take one of these?"

She rushed forward and took one of the bags from me, allowing me to grab the last one. I followed her up the stairs, which she took lightly, and stopped cold just inside the back-screen door.

"Where the fuck did you find an entire *bed*?" I demanded and she beamed at me, impishly.

She'd found an entire full-sized daybed somewhere. An old one with what looked like an iron frame. She'd put it out here on the porch, a classic area rug underneath it. She'd stacked apple crates to one side, closest to the back door and I realized, she'd set it up the way she had because I could see her from the bed inside at night, knowing I would want to keep an eye on her. I shook my head in disbelief.

"You were busy while I was gone."

She nodded happily and pointed up to the loft when we went inside.

"Was that where it was at?"

She nodded.

"How'd you get it down here?"

She raised one finger, then two, then three, then four.

"One piece at a time?"

She nodded.

"You took that whole thing apart and put it back together all by yourself?"

She nodded.

"Good job," I declared, impressed.

She beamed at me.

"I'll be right back, hardware guy managed to scare up some of those fuses. I want to get the electricity going while I still can. A hot shower sounds really good right now."

She smiled even bigger and nodded enthusiastically.

I left her rooting through the bags on the table and went out and around to the side of the cabin that held the metal fuse box. I flipped the catch on its metal cover and opened it up, replacing the blown fuses and hoping like hell that was *all* that was needed. This place was older than dirt and needed a lot of renovation, so…

I flipped the switch and a light came on inside. I heard a smattering of applause from Silence and ran a hand back through my hair, pushing it out of my eyes.

"Looks like we're good to go!" I called. "Should have hot water in an hour or two."

I went around the corner in the back door and stopped. She was standing so very still by the rickety dining table with a box of hair dye in each hand, staring at them with an unreadable expression.

"What's wrong?" I asked, leaning a shoulder against the back-door's jamb.

She looked up at me, her eyes troubled, and held the boxes out almost helplessly in front of her.

"Well, it's your brand, isn't it?"

She nodded, her confusion clear.

"Is it the wrong color?" I asked, knowing it damn well wasn't.

She shook her head, and I pushed off the door frame.

"Well, all right, then."

I went into the kitchen and double-checked that the freezer and fridge were empty. Aside from a few bottles of things like ketchup, mustard, and mayo, it was. Those, I discarded without even opening them. I'd already picked up replacements. The fridge and freezer were already getting cold, but it wasn't like I'd bought much of anything else for them. I'd have to run into town one more time, for perishable items.

"Chile Con Carne for dinner, out of a can; nothing fancy. Good thing you got yourself set up out there, huh?"

She blushed, smiling and almost laughing, and nodded.

"You find sheets for that bed?"

She nodded and went out with her hair dye and set it down, presumably on one of her apple crate shelves and came back in. She trotted up the stairs close to the outer wall of the cabin, up to the loft, and came down, struggling a bit with a big cardboard box. It didn't look heavy, just big and awkward.

I went and took it from her and it wasn't too bad. It had plastic-wrapped pillows on top, and I set it down on the floor by the table for her.

"Go on and make your bed, I'm going to heat up some dinner."

She smiled and dragged the box out the back door and I had to smile. She'd already cleaned and flung open several of the windows along the back of the cabin, which had cooled it down some in here. I opened up two cans of chili and poured them in a saucepan and set them on the electric range to heat.

I watched her as much as I watched the pot, as she spread the sheet over her bed. Didn't seem to me the box had much by way of blankets, but I could pick her up something in town if she needed it. I doubted she would. It was high summer and warm as fuck out. With no air conditioning, it made sleeping at night kind of miserable – I was hoping now that the windows were thrown open, it would be a little more tolerable.

She pulled the pillows with their country-lace pillow shams out of their plastic and fluffed them up, setting them up on the end of the bed closest to the back door. She came back in and fetched her leather bag and went back outside.

I was impressed by the large white piano shawl, embroidered with big pink cabbage roses, that she pulled out of the bottom of it. She set about artfully draping it across her bed and I wondered what else she had in mind for the space out there. She had decorating down to some kind of magic. That voodoo that girls do with castoff items, re-purposing them into something new to make them all artsy and chic; I had no idea how they did it, but she had the touch, that was for sure.

"Silence, come and eat, honey."

She stepped back into the cabin and cleared paper bags and the other random bits and bobs off of the table.

"Thanks," I grunted, pouring chili into two cracked bowls I found in the cupboard.

"Where you going?" I asked, and she held up soap and things for the bathroom, disappearing inside and setting them about where they belonged. I chuckled and when she came back, held out the tooth-brushes and paste I'd bought. She snatched them from my hands, lighting up with glee, and did a spin in the middle of the room like some fairy-tale princess who'd been given the key to her freedom or some shit.

I laughed as she kissed the box and dashed into the bathroom.

"We're about to eat!" I called out. "Mint and chili aren't a good combo. I'd save the toothpaste for dessert if I were you."

She came back out, nodding, and heaved a sigh.

"You want bread?"

She nodded and I tore off a hunk of the whole loaf and handed it over. She sat down with me and took it with a gracious nod.

"Welcome," I said.

We ate in our customary silence, but I couldn't say it was a bad thing. There were times, just sitting with her, that were so comfortable; I got up from those silences feeling better for it. Her presence was a soothing one, the kind of comfortable that was good for the soul. Fuck if I wanted to admit how much I liked her. This not having to be someone else around her was one of the best things, ever.

I sat back in my chair with a satisfied sigh full of gusto, my chili bowl empty, my hunk of bread nothing but a few crumbs beside my bowl. I watched Si take another bite, and she eyed me from where she leaned over her bowl. Her white dress was filthy, streaked with dirt and dust, but I could see why she didn't want to get any chili on it.

"Mind if I shower first?" I asked.

She shook her head and made a slight shooing motion with her hand.

"You good to get the dishes?"

She rolled her eyes and nodded and I had to laugh.

"Not your favorite chore, I take it."

She shook her head.

"What is?"

She tugged on her dress a couple times.

"You might change your mind about that. We don't have a washer and dryer here. It's a good, old-fashioned washtub and board."

She pointed at the sink and out the back door with a questioning look.

"In here, out at the river, doesn't much matter."

She frowned, and mimed hanging up laundry and shrugged.

"I guess I'll have to build a line. Usually we're only out here for a week at the most and we just take our laundry back to the city to do it. Somehow, I don't think that's going to fly. We could be here a while. Shit, I don't even know what I have around here for me. You got at least two or three days' worth of clothes in that bag of yours, right?"

She shrugged.

"You don't know?"

She shrugged again.

"Well, let me know when you get around to checking things out. I know we have a few towels here somewhere. Not exactly bath towels, but beach ones. They should do the trick."

She nodded and shot me a brave smile, like she wasn't judging. She seemed genuinely happier here than she had in the hotel, so at least there was that.

I got up and at least took my bowl to the sink for her. I went through the rickety dresser against the back wall the bed shared, and scored a pair of cut-off army pants I was pretty sure belonged to Driller. I held them up, worried about the fit, because dude was typically narrower through the waist than I was, but it looked like I'd caught up to him. I wasn't as big as I used to be, but I was still shredded.

I tossed the long shorts over my shoulder and though I found one of my old Indigo City Motors tees, I skipped it. It was too fuckin' hot for it.

I let the tap run for a minute to clear the pipes and called out that Si should do the same in the kitchen. As soon as the water ran clear, I twisted the knob to let the shower do the same.

God, that hot water felt good. My muscles loosened under the pounding spray and some of the smaller, weaker aches disappeared. I was used to lifting weights more than I was any kind of labor, but it felt good to be getting back into the latter.

I washed my hair twice; it felt good to get it really clean, but it was bugging me how long it was getting. I was pretty sure I had some clippers around here to deal with the undercut, but I would just have to sport a man-bun for the top, as loathsome as that idea was.

I shut off the water reluctantly, wanting to leave some for Silence, and plucked up one of the two beach towels that lived on the rack in here, pulling it behind the curtain and drying off before whisking it back.

Stepping out of the tub, I frowned and stood in front of the open medicine cabinet. I swung it shut, and written in the steam was *Call me Everleigh.* I huffed a laugh which I quickly strangled and shook my head.

I knew she would have eventually figured out a way to tell me, but I had to hand it to her, this was more creative than I'd bargained for. A little horror movie-esque, but I liked horror movies. I didn't think she'd done it with the intention of creeping me the fuck out, but rather to make sure it got my attention.

Well, that it had.

I picked up and put on the shorts I'd found and had to shrug off the fact they hung lower on my hips than I liked. At least having to go commando didn't bother me. I slung the beach towel over my shoulders and stepped out of the bathroom rubbing it over my hair to find Everleigh sitting at the table, her boxes of dye on it, one of them open and neatly laid out. She was staring at her hands.

"Need some help?" I asked.

She jumped at the sound of my voice.

"Sorry, didn't mean to startle you. So, Everleigh, huh?" She nodded slowly and I said, "It's a good name, the one your parents gave you?"

She nodded carefully and I smiled.

"Told you that you'd figure out a way to tell me."

Her tight posture eased and she tried a smile in return, which made mine grow.

"Let's see about this," I said and walked over, picking up one of the boxes. I let my eyes slide over the directions and nodded slowly.

"Says to start with dry hair, do you need to wash and dry it first?"

She shook her head.

"So, how do I do this, then? Also, let me see if I can find you a shirt, don't want to get this on your dress, do you?"

She shook her head rapidly and stood up. I rooted around in the dresser, and finally asked, "You got a problem with putting this one on, seeing as you're going to shower as soon as your dye is set?"

I held up the one I'd been wearing, an old Black Sabbath band tee with a couple holes in it. I was seriously cringing on the inside about even *suggesting* it, seeing as I'd been wearing and sweating in it for like two days now.

Didn't seem to faze Everleigh, though. She came over to me and took it from my hands and went into the bathroom with it. She came out a moment later with her clothes wadded in her hands, the tee falling to mid-thigh on her.

And I was suddenly having to resist the boner that was trying to stir to life in my shorts.

She went out to her little porch bedroom and tucked her clothes away and came back. I pulled the chair out for her, to where I could move all the way around her, and she sat down.

I asked, "Okay, how does this work?"

She patiently walked me through parting her hair, miming laying dye at the root and painting it out with her finger to make sure it was covered. Seemed tedious, but it wasn't rocket science.

"Just making sure the first bottle covers everything at the root, right?"

She nodded.

"Second bottle is for all the rest?"

She nodded again.

"Plastic sack for the garbage?"

She shook her head and leaned forward, plucking the bag off the table. She pantomimed a rushed version of the dying process, then twisted her hair up and popped the bag onto her head. Finally, she tapped her wrist for time, then made a checkmark in the air with her finger and sat up with an exaggerated expression to mark the time being up. She whipped the bag off her hair and then pantomimed showering.

"How to dye hair in thirty seconds or less," I commented dryly and she smiled and half giggled. It was a good sound that made me smile in return.

"So you do have a voice, a pretty one at that," I said, pulling the cellophane gloves onto my hands. She blushed deeply and stood, mixing up the dye for me in the bottle, putting it into my hands and covering the top with my finger. She made like I should shake it, and I did until she waved her hands at me to stop, then retook her seat with a drawn-out sigh like '*Here we go.*'

"I promise not to fuck it up," I said softly. Truthfully, seemed like it was kind of hard *to* fuck up. It was all one color and really just seemed like you needed to get all the hair and a good saturation.

She sat patiently while I worked and I did my best to concentrate and make sure I got everything. I mean, hell, it was something to do that would kill an hour or two, right?

12

*E*verleigh…

I sat still, my legs pressed together, crossed at the ankle, toes pressed into the hardwood floor. My hands were gripping the corners of my seat, expecting that he would pull sharply on my hair, but he didn't. He was as gentle as could be and was being very meticulous. Still, my back and scalp tingled. I wasn't precisely sure from which, though – from the fact he was being nice to me, or the fact that I was nervous.

My stomach churned a bit with the war of emotion going on in my heart and head. I mean, this man had nailed me to a tree. I was supposed to hate him for that, which was really damn hard because he was proving to be so patient and likable it was crazy.

I tried valiantly to rationalize things to make being around him easier. That he wasn't really Whiskey, prospect, then newly-patched member of the Knights of Crescentia. That he was Narcos, an undercover Indigo City police detective. I told myself the former was all an act; the latter, the man who was gently folding my hair over a piece at a time, making sure the lackluster auburn roots shot through with grey were coated completely, was the real man.

Still, it was confusing, watching bits and pieces of the two personalities overlap. It wasn't like Whiskey wasn't Narcos and Narcos wasn't Whiskey. They were the same man, so of course certain mannerisms, certain tics and personality traits would be one and the same.

"I know you're tense, and you have every right to be, around me, but I'm not going to hurt you, Everleigh. Never again. I promise."

I sucked in a breath at his words, and let it out slow and shaky. I tried to force my shoulders and back to ease, but it was harder than it sounded.

"It's okay," he said, and hurt was in his voice, which ridiculously made *me* feel bad. I sighed heavily. This was really complicated and messy, even if we were both hiding out from King and the Knights and it was for the best.

I wondered if he'd been in contact with Detective Stahl at any point, which made me wonder something else. I looked up and back over my shoulder and pointed at myself and then at him.

"I don't get it," he said at first and I repeated the motion. "You," he said when I pointed at myself. "Me," when I pointed at him. "You're Everleigh, I'm – oh! Duh. Club calls me Narcos, but I think you know that already. My given name is Darrin. Darrin Rutledge."

Oh. He didn't look like a Darrin. I mean, not to me. I didn't know what he looked like, honestly, but 'Darrin' wasn't what I'd expected, at all. I faced forward again and he moved gently to my side to continue what he was doing while I mulled this new piece of information over.

He let out a gusty sigh and said, "Okay, looks like I need that second bottle of dye mixed up, you good to do it for me?"

I nodded and stood up, the backs of my thighs sticking to the chair. It was hot in here, despite the open windows and what cross-breeze we could get from them. I pulled the tee down a bit, self-conscious, but it only tried to ride up when I sat down. I mixed up the second bottle of dye and made motion with my hand that we needed to hurry. It was so hot that my hair was almost dry in places at the roots, and probably wouldn't need much time to cure at all.

He slathered the dye down to my ends and re-moistened the roots and stripped off the goofy gloves. He helped me get the bag on my head and I looked at the back of the box, making the judgment call to go with the lower amount of time it called for. I held up fingers, first one, then the other, and he caught my meaning.

"Right, be right back." He fetched the old-fashioned kitchen timer from the kitchen and turned the dial to the correct time, and then I just sat and waited.

He looked me over and smirked, saying, "It's a good look for you."

I flipped him off and he laughed, cleaning up the dining room table and tossing the discarded boxes and dye bottles. I'd already done the dishes while he'd showered so there was literally nothing left to do but wait.

He smirked at how dumb I looked again when he went by to go back to his bed and I rolled my eyes at him. He laughed and flopped down on his back on one side of the bed, closest to the back door, and let out a satisfied 'ah.'

I'd lit the hurricane lamps and had taken the lantern outside to perch on the apple crate shelves/end table I'd created. We might have electricity finally, but the only actual lights were in the kitchen and bathroom, and the kitchen light wasn't very good.

Well, that wasn't exactly true. There was the blue light of a bug-zapper up by the back door, which, despite the porch being screened in, still crackled occasionally with another victim.

I went out there while the timer continued to tick away and sifted through my things to see what I still had. Some of it had been left behind in the hotel room. I was regretting using the closet and dresser for a lot of my things, now that I didn't have them, and was hoping that I would somehow get them back.

I paused when I found the nightgown I wanted, a simple country affair of light cotton, with a darted, square-cut neckline, and sleeveless, falling nearly straight to brush the tops of my feet. I was careful to hold it out from me, so I didn't get anything on it.

"Your time's up," he said when I stepped back inside, and I realized I didn't hear the ticking anymore.

"Bell's busted on that thing, it just clanged once and stopped ticking."

I nodded and he sat up. "Need me for anything else?"

I forced a smile and shook my head, unsure if he was trying to suggest coming into the bathroom with me or if he really didn't know all I needed was a wash and a rinse. I slipped into the bathroom and shut the door behind me, letting out a breath.

You have trust issues, Everleigh, I thought to myself. Of course I did. You didn't become a selective mute without issues. Problem was, nobody in my life growing up had cared enough to either get me help or accept any of the help that was offered to me. Instead, they just made things worse, made me more self-conscious, made me feel even more defective than I already was.

I started the shower and pulled the tee off over my head before I slipped the bag off my hair. I made a face at myself in the mirror and with my stiff, gooey hair I had to smile and giggle at myself. It was sometimes the little things, you know?

I got into the shower and immediately doused my head, watching the water run a deep burgundy-red edged in rust. If I hadn't seen so much blood from my hands not so long ago, I would say it looked like I had murdered someone. I knew better now, though. I knew what showering off dried blood looked like. I washed my hair twice and conditioned it three times until the water ran more sunset-pink.

My fingers were prunes and the holes in the palms and the backs of my hands were puckered around their edges. I carefully patted myself dry, letting my hair drip into the tub until I could wring it better and get it up into the towel. I wanted to have my body dried off as much as possible before I put my nightgown on, though.

When I stepped out into the main part of the cabin, I was relieved that Narcos was asleep already. I felt kind of bad for him in some ways; he'd put in a lot of work today. I smiled to myself about that. Between the both of us, we'd done quite a bit around here in barely two days to make it both more livable and more comfortable. Granted, more for me than for him, but this was his place. He'd said it more than once, although he shared it with someone, because whenever he talked about it, he kept saying 'we.'

I went out onto the porch and lumped his dirty tee in with my clothes that needed washing before I sat on the edge of my new bed. It creaked under my weight, the springs in the mattress probably older than I was, but it was comfortable enough and hadn't been too hard to move, considering there hadn't been a box spring under the mattress, just a sturdy piece of plywood cut to the dimensions of the inside of the bedframe.

I picked up my brush and set it beside me, using the towel to scrunch my hair. I sat in silence listening to the lazy chirp of insects and the river rushing by, out there; somewhere beyond in the dark. They were soothing sounds, even though my thoughts weren't soothing at all.

What if he's married? Just because he shares this place with his best friend doesn't mean he's not married or doesn't have a girlfriend. What would she think about him being shacked up out here all alone with another woman?

I worried my bottom lip with my teeth and had to ask myself, *Why do you even care, Everleigh? He nailed you to a tree. You're supposed to hate him, remember?*

I was almost ashamed of myself that I was finding that difficult –

hating him, I mean. If anything, I felt so very sorry for his wife or girl-friend, not hearing from him for long stretches of time, not being able to know anything about his life, everything kept secret.

I didn't suppose it was much different from being an ol' lady, though. There were lots of things as an MC member's ol' lady you weren't supposed to know. I know I was a bit of an exception. For some reason, my silence made it easy for King and the rest to forget I was even there. A lot of things that shouldn't have been talked about in my presence were, until they realized I was there. Then, usually, one would mockingly say 'Who's she gonna tell?' and everyone would laugh and I would be sent away or a door would be shut in my face.

Still, I knew too much. I know I knew too much, and it's why I wasn't surprised that King had thought it was me… except it wasn't. It had to have been Whiskey, I knew that now.

Whiskey, who nailed you to a tree so he wouldn't be caught… I thought bitterly, before the voice of reason intervened and said, *or in order to get you out, so you could testify. He* did *come back for you. He* has *apologized.*

That didn't negate the fact that he was likely doing all of it in order to use me.

That was what honestly hurt the most of all. I didn't like being a pawn, just another chess piece to move across the board in order for law enforcement to capture King and his men.

I sighed. I didn't know much about chess, just that smarter people than me played it; that the pawn was the smallest, most insignificant piece on the board, easily sacrificed; and that even though the king was the most important piece, the queen somehow held the most power. I wasn't a queen, though. I was just a teeny little fish in a big gigantic pond with much bigger fish. I was a pawn.

It didn't feel good.

I needed to be careful. I needed to keep reminding myself what I was to him: a means to an end. I needed to stop liking him… which was hard, when he was so damn likable.

I brushed through my hair until it was dry and then turned the lantern down all the way until it doused completely. I got under the sheet and my shawl. For now, I tried to put all the unpleasantness aside and just listened to the water, the trees, and the insect song, letting it lull me into a restful sleep.

No SURPRISE, he was up before me again. When I pushed myself up into a sitting position, I saw his bed was both messy and unoccupied. I frowned slightly and went inside to use the bathroom. The cabin was completely unoccupied, and I didn't hear anything from down below in the garage. I frowned, perplexed, and checked out the front window. No, the motorcycle was still there and I was sure that would have woken me up. Same for the big, old, lumbering truck.

I got myself dressed in my last clean dress, an olive-green peasant dress that hugged just below my bust to my hips with a wide swath of elastic. The cap sleeves of a peek-a-boo lace matched a wide band of the same across my shins, all the way around. It had been yet another of my spectacular thrift store finds, and my auburn hair and the olive tones to the dress made my eyes pop spectacularly against my pale skin.

I ran a brush through my long, thick hair and attempted to tame it, but I was afraid all I was doing was making it frizz worse.

It was muggy today, exceptionally humid and overcast out, but I wouldn't let that fool me. You could still sunburn through an overcast sky when you were as fair as me. I skipped putting on my boots, which were the only shoes I had. My sandals had been left behind at the hotel. I made my bed, laid out my nightgown for later that night, and padded down the back stairs.

I found Narcos at the river… or rather, *in* the river. He whipped a long fishing rod back and forth, flicking the far end gracefully through the air before he let fly and the line streamed on the thick summer air. The end of the line whizzed out over the river and disappeared somewhere along the rippling surface. It was impressive. He made it look easy.

I gently cleared my throat and he jumped slightly and turned to look at me.

"Oh, wow," he said. "That look suits you out here."

I smiled and blushed and reminded myself that 'likeable' didn't always equate a good person. After all, King had been charming at first.

"You okay? What was that look for?"

I raised an eyebrow and I admit I gave him a bit of attitude with my expression. He laughed and I kind of smiled; his laugh was a good one, the kind that said I'd caught him off guard in a good way.

"Right, yeah, keep it to yes or no, dumbass."

My eyes widened and I shook my head and he laughed again. I felt my shoulders drop and nodded. *Okay, okay, you got me.*

"Trying to catch us some fresh dinner for later. You like fish?" he asked.

I liked sea fish, from the ocean, once I'd tasted it. That was the best, so different, exotic from the fish I was used to getting in Indiana, which was predominantly catfish. I wasn't too fond of catfish, but it was okay every once in a while. I didn't have a way of articulating all of that, so I simply nodded.

"Good deal. Hoping to get something. To be fair, I just started. You got any big plans for today?"

I was already sweating and starting to feel kind of gross. I *had* planned to do laundry, but if he was fishing, I didn't want to get soap in our dinner so it could wait. I could make candles today, though, now that the stove was working.

I nodded and pointed back at the cabin and he cocked his head.

"More work on the cabin?"

I waffled my hand back and forth for *sort of* and he nodded.

"Can't tell me, I get it. I'll find out later. Just come get me if you need any help with any kind of heavy lifting, okay?"

I nodded and stepped into the river some, letting the cool water run over my feet, holding up my skirts. He watched me but I closed my eyes and took what relief I could from the heat. He nodded when I stepped back out, and as I made my way back to the cabin he turned back to his fishing.

I told myself that it was better this way, going our separate ways for the day, but damned if I didn't miss the quiet companionship that was developing between us.

13

*N*arcos...

She disappeared into the cabin and I turned back to fishing. I was having no luck, and a handful of hours later, she reappeared, wearing a baker's apron over her dress and carrying a basket.

"Where the hell you find that?" I asked.

She smiled impishly and held a finger up.

"The loft?"

She nodded.

"I really need to sort through a bunch of that shit and take a load to the dump, but as long as you keep finding useful shit, I can hold off."

She pointed at me and raised and lowered a hand. I frowned at first but then caught on.

"You found clothes that might fit me?"

She nodded and I nodded back. She put her hands together like she was praying and laid her cheek against them.

"You put them on my bed?"

She nodded.

"Good deal."

She looked at my rod and cocked her head.

"Nothing sizeable enough to eat, at least not yet. Where are you going?"

She pointed across the river to the woods.

"Be careful. Don't get lost."

She rolled her eyes, then put two fingers in her mouth and let off one of the most ear-splitting whistles I'd ever heard. I grimaced and nodded.

"Point made. You get into trouble, you do that."

She smirked, smug, and skipped along the edge of the river up the way to where it was shallower. I went back to fishing but kept an eye on her, as much as I could until she blended into the wood so seamlessly I couldn't make her out anymore.

She'd smelled of citronella when she'd come near and I had to guess she'd made her candles, which was a good thing. Despite the screens going up, we were still getting bitten. Not as much as we could have been without the screens, but yeah.

I managed to catch two sizable trout back to back in the next forty-five minutes or so and was grateful for it. I knew I had to hit town for those fuses, but I just didn't feel like going today.

She reemerged from the woods with more of those leek-looking things peeking over the edge of her basket and picked her way along the river's edge back to the shallows. She came back my way on our side of the river as I was emptying the guts of the second trout into the water to be swept downriver. She made a face and I chuckled.

"What'd you find?" I asked.

She smiled big and held up her basket. She brought it over and set it on the ground next to me, crouching beside me.

"Leeks that aren't leeks, is that garlic?" She nodded, and I kept on with the inventory. "Poisonous mushrooms."

She rolled her eyes and punched me lightly in the shoulder.

"Ow! Hey!" It didn't hurt at all, I just wanted her to feel better.

She laughed and shook her head, then moved the leeks aside and brought out the real prize.

"Holy shit, how'd you get that?"

She wrinkled her nose impishly and shook her head but the pint-sized Mason jar she held up was chock full of honey and even had a chunk of the comb in it. I shook my head and grasped her wrist gently, inspecting her arm. She took it back and waved a hand back and forth.

"You didn't get stung?"

She shrugged and moved her hair aside, there was a welt on the side of her neck and I sucked in a breath between my teeth.

"Good thing you aren't allergic."

She rolled her eyes and gave me a look that was clearly *'Really, dude?'*

"Right, like you would go reaching into wild bee hives if you *were* allergic."

She nodded her head once, a haughty expression on her face, like *'Pre-cisely'*. I smiled and shook my head.

"You're full of surprises, Everleigh. I really wish we'd met under different circumstances."

Her smile faded, and my own heart felt heavy in my chest as she stood up abruptly. She nodded her head *'Me too'* and turned, ghosting up the path to the cabin steps. I sighed and finished my task at hand so I could follow her.

She'd been productive. Candles in every conceivable type of container were lined up outside on the porch railing, from old soup cans to Mason jars of every size; I think she'd even filled an old metal coffee can, using three wicks for that one. She'd probably made enough citronella candles to last the rest of the summer season and then some. The air on the back porch was already heavy with the candle's perfume as they worked on setting up in the muggy and oppressive afternoon heat.

I went into the kitchen with the fish and over to the old cutting board next to the sink. She was at the sink, rinsing her finds from the woods, and washing the leek-looking vegetables and the garlic thoroughly.

"Fish is probably going to taste better," I said.

She gave a brave smile and made a filleting motion with the edge of her hand.

"Can I fillet them?"

She nodded and I nodded back.

"Yeah, not a problem."

I got to work on that while she tore sheets off a roll of aluminum foil she'd found in here somewhere.

We worked in our usual silence and I watched her out of the corner of my eye. She seemed almost content, moving around the small kitchen, like having the simple task of making something – a meal, or candles – or even just hooking this place up with a facelift was doing her soul some good.

She'd been a bit of a gypsy, a wanderer, when I'd met her running with the Knights of Crescentia, and I could recall that when we were out camping, she'd pretty much been happiest, but what I really think she craved was putting down some roots somewhere, making a space her own and staying for a while. I also got the impression she wanted to do it anywhere but where she'd originally come from, though I had no idea where that was. At least, not yet.

She put together foil packets of fish and vegetables and I asked her, "You want me to get a campfire going for those? Seems like a better bet than making it any more miserable in here by turning on the oven."

She thought about it a minute and finally nodded.

"Cool, I've got it from here, then. You want to set the table?"

She nodded and I put the plate with the foil packets in the fridge and went downstairs. It didn't take me any time at all to build a cook fire in the river-stone fire pit off the back porch. By the time it was going and I headed back upstairs for the fish, she had the table set and was sitting at one of the empty seats, fiddling with an old radio she'd found some-where, probably another treasure from the loft. There was just so much shit up there. I'd honestly been amazed that she'd been able to find anything up there, let alone a whole bed. The loft was jam-packed with boxes full of shit.

"Need help with that?" I asked and she shook her head, eyeing the plate of foil packets in my hands. I smiled and asked, "Hungry?"

She nodded emphatically and I chuckled.

"Okay, food first, and if you haven't got it by the time I get back in the house, I'll have a look at it while we eat."

She nodded, absorbed in trying to make the old radio work and I went down and cooked up our food. When I got back upstairs, she still hadn't gotten it and was looking at the old electronic mutinously.

I laughed and said, "Here, dish up and let me have a run at it."

It was old. As in, 'had a tape deck' old, so, probably the eighties? I fiddled with it and found that it plugged into the wall, but it also took nine-volt batteries. I wondered if that might be the problem, but didn't think it could be. That would be weird… unless the cord or the plug itself was bad.

I thought we had some around here in a junk drawer in the kitchen; we tried to keep batteries on hand, always. I went in the kitchen and looked and found the two the radio wanted, both different brands, but a battery was a battery. I didn't think it mattered much.

I flattened the frayed ribbon and stuck the batteries in. It didn't have the back plate to secure them anymore, but I didn't think that mattered too much, either. The light in the old-fashioned dial lit up and I edged up the volume to static.

Everleigh perked up and I twisted it until some synth-pop bullshit came crackling out of the speaker. She scowled and I kept going. Country came through next, and she grimaced. I smiled and kept going. Classic rock came next and she nodded, eyeing me speculatively.

"I can live with it."

She made the horns and head-banged for a second and pointed at me.

"Am I more heavy and death metal?" I asked.

She nodded and I shook my head.

"The real me likes all kinds of music. Classic rock is good. Some of the new stuff isn't bad. What about you?

She shrugged and kind of left off, pushing a plate of food at me. The leek-like vegetable had a sort of onion flavor to it and was pretty good with the mushrooms and garlic. The fish turned out good and both of us cleared our plates in record time.

She brought over bread and the fresh honey she'd gathered, and slathered a piece with it for dessert. It actually hit the spot.

We both sat back in our seats, satisfied, and she pointed at the radio.

I nodded.

"Sure, I'll listen to whatever you'd like."

I was surprised when she turned it to the AM stations and twisted the knob through news reports, landing on the Golden Oldies station. You know, shit from the 1940's and '50's.

"You like *old-school* old-school stuff, huh?"

She smiled, that secret little Mona Lisa smile of hers and nodded softly and I figured there had to be some nostalgia to it somewhere. I nodded and got up, thinking it must be a grandparent somewhere. She got up, too, clearing dishes, and I stretched with a gusty sigh.

"These the clothes you found up there?" I asked, rifling through what was on the bed.

She came around the kitchen's corner and nodded.

"Cool, some serious Farmer Bob shit," I said, holding up a pair of overalls. "But some of it should work. At least until Driller can bring his ass out here."

She peeked back around the corner and turned her head.

"When will that be?" I asked.

She nodded.

"No fucking idea, but hopefully sooner, rather than later. I'm running out of cash and I'm going to need some if I plan on hauling any of this shit out of here."

She heaved a sigh and eyed the loft, then looked to the floor.

"Yeah, I feel you. Believe me."

She held up her apron and made a scrubbing motion against her lap.

"You want to do laundry?"

She nodded.

I nodded and said, "Sure, we can do that. I suppose that's your way of saying hurry my ass up and get a clothesline up for drying."

She smiled sweetly, wrinkled her nose impishly and nodded. I laughed.

"I'll go see what I've got, but it's starting to get dark, so I may not get it up tonight."

She nodded and I went down to the garage.

There were two 'T' shaped posts planted at one end of the yard, sturdy, but there wasn't any line strung between them to hang anything on. I found some eye hooks still in their packaging and big spool of para-cord that almost matched the dress she was wearing in color. I went out and tried twisting one of the eye hooks into the wood and found it was harder than it looked. I didn't have a cordless drill with the right kind of bit, but I did have a pair of channel locks to grip it with and spare my fingers. It would work, but it would be slow going.

I worked on it until the light failed enough I couldn't keep it up but I'd gone back and forth between the two posts and had it halfway done, enough that I should be able to string some to give her a fair start while I worked the rest in.

When I went upstairs, I found her lounging on her bed, showered and clean, wearing her nightgown, her dress folded neatly on her apple crate shelf and the apron she'd found somewhere hanging from a rusty nail by the back door.

"Look at you go," I said.

She smiled over the top of a book she'd found, reading it by lantern light. I didn't quite know how she did it.

"I'm going to grab a shower and hit the hay," I told her and she nodded.

"Night, Everleigh."

She waved at me, her eyes still on her book and I chuckled.

Best I was going to get.

14

*E*verleigh…

The crack and boom shook me to the very core. I sat up in bed with a wordless yell, my heart pounding, disoriented, wondering if I was being shot at.

"Everleigh!" I heard faintly over the dull roar all around me and I scrambled out of bed, yanking my shawl around my shoulders. The world flashed blue-white, my eyes were blinded by the dazzle, and the cabin shook. I clapped my hands over my ears and shot inside the back door.

Narcos sat up in bed, his arms out to me, and I rushed into them. He lifted the sheet and tucked me in close and held onto me. I clung to him in return, frightened, and he pressed my ear to the center of his chest. His heartbeat was a rapid match for my own and it took some time for me to realize he was talking.

" – just a storm, you're okay."

I nodded, bobbing my head rapidly, unsure if I had been dreaming before being startled awake by the storm or not. Still, the shreds of bad memories and imagined fears of things that'd never been but *could* happen clung to me as I quaked against him.

He settled me against him in a way that was comfortable for us both and let out a breath. Eventually, I turned to face the windows and the water streaming from the sky beyond them while he clutched me back against his chest. His hands stayed positioned appropriately and he simply held me while the storm raged outside the windows.

I vaguely worried about my things on the porch getting wet, but I wasn't about to go out to deal with it right now. Not while I was comfortably warm, and safe. I hadn't felt either of those things in so long, I wasn't quite ready to give them up.

I know, I know, I was supposed to be on guard… but it was hard. With every passing day and every kind gesture he was chipping away at the foundation that held my walls in place. I couldn't find a reason to be terribly concerned about it, the more that I got to know the real him, his true self. So, I lay in the circle of his arms and indulged in the warm and fuzzy feelings that it brought and swore to myself I would reinforce those walls, shore them up, first thing in the morning.

THE NEXT MORNING WAS A FIRST. I woke before him… or so I thought. I drew a deep breath and tried to move carefully from where I was fetched up against his chest, my head on his shoulder when he chuckled deeply and kindly, saying, "Was wondering when you were going to join me. Welcome back to the land of the living."

I pushed off of him abruptly, and sucked in a sharp breath when my hands protested.

"Easy!" He held out a hand to me when I cradled mine awkwardly against my stomach. "Let me see?"

I hesitated before easing one of my throbbing, aching hands in his direction.

"They stiffen up on you?" he asked, examining it.

I nodded and he gently pressed his thumbs into my palm, massaging. I gritted my teeth, expecting it to hurt, which it did a little bit, at first.

"Too much?" he asked, and I shook my head. "Okay, good."

He worked on one hand for several minutes before letting it go gently and waving his fingers at me to give him the other one. I did, and I can't say I felt bad or guilty about it. Having him work on them felt *really* good.

"How's that?" he asked after a while, and I nodded carefully.

He released my hand and I stared at it for a few moments.

"You all right?" he asked gently, drawing in a breath and letting it out slowly.

I thought about it and looked up at him. He sat, his back straight, the sheet in his lap, his green eyes, darker than my own, searching my face.

I decided that I *didn't* hate him. That I couldn't be angry with him, and that I forgave him for what he'd had to do. I mean, it only made sense to, right? We were living together for who knows how long, and he was taking care of me. Letting me change his cabin to suit my whims, letting me roam without constraint and trusting I wouldn't run – although, honestly, where would I go? Better yet, why would I? I had it pretty good here.

I nodded and he smiled and it was as if some kind of truce had been declared. It was a moment of peace, of settling in, that was shattered by the rumble of a motorcycle's engine out front. I stiffened.

"Relax," he soothed. "It's Driller. That's *my* bike; I'd recognize her purr anywhere."

He got up and I drew my shawl around me a bit tighter. He went for the front door and I went for the back.

My 'room' had actually made it through the rainstorm of the previous night relatively unscathed. The candles had pools of water in their tops, which I poured out, and then I relocated them to my little apple crate shelves, which were dry. One corner of the bed was damp from a little bit of a drip from the porch roof. Given the buckets and buckets of rain that had fallen the night before, I was surprised it wasn't much worse.

The sky was clear and the sun already shining through the screen on that corner, so I didn't worry about it much. I simply made the bed and draped my shawl across it once more.

"Everleigh!" Narcos called, and I went back inside, clutching my dress and apron in my hands, intending to change in the bathroom.

Narcos stood with Detective Stahl just inside the front door.

"Well, look at you!" the Detective – Driller cried. "Got your hair did, huh?"

I pointed at Narcos and smiled with a bit of a shrug, gesturing past them both to the bathroom.

"Whoops, sorry," he said, stepping aside so I could get into it.

I shut the door and let out a breath, my anxiety rising – I hadn't realized how much it had calmed down over the last few days. I was sincerely hoping that he wasn't here to tell us that we needed to go back already. I wasn't ready to go back. I just needed a few more… *years*.

I hung my head and snorted at myself, impatient with my cowardice, but I had a lot to be afraid of. I liked being alive, and I wasn't down for whatever creative slow death King would have been dreaming up for me, after having been thwarted in his last attempt at it. I sighed and finished getting dressed and stepped out.

"Seriously, bro, you're saving my life right now. I've never been so happy to see my own clothes in my life," I heard Narcos say and I bit my lips together to try and suppress my smile. I hadn't exactly been enthused about the Deliverance-style overalls, myself. We were just running out of options for him without my ability to get the laundry done.

I left my nightgown hanging on the hook set in the back of the bathroom door and went out the front door to where the boys were standing next to their toys.

"See, now that looks nice," Driller said looking me over and I smiled. "Betcha you missed the rest of this stuff, though." He held up a small duffel bag, the kind you take to the gym, and I perked up. I went over and opened it up to find all of the things that had been left in the hotel when we ran, plus a bit more. I looked up, beaming and gave a little excited jump.

"Figured that'd cheer you up," Narcos said.

I cocked my head curiously, and pointed at him.

"Yeah, King had me get rid of your shit – I took it to this storage locker I have in the city instead. Figured you might still want it."

I lowered the bag and nodded, wishing I could force the 'thank you' I wanted to say out of my throat, which was tight with emotion.

"You're welcome," he said gruffly and I smiled. He cleared his throat and turned back to Detective Stahl.

"So, how long you stayin'?" he asked.

"Sadly, I'm not. We've got some things to talk about, but I need to make the ride back tonight. On my *own* bike, thank you very much."

Narcos gave a half-laugh and asked, "What was your excuse?"

"Broke down and in the shop, you let me borrow yers."

I rolled my eyes, wondering if the other cops really fell for that, then thought to myself, *they're a bunch of citizens at the end of the day, so of course they did.*

"Yeah, I was actually kind of surprised that one worked," he said and turned back towards the cabin saying, "Show me what you've done to the place. I see you got the porch screened in…"

Narcos made us a pancake breakfast, which was delicious but would have been better with orange juice. Driller handed him over a big wad of cash and said, "There's over a thousand there. No one but our club knows where you're at, and even then, they only know you're at our fishing cabin. Ain't none of them been out here or knows where it is. We were planning a ride out to visit, sometime around next weekend."

Narcos nodded and I swallowed hard. I didn't know if I was ready to meet his real club, even if they were all cops.

"Pasquale wanted to know how your hands are doing," he said, and I held them up, front and back. He eyed them and asked, "They hurt much?"

I waffled one back and forth in a *so-so* motion and he pulled an orange pill bottle out of his jacket pocket and put it on the table.

"Naproxen. Sorry it isn't something stronger, but Pasquale said it was the best he could do."

I smiled, but honestly, I figured they'd be handier if my period struck than they would be for my hands.

"Been into town yet?" he asked me.

"No, but it's full of busybodies," Narcos answered for me. "Baker and his wife saw her on our way in when we stopped to eat, and just about everyone I've come across since, in the couple of times I went into town, has asked about her."

"What'd you tell them?"

Narcos grimaced and said "I said she was my girlfriend. I figured they'd never buy 'sister'; we don't look nothin' alike."

"No shit you don't, she's way too pretty to be related to your ugly ass," Driller said without missing a beat.

My mouth dropped open and Narcos just laughed and said, "Fuck you."

I shook my head in amazement and stood up to clear the table and wash the dishes. I stacked them neatly, and fetched my apron before anything. I liked this dress and I didn't want to screw it up.

"I see you did some major redecorating," Driller said to me and I forced a smile and nodded. He smiled back genuinely and said, "It's nice, I like it. Got any other plans while you're here?"

"I figured we'd ding out the loft if it was raining, the garage if it's nice. Doesn't look like the river is going to be a good place to wash clothes today, Everleigh. You look at it?"

I shook my head, and went out the back door and stood at the screen across from my bed, to glimpse the river through the trees. It was slightly swollen, rushing and brown from the churned-up sediment. I sighed and went back inside.

I put my hands on my hips and looked around, and finally up at the loft.

"There's a Goodwill-type of shop in town, donate what they'll take. When it comes to the trash, there isn't really a dump around here, but there's a scrapyard about six miles outside of town. Might be able to get a little cash from that. If the town already knows about her, might as well take her with you, but don't share where you're from. If you have to pick a place, say Baltimore."

"Fuck, man. I miss my damn colors. My *real* colors," Narcos complained.

"I brought them, but leave them here."

Narcos shook his head and asked, "How'd the brass take us disappearing?"

"Pissed them right the fuck off. Pretty sure I'm going to lose my shield for insubordination by the time this is all over, but I don't give a fuck."

"Nah, you won't lose your shield," Narcos said. "You're just dead in the water for any type of promotion."

Driller nodded, but he didn't look like he thought he was missing out on much.

"I'd be shit at a desk job," he remarked dryly.

"Bullshit," Narcos snorted. "You're better suited to that shit than I am. I tell you what, though – "

"Robbery is looking better and better?" Driller asked.

"After this shit," Narcos said, casting a look behind him to where I had drifted to the sink. I got the impression he was looking less at me and more at my hands when he said, "Yeah," in the most resigned tone of voice I'd ever heard from him.

I bit my lips gently together after turning back around from the men and their conversation. It had looked like doing what he had done really had nearly broken him and my eyes became misty thinking about that.

He really *was* one of the good guys.

"You got any leads on who the mole in the department is?" Narcos asked.

"Not yet," Driller said.

"Seriously?"

"Still trying to figure out what to leak to who. Give us a little time.

Knights of Crescentia are fuckin' pissed. Joker told them all about you being a cop and the fact Everleigh's turned."

I scoffed and rolled my eyes.

"Right," Driller said, reading me loud and clear. He nodded as he voiced my thoughts, "What did they expect?"

Narcos grunted in agreement.

Their conversation turned back to the cabin and the small improvements we'd made over the last few days. I finished the dishes, drying them all and putting them away. I was still going to do the laundry, I was just going to have to do it here at the sink. First, though, I wanted to go through the bag Driller had brought and put my things away as best I could.

I found my sandals and stowed them beside my boots beneath the bed. I pulled out the wooden flat for apples that was only half the height of one of the crates and stashed my extra bras and underwear in it, grateful beyond measure to have them. I was wearing my last pair!

I heard Driller and Narcos talking down below, but they were far enough that I couldn't make out what they were saying. I peeked over the edge of the porch rail and smiled when I saw they were finishing stringing the clothesline for me. I was going to need that, so I was really pleased they were working on it while they talked.

I didn't have enough room to put everything away; what I couldn't find room for in my apple crates, I stored back in my leather bag so that Driller could have his back. My leather bag, I shoved under the bed, and stood up, startling when I caught Driller standing just the other side of the screen door.

"Sorry!" He put up a hand and laughed. "I was trying *not* to scare you. I've got to get back on the road."

I pouted some and backed up so he could let himself in. He shook his head grinning and said, "You even found an area rug?"

I nodded, pleased with myself. I couldn't wait to bring in some potted plants and light candles, it would really be amazing out here, then.

"You and he… you, uh, doing okay?" He searched my face, his own expression hooded, but worry and nervousness shining through despite his best efforts to hide it from me.

I put a hand on his arm and smiled, nodding. He looked relieved and said, "It wouldn't have been my first choice, but it was literally the *only* option at the time. You believe that, don't you?"

I nodded and did something unprecedented: I went up on my toes and I hugged him. Both he and Narcos had been nothing but good to me when they didn't necessarily have to be. He hugged me back and said, "Seems like you been taking care of my boy as much as he's been taking care of you."

I went down, flat-footed again, and gave a little shrug. I mean, I tried to be kind when people were kind to me. Hell, I tried to be kind even when people *weren't* kind to me. I did draw the line somewhere, though. *Like when your old man has you nailed to a tree.*

I probably should have left far before his drug-addled, psychotic brain had let him get that far, but… well, the more you know…

"You take care of yourself, Everleigh. I'll see you in a week."

I nodded and he smiled, patting me on the shoulder a bit awkwardly.

"Can't wait to see what else you've done with the place by then."

I smiled and gave a bit of a curtsy in thanks. He laughed, tipped an imaginary hat, and disappeared into the cabin. I closed my eyes and listened to his booted steps cross the floor and fade across the walk-way. A minute or two later, his motorcycle started up… and the rumble of the engine drifted further and further away.

"Wished he could have stayed longer?" Narcos asked from just beyond the screen door. I sighed a little and nodded. He smiled, a bit of nostalgia playing along his lips, nearly hidden by his unruly beard. "Yeah, me too."

I gathered my washing and he came inside the porch and asked, "Doing laundry at the sink?"

I nodded.

"I'll go grab the washboard for you, and I'll help. It's harder than it looks."

He wasn't kidding. Around halfway through the first article of clothing, the water still not running clear, he said, "Fuck this, load a bag or a crate. There has to be a laundromat in town. We can do the washing and bring it back here to hang. This is bullshit."

I nodded in wholehearted agreement. I may have been one with nature and all of that, but apparently I wasn't ready to be a full-on pioneer woman.

I put all of the laundry into one of the trash bags he'd bought and put another empty, clean one in with them to bring the clothes back in. I made sure to grab the laundry soap he'd bought and he took both from me and led me down to the truck. I grabbed my sandals from under my bed and hung my apron back up on the way by.

The old truck was in pretty bad shape, both the exterior and the interior. I sank into the bench seat and had to watch my feet, as there were holes in the passenger side floorboard. I kept my sandals clutched in my hands, afraid one would fall off and through the floor.

"Yeah, I need to put a piece of plywood or something down there. That's ridiculous."

I heaved a sigh. There was a lot that needed done in that place. The truck was the least of our worries. He glanced at me and laughed a little before saying, "My sentiments exactly."

I smiled at him and the old truck rumbled to life. The drive into town was pretty idyllic. We didn't find a laundromat, but when Narcos came out of the hardware store with the extra fuses, he hopped in the truck and said, "You ain't going to believe this."

I looked at him and cocked my head.

"Mitch called his wife, Nora. She told him to send us over to do our washing."

I blinked and crossed my eyes. Who did that? Invited strangers into their house like that?

"Good thing we are who we are, isn't it?" he asked, starting up the truck. I nodded and he said, "Yellow house, one street over from the smokestack." I made a choking noise and he laughed. "Right. Doesn't get more small-town than directions like that."

We found the house, no problem, an older woman in old lady jeans and a yellow sweatshirt with gray kittens and one of those white faux-collars waving from the front porch. She came stumping up her brick walkway to the white picket fence around her front garden calling out, "You must be Darrin and Everleigh!"

I smiled and nodded as he cut the truck's engine.

"We are!" he called past me, and I got out of the truck.

"Oh, my! Isn't this just the prettiest thing on you," she declared, fluffing my lace cap sleeve and taking me in. I blushed and dipped a little curtsy, and she laughed.

"Well, come on in! Bring your things and let's get it washing."

"Thank you, Ma'am. We sure do appreciate it. I can give you some money if that would be all right."

"Oh! It's only one load!" she cried, waving a hand at me, taking in the bag in my hands, which Narcos had passed to me.

"Appreciated," he said stepping up beside me. He'd changed into a gray tee shirt and a pair of worn jeans and looked sexy as sin. "We just need to wash. I put up a line this morning with my brother."

"Oh, is he staying out there with you?"

"No, Ma'am. Just came by for a quick visit on his way home."

"I heard two men bought the old Mercer place a few years back."

"Yes, Ma'am. That would be me and my brother. We just decided it was high time we started fixing it up. Everleigh, here, came with me because, well, she must really love me." He smiled at Nora, but the panicked look of *'I'm sorry!'* he cast me behind her back made me giggle.

She turned around and I nodded vigorously. *'Oh yes, absolutely. Love him to pieces.'* I tried to put it in my eyes and my face and she smiled warmly and held her screen door open saying, "Aw, now isn't that lovely?"

Nora was lovely and talking to her in her kitchen was a delight. She tried to feed us fresh scones, and honestly, she didn't have to try very hard. They were amazing and I had a mind to revisit that beehive to bring her fresh honey as a thank-you gift.

"You know," she said as we were leaving, "There is a Salvation Army in town, just off Coal Street. You might want to try there if you're lookin' for a place to donate anything, like you said."

"Thank you, and thank you so much for letting us use your washer. We would have been at it all day with that old washboard."

She smiled sweetly as I got into the truck and Narcos handed me the clean bag of washing.

"Y'all come back any time you need to." She patted his arm and he smiled, nodding.

He got into the truck and I smiled at him and he asked, "Need anything from town?" as Nora turned from her porch to wave.

I waved back and made motion like eating. She'd been so sweet when she'd learned I couldn't talk and had been surprised when I didn't know sign language.

"Right, we need to do some stocking up," he sighed and pulled away from the curb.

Our town adventure took longer than we'd thought, but it had been worth it. We'd stopped at the general store and had gone on to the butcher and the baker. When we got home, the clothes were still wet, but I now had clothespins to put them up with, thanks to a second trip to the hardware store.

I hung the washing, he cooked dinner, and we ate to the slow melody of the old-time music my grandfather had loved so much.

It had been a good day, I was happy, and so I began to sway lightly to the music at the sink. I spun lightly to put things away and caught Narcos watching me from over by the back door, coming in with dry clothing heaped in an old milk crate we'd emptied, sorting through things in the garage. We'd washed it thoroughly to use as a laundry basket for now, until we could either buy a proper one, or I could make one.

He slid it onto the dining room table and I smiled, put the plates away and wandered over to help fold clothes. He took me gently by the hand when I reached to pluck an item off the top and I stilled, looking up at him. He smiled and drew me out into the middle of the room, pulling me close and dipping me back.

I laughed and we danced through Frank Sinatra's version of Bobby Darrin's *Somewhere Beyond the Sea*.

I spun beneath his arm and he drew me in. He was actually pretty good at dancing and I felt myself relax, easing into his arms, his smile disarming, a moment passing between us, our steps slowing, my heart giving a painful, apprehensive squeeze even as it begged for him to close the gap between us. His eyes, heavy with desire, traced every curve of my face before settling on my lips with such an expression of pleading wanting.

Please... my mind and heart begged, my lips parting slightly in invitation. He sucked in a breath and closed the gap between us, his lips descending on mine gently, perfectly, but far from chastely. He kissed me, lightly at first, his tongue flicking out to taste my bottom lip and I groaned, melting against him, my body molding itself to his perfectly.

He broke the kiss first, his breath coming in ragged pants as I looked into his eyes and whispered, "More?"

15

*N*arcos…

Her voice was light, breathless with wanting me, and so musical to my ear. She went from wood nymph to sexy siren in the span of that one breathy syllable and I couldn't deny her. Hell, bastard that I was, I couldn't deny myself. I needed her like plants needed sun or rain to grow. She'd become food for my battered and weary soul and her forgiveness… Jesus, there was nothing else like it in the world.

I held her close, her fingers tangling in my hair, her body rising as she stood on tiptoe to press her mouth to mine. I kissed her back, my tongue exploring the sweetness of her mouth, my hands sliding along the hourglass curve of her ribs, the flare of her hips, my fingertips rucking up the skirt of her dress.

She moaned into my mouth as the material slid up her shapely legs and I groaned into hers in return. She did everything for me. She was beautiful, she was sweet, she was kind and gentle and forgiving – all of these things I wasn't.

That's what they meant, though, wasn't it? When men introduced their woman to you as their better half? I think I finally understood it like I never had before, because if she were my other half, she was certainly the better one.

She gave a little leap and I wasn't quite ready for it. I compensated quickly, though. Her long legs twined around my hips, her arms around my shoulders, her lips finding mine once more. I slid my arms around her back and felt her sex press against my thickening, hardening cock imprisoned in my jeans.

I had to fix that. I had to fix that, like, right then. I laid her across my bed and dry-humped her like a teenage boy. All the while, I worked at my belt and fly, trying to get my damn pants off. It wasn't helping me that her hands were first pulling at my tee, then warm and soft against the skin of my flanks. She sent them stroking over my ribs and my back, delving beneath my waistband, against my ass. She was pulling me into her, her hips rising and falling of their own accord as she let out these little moans into my mouth which I devoured like a starving man.

I had reached –and exceeded– my limits when it came to her and maintaining a professional boundary, and I couldn't help myself. I could and would throw my entire career away for her because I knew, deep in the bottom of my very existence, it was the right thing to do. That she was worth it.

"Tell me you want me," I growled, after tearing my mouth from hers.

"Yes," she gasped. "Yes, please, *now*."

It wasn't the most graceful or sexy move ever, flopping my cock out of my pants, smacking her pussy with it through the thin cotton of her panties, but she either didn't notice or didn't care, her voice like an angel's choir when she cried out in need. I slipped her panties off, whisking them down her legs and dropping them to the floor, and just managed to drag my shirt off over my head before I collapsed over her again, nothing between my dick and her hot, wet, velvet heat except my quickly fraying patience. I pressed hard with my hands against the mattress and let my gaze sweep over her.

"Oh, God, Everleigh. You're so fucking perfect."

She smiled up at me, and reached for me and I lowered myself over her once more, only this time, I rocked my hips against hers, trying to find purchase. The third time was the charm as I slid into her, too quickly at first, her body jerking beneath mine as she sucked in a sharp breath. I stilled and asked, "Did I hurt you?"

She shook her head and dragged my mouth back to hers and I eased into her body with mine, further.

She moaned and arched beneath me and my hands found her hips, pulling her onto me as much as I thrust into her. She pressed her hands to her mouth to stifle her next moan, and I shook my head.

"Don't do that, don't ever hide that perfect angel's voice from me, babe."

She arched beneath me, provocatively, and cried out a little as I found that spot inside her and started working it with slow, measured, angled thrusts, the head of my cock tingling, my balls tightening, that slow build I was used to moving instead with the speed and ferocity of a freight train.

I was so used to having more control than this, but this woman, this beautiful creature of fable and fantasy… she disarmed me in so many ways with those luminous green eyes. I cried out as she tightened up around me and drove myself deeper, bringing an echoing cry from her.

She touched every part of me she could reach, her hands stroking over my skin in light, butterfly touches, as if she was trying to convince herself this was real.

I had every intention of making her believe.

I hooked an arm behind her knee and placed one of her shapely calves against my shoulder, turning my lips to her leg, nipping her soft skin lightly with my teeth. She gasped, her even panting a seductive song as I kept a slow, even rolling rhythm with my hips, the head of my cock brushing against that slightly-roughened patch on the roof of her pussy.

Those luminous green eyes of hers were shuttered, her eyes closed as she surrendered to my touch completely. Her head falling back against the sheets, her long auburn hair a corona of deep fire around her face, she was an angel fallen to earth, and I didn't know how she'd found her way to my bed, but if she'd let me, I would keep her here forever.

It was getting harder and harder for me to keep myself in check. I wanted to come so badly, but I wasn't about to come first. I tried, I mean I *really* tried, but in the end I thought sure I'd failed. I drove into her deeply and both of us cried out. Her arms went around me, pulling me atop her body and I went willingly, caging her within my arms, cocooning her protectively.

Pleasure throbbed through my body, echoing my heartbeat and my ragged breathing, coursing through me thoroughly. I was about to apologize for coming first, for coming without her, but then she gripped me again in a gentle little aftershock and I realized we'd both pitched over the edge at the same time, had taken the plunge together, holding on to one another, in a perfect harmony that I don't think I'd ever experienced before, nor was I really certain I would again.

She put her hands on my bearded cheeks and turned my face to hers. I looked into her eyes from inches away and she gave me the sweetest, most tremulous smile and drew me down for another kiss, and I just lost myself in her. I was so completely under her spell that I would do anything I needed to become her knight, her champion. I would spend the rest of my life making up to her the evil, the terror I'd put her through, and nothing, I mean *nothing,* would so much as come near her again. Any harm that came her way would have to go through me first… whether she told me to get the fuck out of her life later on or not.

I pulled back from the kiss and searched her face, and fear slid through her eyes at the serious look on mine. I caressed her cheek and shook my head gently and said, "Nothing's ever going to hurt you again, babe. If it does, it will literally be over my dead fuckin' body."

She sucked in a sharp breath and placed one hand on my shoulder; the other she rested lightly in the center of my sweat-dewed chest, over my heart. She shook her head gently and whispered, "Don't make promises you can't keep."

"Oh, I'm keeping this one."

She shook her head and her eyes became dewy with unshed tears, her chin trembling slightly. I cocked my head slightly in question, and she murmured, "I don't want you to die because of me."

"I'm not going to let that happen, either, babe. My brothers won't. You're safe," I smoothed a stray lock of her long hair off of her forehead. "Life is going to be different for you after this chapter of it comes to a close. It's going to be better."

"You really think so?" she asked and her voice was so frail, the hope as delicate as a snowflake freshly landed on a blade of grass. Everything about her felt so fragile right that moment, but I wasn't making any promises I had no intention of keeping. I wasn't that guy. I would never be that guy again.

As soon as this case was done, I needed the fuck out of Narcotics; I needed to slow my roll. I couldn't do it to her, go back undercover, leave her wondering and going weeks without seeing me, not being able to tell her about my day or my time away from her. She needed full transparency and I couldn't give that to her as a Narcotics detective and I wouldn't.

"I really think so," I told her.

"You really mean it, don't you?" she whispered. "All of it."

"Yeah, Everleigh. I really mean it. All of it."

She wrapped her arms around my neck and buried her face in the side of my neck. I held her as best I could while also trying to hold myself off of her, but it was awkward and hard to keep up. Just as I was about to say something, she relinquished her hold on me and murmured she was sorry.

"For what?" I asked.

She shook her head and pressed her lips together and wouldn't be budged. I moved off of her and out of her and to her side. We lay next to each other, staring into each other's eyes, and even though she'd found her voice with me somehow, the silence that stretched between us was so full that no words needed to be spoken.

I loved that about her, like I loved a lot of things that I'd learned about her the last few days. She'd been through some awful shit. Trying shit, that would have broken a lesser woman to pieces, but she somehow stayed whole. Not only that, she somehow managed to still hold a sense of wonder in everything around her. She was resourceful, intelligent, beautiful, thoughtful, and just my type of perfect but I knew if I tried to tell her any of hat, she'd refute my claims, because she was also so very humble.

"Sleep with me tonight," I asked her, and she smiled and nodded.

"Outside?" she asked.

"Sure, I'm happy to do it at your place," I said and winked and she laughed. It was a good laugh, high and clear and sounding so free.

I laughed with her and drew her forehead to my lips and kissed her softly there. I was sure her eyes drifted shut and she just melted into me in the sweetest way.

God, I would die to protect her, and fuck any motherfucker who would try to stand against me.

16

*E*verleigh…

I didn't know what had possessed us, but there was no going back now. Problem was, I didn't want to go back. Ever. I wanted to see where this would lead but I was afraid. Not for me, but for him. I mean, weren't there rules against sleeping with a witness during an active investigation? Granted, I was a willing participant, and I do mean –absolutely– willing. It was a lovely summer evening, the dulcet sound of insect song and rushing water the perfect backdrop for what I was doing. The citronella candles burning around us cast his skin in golden light, and my fingertips lovingly traced his tattoos as he looked up at me.

I was straddling his hips, nude, letting the outdoor air wash over my skin as I reached between us and raised his cock up off his stomach so I could slip him inside me.

I couldn't remember ever being so aroused before. I mean, I was positively dripping wet with my eagerness to make love to him and he was so gentle, so perfect, and so kind about it. He was easy on me, his hands splayed across my hips, smoothing over my skin like he'd never felt anything so soft.

My nipples pebbled in the slightly cooler air out here and I threw my head back and gasped, working my body up and down his shaft, gripping him with my pussy as I rolled my hips. I felt like I was part of the divine like this. Like we were performing for the ancient gods and goddesses, the moon our witness to this rite, this offering of our joined bodies.

I felt as free as I'd ever been, and worshiped by this man beneath me, all-powerful, a goddess in my own right. It was beautiful, a powerful feeling like no other. Spectacular and winsome, I wanted to feel like this forever and the promise of it was reflected in his eyes, but I'd had promises before, and promises were meant to be broken.

"Like that," he whispered. "Just like that, babe."

"Yeah?" I whispered back, gently.

"Oh, yeah. I want to remember you like this forever. Every time I think of you, I want to see you just like this, wild, beautiful, and free. Body bathed in golden light, fire in your heart showing just behind those cat-green eyes of yours."

His words stole my breath, his body took mine to heights it'd never been, and I wanted it. I wanted to stay just like this forever and ever, and so tonight, I let myself believe.

"God, Everleigh, you've got me under your spell," he growled when I bent over him, and he buried his hand in my hair and dragged my mouth to his. He kissed me with such a fiery passion it sparked flame through my soul, spreading through my veins, and I swore I rose like a phoenix from the ashes and I soared.

"Oh, God, yes!" I gasped, and I came, my pussy gently pulsing around his cock. Not as intense as before, but lasting; it felt like I flew for hours without ever having left the ground.

I drifted lazily in the afterglow, hazy, warm, safe and held fast in his arms and I vaguely remember my voice asking him, "What happens tomorrow?"

He chuckled, the vibration of it thrumming through my body and he said back, "Tomorrow you'll still be you and I'll still be me, and I'll still be here with you, and I'll still feel the same. You'll be safe, and we'll make this place better, together. Sound good?"

I nodded against his shoulder, my body limp where it was draped over his, my eyes too heavy to keep open. I mumbled, "Sounds good," and it was the last thing I remember until the sun came up the next morning, casting fire through my eyelids.

I moaned and shifted and realized I was in bed, alone, but then something blocked the sun and cool glass was pressed into the palm of my right hand.

"Morning, babe. Here, drink this. I'm afraid you might be a touch dehydrated."

I cracked one eyelid and immediately fell in love with the sexy smirk on his lips, half-hidden by his beard, which I loved but was in desperate need of a trim. I pushed myself up with my other hand and hissed at the twinge in both it, and between my legs.

Good sex will do that to you, Everleigh. I smiled and drank down half of the quart Mason jar full of water he'd given me.

"That's my girl," he murmured. "How you feel?"

"Well-fucked," I smiled warmly and he laughed.

"Glad I could be of service." He cocked his head to the side and traced his middle finger across my forehead and behind my ear, taking the hair that'd been in half my face with the gesture so that he could see me. He heaved a satisfied sigh and whispered, "There's my beautiful girl."

I felt myself blush and his smile grew.

I shook my head and said, "I don't feel beautiful."

"Mm, why do you say that?" he asked.

I heaved a heavy sigh and said, "I just feel… broken."

"Well, I feel special that you've decided you're comfortable enough to speak with me."

I smiled and asked, "How much do you know about selective mutism?"

"Nothing, other than there's nothing physically wrong with your voice. You *can* talk, you just choose not to."

I shook my head and bit my lips together for a second before I started to cry. It was so frustrating and humiliating talking about it. I cleared my throat, which was trying to close on me, my anxiety starting to bubble to the surface. I forced the words out and tried not to choke on them.

"Th-that's not exactly it. It's not that I *choose* not to, it's literally that I *can't*. It's a severe form of anxiety, of f-f-fear and it's like it chokes me. It strangles me and cuts off my voice, my air, and I c-c-can't!" I covered my face with my hands and not for the first time thought to myself savagely, *Why can't you just be normal!* Except the words took on my father's voice, my mother's scornful tone and the mocking cries of the children I'd gone to school with on the playground and finally in the halls.

The only person who hadn't treated me like a freak had been my grandfather, and he'd died when I was thirteen. My last escape, my only beacon of light in an otherwise dark existence had disappeared.

"Shhh, it's okay," he soothed, smearing the errant tear that escaped my lashes across my cheek. "You don't have to explain anything to me that you can't or don't want to, babe."

"I-I-I want to, though."

He nodded and smiled at me and it was one of those perfect smiles that meant exactly the right thing at exactly the right time.

"So how come you're talking to me now, huh?"

I shrugged a little helplessly and said, "I guess that part of my brain that's defective is comfortable with you. I have to be completely comfortable and at ease for the words to come."

He nodded slowly and I could tell he was thinking.

"Didn't anybody try to get you any help for this as a kid?"

I shook my head.

"Where are you from, anyway?"

"Indiana."

He nodded some more, his eyes unfocused and distant as he puzzled through something, and I waited with bated breath for what he would say. He finally came back to himself and smiled at me and said, "I'm not sure what to do to make things easier for you."

I smiled and shook my head and said, "I get along just fine."

His smile grew into a grin and he said, "You got that right. You're one hell of a woman, Everleigh. A force to be reckoned with. Voiceless, sure, but still the loudest personality in the room. I knew it the moment I saw you."

I wrinkled my nose and said, "You don't have to compliment me every five minutes. I don't need it."

He chuckled and smacked a kiss against my lips and said, "Oh, I think you do." He got up with a gusty sigh and said, "Feel like a day off from this place?"

I frowned and drank more of my water, lowering the jar and asking, "What did you have in mind?"

"A hike. There's a swimming hole, complete with a little waterfall, around a mile or so up the river."

I raised an eyebrow. "I wasn't brave enough to go that far."

"Good, you shouldn't go that far, not without me, anyway. You ever want to, I'm happy to go with you."

I smiled and said, "You're so accommodating."

"I'd follow you into hell if you asked me."

"Why?"

He shrugged and said, "I think it started off as guilt, but now? It's something else. Something better, but I don't really have the words for it."

I shifted slightly uncomfortable with the turn in conversation. He saw it and smiled again, switching topic back to hiking.

"You got better shoes, and maybe, not skirts for this?"

I nodded. "The boots I came here in, and I have a pair of shorts and some blouses."

"That'll do. Hungry?"

I was starving. He laughed at the look on my face and said, "I'll fix breakfast."

"Thank you," I murmured and he went inside the cabin.

I finished my water and got out the clothes I would need for this trek. I did go in and take a quick shower, mostly to rinse off the sex of the night before. The best sex was always messy and left you sticky the next morning, and the sex we'd had was definitely fun and, as such, had ended up being exceptionally messy.

I dressed quietly and went out to warm toast with butter and honey and a plate full of eggs and bacon. I smiled appreciatively as I wound my hair up on top of my head in a tight bun and used a hair elastic to secure it.

"Smells good."

The smile he bestowed upon me when I spoke was enough to send a rush of pleasure through my body, an echo from the night before. I smiled and blushed faintly and slipped into my seat at the table.

"Feel okay?" he asked.

I nodded.

"A little sore, but if you aren't a little bit by the next morning, I feel like you didn't do it right, you know?"

He laughed and said, "There's the wild child."

I wrinkled my nose and asked, "What do you mean?"

He chewed his bite of food and swallowed before saying, "A pretty girl like you doesn't manage to hook up with the likes of the Knights of Crescentia by accident. You have to have a bit of a wild streak in you to stay with a biker."

I nodded carefully, realizing he wasn't judging, just merely making an observation.

"I come from a town a little bigger than this one," I said. "Which is to say, 'boring', or at least, it was to teenage me. I couldn't wait to get out, and neither could my best friend Mariah. This biker gang, the Steel Wraiths, rolled into town and spent a rowdy night in Mariah's bar. We weren't even old enough to drink or serve liquor, but again, small town."

"How old were you?" he asked me.

"I was just a few days shy of eighteen, Mariah *was* eighteen."

"You graduate high school?" he asked and I pursed my lips and shook my head.

"That's surprising," he remarked. "You're smart as hell to know what you do out here. What's edible and what's not."

I smiled. "I learned all of that way before high school," I said. "My grandfather taught me what to forage for and how to hunt until he got too sick to do it anymore."

"And the thing with the honey?" he asked. "Was that your grandpa, too?"

I smiled big and nodded. "He used to keep hives but he taught me how to deal with wild hives, too."

"That's an impressive skill."

"Not particularly useful outside this scenario, though."

"I guess not," he said ruefully. "Sorry, I didn't mean to get us side-tracked."

"It's okay."

I told him about how Mariah and I blew town with the Steel Wraiths and how we'd ended up connecting with the Knights of Crescentia. He listened carefully, a pensive look on his face and nodded when I ran out of things to say.

"Sounds like life back at the old homestead was real bad for you."

I nodded. "I'm guessing you're saying that because life with outlaw bikers was so much better by comparison." I rolled my eyes some, but there was some merit to the assumption.

He nodded and said, "When those outlaw bikers are like King, yeah."

I looked away and sighed, saying, "He wasn't always like he is now."

"Oh, I don't doubt it." He leaned back in his chair, the creaking sound it made bringing me back around to look at him. "Abusers are always charming at first, telling you what you want to hear, making you feel important… then when they get comfortable, and their true selves start to come out, the gas lighting starts and the manipulation and the bull-shit until it gets so heavy – "

"You're so afraid and so hopeless, you think you can never dig out. You're afraid of what they might do if you tried and who they might hurt if you leave and they can't find you… I know," I said softly.

"You're a real smart girl, Everleigh."

"That's the problem, though… I am a girl." I sighed.

"Part of it, I'll agree. Not all of it, though. Part of it falls on your folks. How you were raised."

"Or wasn't, in my case," I said sardonically.

He nodded carefully.

"Rome wasn't built in a day, babe. This is just the first day in the rest of your life."

I cocked my head slightly and regarded him, really thinking about what he was saying.

"I suppose so," I said, strangely bolstered, emboldened by the thought.

"Carpe diem," he said with a shrug.

"Seize the day?"

He nodded.

Don't mind if I do.

I smiled, and said, "Let me grab my basket and put a few things together."

"What, like a picnic? Good idea."

I smiled and put together some sandwiches, wrapping them in aluminum foil since that was all we had. I filled a couple of quart Mason jars with water; we had, like, a million of them around here, and put lids on them, screwing them down tight with their accompanying rings. It was supposed to be hot today, like it had been every other day since our arrival. It was definitely the dog days of summer out there and I almost couldn't wait for fall to arrive. I loved my boots-and-sweater weather. It was my favorite season, and all too short.

"Let me grab a couple towels," he said and disappeared around the corner towards the bathroom. I slipped an empty jelly jar into the basket to collect the honey for Nora in, and when he handed me the towels, I tucked one around the jars to stabilize them, and the other I draped over the top of the basket.

"All set then?" he asked, and I nodded and took his offered hand. He linked his fingers gently between mine and brought the back of my hand carefully to his lips. He looked solemn as he gently laid his lips against the mark in the back of the hand he held and closed his eyes. A look akin to grief crossed his face and I stepped closer and sighed.

"You had to do it, or we'd both be dead. I get that, now," I murmured and his eyes, a darker green than my own, more earthy, more real, locked onto mine. He didn't speak, and I knew the feeling, I could read the fear and anxiety on his face and in his eyes. I mean, what do you say to the person you nailed to a tree a couple of weeks ago, then nailed in bed last night? 'Complicated' didn't even begin to cover it.

I gently took my hand from his and laid it against his bearded cheek. I wished there was some kind of way to say this without words, because words just didn't seem to do these kinds of emotion justice.

"I forgive you," I said. "I don't know how long it will take for you to forgive yourself, though, and that seems to be the bigger problem here."

He sighed and let out a shaky laugh, his smile quickly dissipating. He searched my face and said, "Honestly? Probably never."

I nodded and tucked myself against his chest, loosely putting my arms around his waist. He sighed and put his arms around me and held me close for a minute before rubbing my back lightly through my blouse and taking a step back. He held me loosely by my shoulders and said, "I promise, no one will ever hurt you like that again."

I smiled and said, "I know, you've said."

"I mean it. I need you to know that I mean it. I mean *really* mean it, Everleigh. Never again. It'd have to be literally over my dead body."

I put my fingertips against his lips in a soft touch, "Shh, don't talk like that. I more than kind-of like this, whatever this is we've got going on between us. It's nice. It feels… I don't know… *real.* Like, realer than anything I've felt before."

He nodded and I took my fingertips away.

"I was thinking the same thing," he said and swallowed.

I smiled, uncomfortable with deeply-emotional revelations of any kind. I said, "I'm really looking forward to cooling off. I'm happy to follow your lead, so lead away."

He chuckled and nodded, hooking a hand behind my head, his thumb caressing lightly just behind my ear and he leaned forward and kissed my forehead. My eyes drifted shut and I shivered lightly as a sense of peace and well-being descended on me. It was gone as soon as he took a step back and I fought not to sigh. Instead, I smiled and motioned toward the back door, "After you."

"Ladies first," he murmured, holding it open for me.

"There's a lady here?" I asked, quirking an eyebrow.

"Ah, she found her voice and now you got jokes. Nice."

I wrinkled my nose and grinned at him, and stepped onto the back porch. The heavy mood of the moment before was lifting and lightening the more we stepped out of the shadows of the cabin and its porch and into the sun. By the time we reached the river's edge and trekked to the easy-to-cross shallows, we were laughing again, baiting one another with harmless barbs, engaging in witty repartee.

It'd been a long time since I'd felt so relaxed, so completely at ease with another person, let alone a man. The last person I could so easily talk to was Mariah, but I hadn't seen her in at least two years.

It was refreshing, a welcome change, and one I hoped wouldn't be fleeting, even though I didn't hold out much hope that it could be anything other than a brief interlude of happiness for me. Nothing good ever seemed to last and I didn't want to fool myself into thinking it would, or could. Instead, I tried not to let the anxiety, the constant sense of foreboding I always had anytime I thought of the future, ruin what I had right now.

"Wait!" I cried, and he stopped and turned, once we had crossed the river.

"What is it?"

I smiled and bit my bottom lip, excited to share this part of me with him, he cocked his head, a half-grin taking up residence on his own lips, a smile I found incredibly sexy and endearing and one I noticed him turning on me with more and more frequency.

"This way; I'll show you." I held out my hand to him and he back-tracked to me and took it. I didn't hesitate, stepping off the riverside trail and into the woods beyond.

"Where are we going?" he asked after a few minutes and I laughed lightly.

"We're almost there, I promise. Do you hear that?"

He stopped, dragging back on my hand and listened, a puzzled look on his face furrowing his brow, which smoothed when his eyebrows went up and he realized what he was listening to.

"Oh, I don't know, Ev…"

"Relax, you won't get stung, just come here." I tugged on his hand and he followed. I just needed him to take something like six more steps to our left to bring the tree and the hive into view.

"Holy shit," he muttered and I smiled.

"Just stay right here, and *don't move,*" I told him. I knelt and flipped the towel covering the basket off the top. I dug out the kitchen knife I'd stashed against the side and the jelly jar, and took off the latter's ring and lid.

"Hold these for me?" I handed them up and he took them, his eyes a bit wide, looking at the huge hive in the cleft of the dead tree.

"Everleigh, I really don't think – "

"Relax," I said and stood up. "It's fine, really." I turned and went and did my thing. My grandfather had always said the more fear you exuded, the more you fussed, the likelier you were to get stung, and so I approached the hive slowly and deliberately, the way I'd been taught.

Of course, my grandfather had mostly worked with hives he kept in boxes, but when bees moved into houses and attics, he went and rescued the hives, until he couldn't do it anymore. I'd tried to keep up with his hives when he'd died, but I couldn't.

I swallowed, my eyes misting. I felt closest to him when I put the knowledge and lessons he'd given me to good use, like now.

I carefully cut a bit of comb, thick with honey, from the edge of the hive and put it into the jar. I cut another bit of comb and squeezed the honey from it, the bees buzzing around me. I listened to them for agitation, careful not to upset them terribly. I managed to get away without being stung, this time. I'd been less lucky last time, but I had still been lucky in that neither time I'd visited the hive had the bees swarmed on me.

I turned back to Narcos triumphantly, and carefully and slowly stepped down off the gnarled root I used to stand on to get to the part of the hive I harvested from. He watched me, silent, apprehension on his face as I walked slowly back to him.

"Wow," was all he said as I handed the jar to him.

"Cap that for me, please? I need to rinse my hands back at the river, I'm afraid I'm a bit sticky." I winked at him and he laughed lightly and secured the lid on the jar.

"That was a trip," he said. "Where'd you learn how to do that?"

"My grandfather was a beekeeper."

"Huh."

He tucked the jar back in the basket and draped the towel over it, taking up the basket without being asked.

I held out my hand, my fingertips coated in thick, golden honey.

"Want a taste?"

He gave me a devilish look and took my middle and ring fingertips into his mouth, sucking them gently.

I'd been teasing, sure, but he was much better at it, the look in his eyes powerful and raw, leaving an ache at the apex of my thighs that had nothing to do with any residual soreness from our lovemaking the night before.

"Mm, never had it fresh from the hive before," he murmured.

"Glad I could be a first for something," I whispered, breathless.

The look he gave me was seriously intense when he said softly, "You're a first for a lot of things when it comes to me, Ev."

"Yeah?"

"Yeah." He stepped into me and lowered his mouth to mine, the kiss sweet and thick with the honey he'd just sucked from my fingers.

I made a small noise into his mouth, my knees weak, my heart thundering in my chest. I swooned, and he caught me around the waist with one strong arm as I held my sticky hands and kitchen knife out from us.

This man was amazing, and I much preferred him to Whiskey, wishing I could have met the real him much longer ago and without all the fuss and danger that was the Knights of Crescentia. I kissed him back with every bit of passion and arousal that I felt when I was with him and wished that this could be a forever kind of love, that a happily-ever-after with him could be a thing… but I knew better.

If you lost a shoe at midnight, you were drunk, not a fairy tale princess. Fairy tales didn't exist, not for girls like me. For now, though? For now, I would just let myself pretend.

17

*N*arcos…

She was incredible, so giving, so fearless, giving of herself completely despite how much, how many times, she'd been screwed over. She wasn't afraid to try, to believe in me, even though I know she had every reason to doubt me, not just by the way others had treated her, but by how I'd treated her, myself, in the guise of Whiskey.

She melted into my embrace so willingly, so trustingly, and it was so beautiful it almost made my heart ache. It definitely galvanized my resolve to keep her safe. She riled every one of my baser male instincts like no other woman and it scared me, a little. There was no telling how any of this would end up, and I didn't want to make promises to her that I couldn't keep… but at the same time, I wanted to promise Everleigh everything. The moon, the stars, the very sky itself – all she needed to do was ask and I would move heaven and earth for her.

Thing was, I knew she would never ask. It wasn't her way. Of course, with me, she didn't have to ask. That wasn't *my* way. You didn't become a cop out of selfishness, no cop ever started out that way. The streets jaded us, consumed some of us, but me and my brothers refused to go down that road. We weren't weak, we held ourselves up, held ourselves to a higher standard, and we held each other accountable.

She didn't have anything to worry about now, but I didn't think it would be any kind of easy convincing her of that. She'd heard a lot of lip service, I could tell, so I wasn't about to be one of those guys. I was going to show her, rather than tell her, and hopefully, eventually, she would know, she would learn there really were trustworthy men out there, even despite our definitely-rocky start.

I'd never wanted a forever with anyone before, but she'd ensnared every one of my senses and now I couldn't fathom any kind of forever without her. It was a serious mind blower for me and I wished I could talk to my brothers about it, see if it was the same for them, see what they said. I felt in over my head with Everleigh, but at the same time, there was no place, no one, I would rather be with.

I broke the kiss by planting several little butterfly kisses along her jaw and down the side of her neck. I placed one last, gentle, chaste kiss against her shoulder where the neckline of her peasant blouse had slipped off, and straightened.

She looked at me, speechless, but for the first time, I think, out of something much different than her usual anxiety or fear. She didn't need to say anything to me though, those luminous green eyes said it all. I pulled her into my arms, wrapping her up in them soundly and she laid her ear against my chest, her own arms twining around my waist, even though she held her sticky hands out and away from me, my holding onto the basket made things a little bit awkward on my end, too.

She took a big, cleansing breath and sighed out, and it was the sound of a woman laying her burden down, of a woman who had finally come home. I loved that sound. I loved that I could bring it out of her, and I think, to be honest, I was just plain in love with her, as scary as that sounded to me for so many reasons.

"This is nicer than anything I could ever have imagined," she finally murmured and I smiled, laying my cheek on top of her silky hair.

"Isn't it just?" I asked.

"It's also very hot, and sticky," she continued, "and the bees are going to be attracted to the honey, so we'd better move."

I laughed and let her go and she stepped back.

I winked at her and said, "To be continued."

Her eyes turned bright and she said, "I really like the sound of that."

We walked together back to the riverside, and she rinsed the knife and her hands in the fast-moving water. She put the knife away in the basket and made to take it from me, but I shook my head as we resumed our initial hike.

"I've got it."

She took my free hand and we walked on.

"What about you?" she asked, suddenly.

"What about me?" I asked.

"Where do you come from?"

"Born in Baltimore, raised in Indigo City."

"Really?"

"Yeah, why? Is that hard to believe?"

"You seem really at home out here, I can't picture you thriving in a city."

I was a bit mollified. She stepped up on a fallen log and balanced her way across it, her arms out, yet she wouldn't let go of my hand. I smiled and raised my arm up to help her as she navigated her way across the crumbling bark.

I nodded and said, "My granddad was a fisherman; I learned from him. If he wasn't fishing off the wharf or out on his boat in the bay, then he was knee-deep in the closest river. Deep sea or fly fishing, it didn't matter. He was like a junkie."

"Yeah?" I asked.

I nodded, a bit solemn. "Yeah. He also had a really unhealthy addiction to gambling. Lost his boat, died pretty bad; owing the wrong kind of people."

"Is that why you became a cop?" she asked, quietly.

I nodded. "Part of it. I wanted to stop those kinds of people."

She nodded. "Then how did you get into undercover and drugs?"

"I just went where the job took me, to be honest. Drugs and gambling are kissing cousins. Both of them are under the same umbrella; that's Vice."

"I thought Vice was just hookers and johns."

I chuckled but had to sigh. "A lot of those hookers are hooking because they're addicted to drugs and trying to feed a habit. A lot of them are being trafficked. There's a lot of money to be had when it comes to exploiting sex workers."

She looked unhappy, a shadow passing over her face, through those eyes, and I wondered what thought had traveled through her mind and dimmed her sparkle. She heaved a sigh and said, "I guess I should feel lucky that wasn't me–"

I stopped her and said, "Look at me, babe."

She looked at me, and I untangled my hand from hers and grazed her cheek with my thumb.

"There's nothing 'lucky' about what you've been through, living like you have been, with King, or with the MC you were with before his." I paused, and tried to figure out how to put it. "Just because someone's had it 'worse' doesn't minimize your experiences in the slightest. You've been through trauma, and trauma is trauma."

She nodded and said, "I know," turning her face into my touch, her eyes closing as if she wanted to commit every little good thing we did together to memory, as if it wouldn't happen again, as if it needed to be savored.

It pissed me off, but I kept a lid on it because I didn't need her thinking I was mad at her. Far from it. I was mad at the people that had put her into so many positions, time after time, to make her feel like she didn't deserve anything good. The ones that made her feel like that was what life was, going from trauma to trauma, bad experience after bad experience, with only brief breaks of happiness in between. They'd left her so bereft that she had to find what little joy she could in the tiniest things.

That last bit was what made her so damn impressive, the fact that, despite the shit that just kept being heaped on her slender shoulders, she managed to find any happiness in life at all.

It was a rare and beautiful thing that someone could go through so much, yet hold so much hope in her heart.

I knew I certainly couldn't do it.

I knew that I had become a pretty bitter bastard the longer I'd stayed under, and that I couldn't work fast enough or hard enough to reach that light at the end of the tunnel. I just hadn't expected that light to be her, and she'd been walking beside me this entire time.

"I remember the first time I saw you," I said, as we resumed walking.

"Yeah?" she asked.

"Mm-hm."

"At the bar, right?"

I shook my head. "Surveillance photos, actually."

She laughed. "That doesn't count."

"Doesn't it?" I asked. "Even from the photos, I feel like I got a sense of you, you know?"

She shook her head. "No. I mean, how could you? I don't think seeing a person in a picture or on TV counts."

"Okay, fine, then. It still wasn't the bar."

She frowned. "Then where was it?"

I chuckled. "The jail. I was in the visiting room when you came to see King."

"You were?"

"Yup, talking to Driller. He was sitting right next to you at the glass. I was right next to King the whole time."

Her puzzlement grew, her brow furrowed as she tried to remember. I had to smile, and stopped our trek and said, "You picked up the phone and put your hand to the glass and didn't say a word, but your compassion was clear. It was a trumped-up charge, for sure, but we needed him jailed in order to facilitate a meet. My 'saving his ass...'" I put it in air quotes. "It was all a joke, every dude in that fight was a cop. He was never in any real danger. Just needed to initiate contact in a believable way."

She wrinkled her nose in that adorable impish way and said, "I didn't really feel too bad about the set of raccoon eyes he walked away with," she said. "I felt bad about *not* feeling bad, if that makes sense." She thought about it for a second and said, "And I felt bad about his getting locked up, because he may have done a lot of things, but what they arrested him for? He didn't. I figure if you're going to be punished, it should be for something you did, right?"

"He really did kill that man, didn't he?" I asked.

Her expression became solemn then, and she nodded. A flicker of guilt crossed her fair face and I sighed.

"I should have come forward," she said.

"You were scared," I said with a shrug. She nodded, but only looked more miserable, almost guilty. "Hey, it's not your fault."

"I didn't want to die too," she said plainly. "I watched him shoot that man, and it didn't faze him." She shivered despite the heat. "Like, at all."

"He's killed a lot of people, babe. He may have shot Jory Marsh, but he's killed a lot more than that with that poison he's peddling."

She nodded and whispered, "I know. It was just easier not to think about it like that."

"I never expected, in a million years, that he would think that bust had come by way of you," I said. "What he did to you was my fault, through and through."

"What *did* happen?" she asked.

I thought about it, and decided, even though I *shouldn't* tell her shit, that she was on our side, and, given what she'd been through, she deserved to know.

"This conversation never happened," I said and she rolled her eyes slightly, that Mona Lisa smile crossing her gorgeous lips that I had such a hard time keeping myself from kissing.

"Who would I tell?" She asked. "You?" I chuckled and she made an 'X' over her heart with her finger.

I shook my head and captured her hand gently with mine, saying, "Don't do that."

"What?" she asked, her eyes wide.

"Cross your heart and hope to die. I so very much like you alive," I said in a low tone, the words just between us, even though there was no one out here to hear.

She swallowed hard. "I didn't even think about it like that," she said evenly.

I placed her hand against my chest and she spread her fingers over the material of my soft tee-shirt. I kept it there, my hand over hers, lightly, reveling in the feeling of her touch, so new, yet so familiar already. I loved when she touched me as much as I loved touching her.

"I was being a good cop. I told my handler, Driller, what was going on. He passed it up the chain. Someone above him got it in their head to make a bust, didn't pass it to Driller, I didn't get any advance warning – it was a shit-show all the way around. I thought for sure my cover was blown, even though I wasn't at the meet or the bust. I had no idea it somehow landed on you."

She shook her head. "It wasn't your fault," she murmured.

"It was…"

"No, it wasn't." She swallowed hard and blew out a breath and said, "I think it was Grave Bass."

"Grave Bass?" The guy was a big dude, played bass guitar. Not sure how he got 'Grave' as part of his road name. I did know he had a temper, but he was smart about it. He didn't fly into fits of rage and fuck things up. No, he did shit dirtier than just knocking your damn teeth in. I could see it, but what I couldn't see was *why*.

She didn't answer.

She wouldn't make eye contact with me when she shook her head, and I could literally see her sliding back into her shell, cringing on the inside, away from an unpleasant memory.

"Hey, easy, deep breath. It's just you and me out here, the sun, the water and the woods."

Her gaze flicked back to mine and she looked grateful for a moment, before she rushed out, "I can still feel his hands on me when I think about it."

I froze up but tried to lock it down, to make my face unreadable before it was too late. She touched the side of my face like I had hers, stroking her thumb just along where my skin gave way to the unruly scruff that my beard had become. In some ways, I couldn't wait for it to go, in others, I wished I could keep it, just not in the state it was now.

"Did he hurt you?" I demanded.

"I'm okay," she assured me. "I just don't like thinking about it."

"Did he rape you?" I asked, and my voice sounded hollow, even to me. I was gutted just thinking about it.

"No, but given the chance, I think he would have." She swallowed hard and rushed the story out. She'd been coming back from the bathroom at the back of the bar and Grave Bass had stopped her in the narrow hall on his way back to the john. He'd pinned her in the corner by the old, all-but-defunct payphone and had cupped her pussy through her skirt. He'd said a bunch of seriously lewd and ludicrous shit and had scared the ever-living shit out of Everleigh.

He'd been drunk, but that hadn't excused it. You *never* touched or hit on another brother's old lady. You *never* fucked with a man's property like that. It was enough to net yourself the ass-whoopin' of the century, at a bare minimum. At the worst, it put your ass out-bad with the club. Depended on the club and their tolerance for drama. King and the Knights of Crescentia had *none*.

You could look, within reason, and your thoughts were your own. If you didn't get caught looking too much, and you didn't voice those thoughts or act on them, then who was to say? Grave Bass had grossly overstepped.

"You didn't tell King, did you?" I asked, finally.

She shook her head and gave me the answer I was expecting, "With how tight the brothers are, and how much he'd been using, I was afraid it would somehow end up my fault. You know?"

I nodded. I did know. It was a man's world through and through, and a woman, even the president's woman, was at the bottom. We all knew shit rolled downhill. She looked away from me again, her bright green gaze somehow dimming as the shadows of memory flitted behind them.

She stared at nothing when she said, "I thought if I kept it to myself, everything would be okay."

"But Grave Bass probably sobered the fuck up, got real insecure about it, and put a bug in King's ear and let King's drug-induced paranoia take care of the rest," I supplied.

"That was my thought, yes."

"Coward wasn't even fuckin' there," I muttered.

I closed my eyes, pained for her, and she shuddered, her hand slipping from beneath my hand, from against my chest.

She said quietly, "Are we anywhere near this swimming hole of yours? I could really use to get in the water."

I couldn't blame her. If I were her, I'd want to wash the stain of those memories away, too. I smiled with a bit of a false brightness as I tried to swallow and digest everything she'd told me and said, "Yeah, actually. We're here."

18

*E*verleigh…

The water was cool and refreshing, but after only a few moments in it, it grew to be *almost* too cold. I was letting it hold most of my weight, but was twined around Narcos' fit, inked body, my legs wrapped around his waist, my hands on the swell of his shoulders. His big hands resting against my back stabilized me as we talked over the sound of the river tumbling over rocks into this pool.

It wasn't just a swimming hole; there was a waterfall, too, and it was unbelievably beautiful here. I loved it.

"We need to talk about later this week," he said, and I felt my mood sink a little.

"What about it?" I asked, pointedly.

He chuckled and said, "Look, I don't want to deal with it this soon, either, but it's happening, whether we like it or not."

"I know," I said unhappily, and he sighed, shifting one hand from my back to my hip as he spun us lazily in the pool.

"I don't know how many of the guys Driller's bringing with him, but it's a long ride and they're probably going to want to stay the night. Go over some things when they get here, and a few more before they take off the next morning."

"And?"

"And – that means we need to have someplace to put them up, or you up… This has become your space for the time being, so what'll it be? We moving you up into the loft, or are they crashing up there?"

"There's a lot of stuff up there," I said.

"I know, which is why, either way, we got our work cut out for us over the next couple of days."

I chewed my bottom lip and thought about it and finally said, "I'd rather they stay in the loft; I'll stay on the porch with you."

He shook his head sadly and said, "You're a witness…"

I blinked and realized, *Oh shit… he could lose everything, being with you, Everleigh.*

"Oh…" I trailed off and felt the blood drain from my face.

"Hey, no, don't do that. I didn't mean it like that."

"No, I get it," I said quickly. "Being with me, you could be sanctioned, fired, or whatever. Lose everything you've worked for… I don't want to see that happen."

I let him go but he didn't let me go, just walked us both to where I could stand in the pool, too and we could talk. Although, I suddenly didn't so much feel like talking. I suddenly just wanted my clothes, and to go back to the cabin.

"Don't for one minute think I am treating this as just some sort of fling, babe. That isn't what this is," he said, suddenly so very serious.

I met his eyes with mine, slightly defiant, which was more just me trying to be guarded. He sighed again, and looked unhappy – though not with me, more at himself.

"Do I want to lose my job? No. Do I want you? With everything I am." He put one hand against his chest, the other resting still against my back as I shivered in the river water. It was cold, not being tucked against his warmth, like I was.

"You can't have your cake and eat it, too," I murmured and he frowned at me.

"The fuck I can't," he said. He searched my face and looked uncertain for a moment. Finally he shook his head and said, "Look, I know I don't have any right to ask, and this is totally up to you, but as much as I fucking hate the idea… I can only think of one solution."

"Let me guess: hide what we have between us until after the trial is over?"

He nodded and he looked like he genuinely felt like shit for even asking. I pressed my lips together and took a deep breath. It *was* a shit thing to ask, and I *was* angry, but I couldn't say that I was angry specifically at him. I was angry at the whole situation, at the whole world for letting me down, time and time again, but if it was one thing I'd become good at over the years, it was plucking myself up after one of these pity-parties and forging ahead. It was just a matter of deciding, in my heart of hearts, what was best and how to proceed.

I closed my eyes and twin tears slipped beneath my lids and spilled in scalding lines down my cheeks.

"Don't clam up on me now, babe. Talk to me."

"I'm just so tired of *everything*," I said, my voice trembling. "If it's not this, it's that; if it's not that, it's another thing, and I am just so tired of going through it."

He captured my face between his hands and tipped my head back so I would look at him. I opened my eyes and sniffed and he looked me over, his eyes fierce, his expression set in undeniable determination.

"You aren't going to go through it alone, babe. I'm here, I'm right here, and I'm not going anywhere."

I looked at him, desperately wanting to believe, but I'd heard such empty assurances before, and here I was, with him, not them… *And there's no place you'd rather be.*

His expression cooled and hardened into steel as he read my face. His shoulders eased from their tense posture, though his hands, where they held my face, had never gripped too hard, had been as gentle as if he handled a kitten. He trailed his fingertips down the sides of my neck and rested his palms on my shoulders.

"I'm not going to tell you again unless you really need the reminder," he said quietly, and shook his head. "No, I'm just going to put up. I'm here, Everleigh and I'm not going anywhere. Whatever happens, it's not just you going through it. *We* are going through it. Together. Always. I'm not giving up on us for anything. You're not disposable to me." His arms slid around my shoulders and I fit myself against his chest as the tears welled and spilled, as if my damn face had suddenly become a running faucet.

I clung to him in the pool and let his warmth comfort me, and as much as I wanted to hide behind my walls, as much as I wanted to duck behind my shield of experience and hold my doubt tight and close to my chest, I was weak because I *believed him.*

"It'll be okay," he breathed into my hair.

"Don't make promises that are so hard to keep," I mumbled, as my last moment of misery passed like a leaf riding the surface of a stream.

He chuckled and sighed, holding me tighter and said, "You have every reason to be bitter, but you aren't. Every reason to tell me I'm full of shit, but you don't. You're something special, babe. I don't know how I made it this far without you. I feel like with every act of trust you put into me, you save a part of my soul. Wash away some of the dirt."

I pushed back from him and frowned. "You're probably the best man I've ever met," I told him honestly, and he laughed at that.

"Should meet some of my brothers, they're by far better men than me."

I found that extremely hard to believe.

19

$\mathcal{E}$verleigh...

Four days later I stood under the warm shower spray, aching and exhausted. We'd just finished cleaning out the loft the day before, and I'd spent the first bit of the morning dusting and sweeping it out. I'd felt gritty and covered in dust, so while Narcos was bumping and throwing things from the pile in the back yard into the back of the old truck, to make a final scrap run, I was trying to clean up myself instead of the old cabin.

We'd worked hard the last several days, making one trip into town to the second-hand store to donate what we could. The little shop had been full of treasures for me, and Narcos had let me splurge on his dime, buying me two dresses, a blouse, and three different skirts without a single word of complaint. He'd even bought me the big, floppy straw hat with the dusty fake flowers that I had been eyeing, telling the clerk to bring it down and add it to the pile.

I hadn't wanted it to wear, but rather, I had a vision for it, one I set to work on while we did our washing at Nora and Mitch's house. I'd given Nora her gift of honey and Narcos had gone out to help Mitch with a project. I was at ease enough with Nora that I told her my plans for the hat, and she'd beamed and said she had just the thing. She'd given me the materials out of her sewing stash and wouldn't hear of taking payment.

It was a project I worked on in the evenings until I was too tired to keep my eyes open and Narcos pulled me away from it gently, into his arms so I could fall asleep against his chest.

That was, honestly, becoming the best part of my day, and I was stressed that his brothers would be here soon, and I would have to do without that comfort.

I stuck my face into the spray and thought for a second that I heard something, but figured that it was just Narcos, coming in to use the bathroom. When I heard a stream of water hitting water, I smiled to myself and thought, *Couples achievement unlocked.* It was a milestone, albeit one that, once you'd had sex with another person, was kind of silly.

He knew not to flush when the shower was running; I'd accidentally found it out the hard way when I'd used the toilet while he was in the shower. I thought it'd been a myth, but apparently, old plumbing –

He flushed and I shrieked and cried out "Hot!"

The shower curtain whisked back along the rod and I was faced by one stern and angry-looking prosecutor.

"You can *talk*?"

I screamed and grabbed for the curtain, trying to hide behind it–

But he wasn't looking at my body. His dark eyes were drilling into mine–

And my throat was seizing shut, tighter than a Venus fly trap, trapping my words inside–

All that was coming out when I tried to speak were frightened screams.

He reached out and took my wrist in a firm grip and kept going on about me talking and I just kept screaming, not knowing what to do, the panic taking over, sucking me under, I was drowning in fear and adrenaline –

And suddenly he was just… gone…

And in his place was Narcos, and I burst into tears.

"Hey, hey, hey; it's okay, I've got you, babe. Shh, shh, shh."

I held onto him, rattled to the point I couldn't even get words out to him if I tried. I bit my bottom lip until I could taste the slightest bit of copper, and then eased off with my teeth. Sometimes, a little bit of pain helped ground me, helped bring me out of the frenzied loop of panic that shuts me down, but this time – it wasn't working.

What *was* working was the solidness of Narcos' arms around me, the softness of his tee beneath my cheek, the hardness of his body covering mine as voices rose, out in the rest of the cabin. He reached over and shut off the water, and lowered me to kneel in the tub, while the voices outside grew louder before ceasing altogether.

I swallowed hard, and held myself tight to Narcos' chest as he reached up and pulled the beach towel off the rack and wrapped it around my shoulders.

"Easy, babe. You're okay. You're solid. I don't know what the fuck Yale's problem is."

I swallowed again and looked up at him, my eyes wide, and he looked down at me. "Yale would be the guy that busted in on you."

I frowned and then it clicked: *The prosecutor is part of his real MC?*

"You got clothes in here?" he asked, as I knelt in the bottom of the tub in just a beach towel, my hair sopping wet and his tee turning from light to dark grey as it soaked up water.

My brain finally caught up to what was happening as it broke free from my fright, and I shook my head violently, as much to say 'no, I didn't have any clothes in here' as it was to try and clear it.

"Okay, wait here, I'll get something for you."

It would be easy, I'd laid everything out on the bed. He smoothed his hands over the towel, along my back, arms, and shoulders, drying me as much as soothing me, and stood up from where he sat on the edge of the tub. He helped me to my feet and shut the seat and lid of the john and had me sit, wrapped like a child in the oversized towel.

"Be right back with some things, you hang tight." He squeezed out the gap he cracked in the bathroom door in a bid to preserve my modesty, but I saw no less than two unfamiliar faces look my direction, the third belonging to Driller.

I hated the looks of pity; I hated being pitied, even though I could agree I had my moments where I was pitiful. I felt my cheeks burn with humiliation as their voices, too muffled to understand, came through the door. I knew they were talking about me, of course they were talking about me. How could they not?

They probably thought I was nuts. Too damn nuts to testify… *Oh, God… what if I'd just ruined everything? What if I screwed everything up so badly just then that they wouldn't let me help, they wouldn't let me say what I knew, and everything fell apart, and King and the rest of the Knights got away with killing that man, with trying to kill me?*

What if…

The door opened back up and I jumped, but it was just Narcos. He set my clothes on the edge of the sink and knelt in front of me, looking up at me, heaving a sigh.

"What can I do?" he asked.

I shook my head. *Nothing, he couldn't do anything.*

I couldn't either. I just needed to ride it out, to feel the awful feelings and wait until I was a bit calmer.

"Okay, you take your time. You get dressed, and you come out, but *only* when you're ready. Okay?" I nodded and he thought about it a second and said, "If you need me to come back in here for anything, you knock three times on the door, okay?"

I nodded emphatically and grasped onto the kindness with both hands, holding it to my chest.

"I mean it. Take your time, take as long as you need," he said, and knelt up, kissing my forehead gently before he stood. I closed my eyes, the press of his lips against my skin doing wonders to calm me, but at the same time, all too brief. He stood up completely and went to the door. I made like I was knocking three times in the air, my expression solemn and he nodded.

"Knock three times if you need me," he said, and I nodded, and then I was alone.

I closed my eyes, let myself have a brief, quiet cry, and then got up to fix myself and get my shit together, feeling a bit stronger, a helpless anger replacing the anxiety.

I looked at myself in the mirror.

Other than being a touch pale from the encounter – and looking like a complete drowned rat – I didn't look much different on the outside.

I hated that. I felt like my anxiety had completely changed my land-scape on the inside and that there should be some sort of reflection of something so jarring on the outside, but there wasn't. There never was.

I set my clothes aside on the john, dried myself, wrapped my hair in the towel and washed my face.

I stared for a long time at myself, looking scrubbed and clean, and had to sigh. Sometimes, I really wished my outside matched my inside. If it did, then people might understand.

Sometimes, I really hated my life, my existence. I felt like a magnet for abuse and I was so fucking tired of it. So tired. I stared at my hands, at the shiny pink scars, front and back, through the palms and out the backs of my hands, and closed my eyes.

I was tired of it, and it was time for me to stop doing the same thing over and over again, which was live passively through it, bouncing from one bit of bad to another like a pinball in a machine, going from bad to worse and back again.

The worst had pretty much already been done to me, hadn't it? There wasn't much worse to go to from here, except maybe death, and I wasn't keen on dying. I was a live-er, not a die-er and I wasn't about to go down without a fight. I just needed to convince the men out there that I had some fight in me and that I wouldn't crumble.

Good luck with that, Everleigh.

arcos…

Well, so much for that, I thought to myself as soon as I stepped out the bathroom to the spectrum of looks ranging from cool and appraising to downright tempestuous from my brothers.

Driller looked, I don't know, resigned? Golden looked amused, Skids gave me a cool, detached cop-face, and Yale? Yale looked *pissed.*

"Are you, seriously, fucking my witness?" he demanded, and I knew shit wasn't right with him. I don't think I'd ever seen him lose his shit so completely. He was always a man in control, but something was going on back home that had his fuse fucking *lit.* It'd been burning for a while, considering how he'd snapped off on Everleigh just for talking.

"Think she's going to *be* your witness if you treat her that way?" Driller asked, and scowled.

Yeah. He knew; he had my back; we were at least cool. Best friends for-fucking-ever.

"You knew about this?" Yale demanded.

"Come off it," Golden said, and rolled his eyes.

"Didn't expect to see you here, Pres," I greeted Skids.

Skids shrugged laconically.

"Shit's real deep. What kind of leader would I be if I weren't here?"

I walked over to the table and pulled out a chair. "How about you stop seething for thirty fucking seconds and catch me up; you fuckers know I've been livin' dark out here. And I ain't no mushroom, so don't even think about feeding me some shit, either."

The guys all drifted over and sat. Six seats, one left for Everleigh. I'd be lying if I said I wasn't worried about her, but I refused to make shit any worse than it already was, by looking at the door she was behind too much.

"The defense has come out swinging," Yale said with a harsh sigh. "Trying to force my hand, speed everything along. I'm assuming it's because they know Everleigh *can* talk – "

"She can talk, but she can't," I said, unhappily.

"She *can*, I just heard her." Yale scowled at me.

I shook my head. "She probably thought you were me," I said, shifting slightly.

"Again, I ask, *how long have you been fucking my witness*?" Yale demanded starkly, his eyes stormy.

"If it's good enough for Youngblood…" Golden said, and it was gentle for him. He gave Yale a pointed look.

"That was different," Yale said defensively, and Driller arched a brow.

"How so?" my best friend demanded.

"Knock it off, the lot of you," Skids growled. "This isn't getting us anywhere productive."

"She's capable of speaking, but only under certain circumstances," I said with a sigh.

"Those circumstances being?" Yale crossed his arms, and shit had to be rough, had to be getting to him, because even though he could be a dick, he wasn't usually this big of a pain in the ass.

"Calm, secure; she's got to feel safe and completely at ease," I said.

"Which she's not going to be, in front of King or a courtroom full of people," Driller said unhappily. "She hasn't said a damn word in front of me, that's for sure."

The bathroom door opened and we all turned. It took several moments, but finally, Everleigh peeked around the corner. It was so childlike and innocent and it damn near broke your heart, the expression on her face. It was like she was checking to see who was mad and how mad they were at her, like she was expecting to be yelled or screamed at, or worse, that someone was apt to tow her out from around that wall and beat the living daylights out of her.

"You're safe, babe. Coast is clear, I promise."

She bit her lips together and looked miserable anyway. It was as if someone had rubbed off some of her sparkle and I hated it.

She stepped out carefully, wearing a white, fitted tank top with those thin straps and one of her gypsy skirts that brushed the tops of her feet. The skirt was a light cream at the top and got progressively darker in brown toward the bottom, the different bands of the skirt set with these tiny round and diamond shaped mirrors that sparkled and flashed in the sun coming through the windows.

She was lovely and I held out a hand to her to try and entice her to come nearer.

She hesitated, hanging back, her shyness full force despite the fact that only two of my brothers at the table were unknown to her.

"It's okay. I apologize. It's no excuse, but I have been a bit frayed; this case is very complicated." Yale at least tried.

She nodded carefully, forgiving as ever, but still wary as she padded nearer. She took my hand and I decided, *Fuck it. The cat was already out of the bag.* I pulled her down into my lap. She sat atop my thigh, and with a hard swallow, put her arms around my shoulders to steady herself.

"Look at me," I murmured and she met my eyes with her own. "Just take your time, and talk to me… you okay?"

She swallowed hard and opened her mouth, but closed it as she glanced down the table at the expectant faces there.

I stopped her.

"Don't look at them, baby. Look at *me*."

Her eyes snapped back to mine and I tried to put everything she needed into my gaze.

"Just one word, babe. How are you doing? Good? Bad? Scared? Sad? Just one word, tell me what's up."

She swallowed, determination flooding her expression as her jaw worked, once, twice, then… "S-s-scared," she whispered.

I smiled and she flushed beet-red, and I nodded.

"It's okay to be scared, brave girl."

She shook her head and I tucked the hair she'd used as a curtain to shield her face from the rest of the table behind her ear.

"It's the very definition of bravery to be scared as shit to do something, but going ahead and doing it anyway," Skids said. "For us, it was one word; for you, it was a whole lot more. You did good."

"I'll try to keep it to 'yes' or 'no', okay?" Yale said, and though he was tense, his tone had gained more than a few measures of control. Everleigh nodded and he asked, "Does King know that you are capable of speaking?"

Everleigh nodded.

"You've spoken to him before?"

She nodded again and I caught her eyes as she bowed her head in something like shame.

"I think she trusted him, once. They were in a relationship."

"You know what happened?" Golden asked.

Everleigh bit her lip and took a deep breath and our eyes met. I nodded slowly and said, "He started using more, drinking more. The real him started to come out, and I think, ultimately, nailing her to a tree probably did some irreparable damage to that relationship."

Everleigh nodded emphatically.

"Yeah, I suppose that would," Skids said, drawing a deep breath and huffing it out. He looked Ev in the eye and said, "I'm sorry that happened to you."

She nodded solemnly and I asked, "So what's this mean, in the grand scheme of things?"

Yale sighed and said, "It means, she's going to have to get up and testify, otherwise she's pretty much a useless witness."

Everleigh's jewel-bright eyes widened and she looked stricken.

"Do you think you can do it?" Yale asked point-blank and she took a deep breath and we could all see she thought about it, and I mean really *thought* about it.

"I'll be right there in the courtroom, babe. We can practice as much as possible between now and the court date."

She nodded but looked apprehensive. But she was willing to try. As hard as it was for her, she was going to try. She was brave as hell for it, too.

"Y'all figure out where the leak is coming from out of the department, yet?"

"Ugh, God…" Driller looked a little green. "Been working with the rat squad, do you have any idea how much fun *that* is?"

Chuckles went around the table.

"Worth it to catch a rat," I said.

"Too true, and we've come up empty for the most part. I hate to say it, but it was a dead end."

"Which is why we have to move you two," Golden chimed in.

Everleigh sat up straighter and turned her full attention on him.

He smiled a little sadly and asked, "You like it here, do yah?"

She nodded and he shrugged and said "Sorry, darlin', but it's not safe here for you anymore."

"Ah-huh, is that why the backup?" I asked.

Driller, Yale, and Skids nodded.

"It was Skids' idea, actually," Golden continued.

"What was?" I asked; Everleigh had gone rock-still in my arms, her fingertips biting into my shoulder.

"Had Driller let it slip out in the open about the fishing cabin, and that he owned it, but not where it was," Skids said.

"Before that, he had me make a trip down to the assessor's office, and drop notice that if anyone should come looking for information with my name attached to it, that they should give us a call."

"Rat squad sitting on the office?"

"Yup."

Everleigh stood up abruptly and was out the back door in a flash. I stood up and so did the rest of the guys. I waved them down and said, "Let me go talk to her."

"Guess she really likes it here," Yale muttered and I nodded.

I found her standing by the river, her chest heaving, bent double with her hands on her knees as if she'd just run a marathon.

"Easy, just take it easy, it's only me," I said when she'd like to hit the roof when I came up on her.

"Why would they *do* that?" she asked, her tone agonized.

I shook my head. "Sometimes, it's what you have to do. When all else fails…"

She shook her head violently, as if she didn't want to hear it, and it clicked for me: she was *angry* and she didn't have anywhere to put it.

She'd told me how she'd grown up. How her dad was an abusive fuck and how her mother just let him do it, sided with him over her own daughter, told Everleigh to stuff it down, to be a good girl, to not rock the boat, etc., etc.

She'd been a girl with a stutter and he'd beat her ass for it more than once, until she'd just stopped trying to talk altogether. She'd grown out of the stutter, but her anxiety about speaking in front of anyone, well… it'd reached epic proportions. Left her scarred, left her broken in some ways, and made her so much stronger in others.

I couldn't blame her for hopping on the back of the first bike to roll through that shit town of hers. I also couldn't blame her for not looking back. No matter how bad it'd gotten, back there was worse for her, so she only looked ahead.

"I know you love it here, babe, and this isn't forever. You knew we'd have to go back eventually…"

"No, I know," she said. "I just… Why did it have to be so soon?" For this, she did start to cry.

"I feel you, there," I murmured and went to her, and she folded herself against me so beautifully.

"Where do we go from here?" she asked, voice muffled by my still-wet tee-shirt.

"I don't know," I said. "We're going to have to go back inside to find that out. I can tell you one thing, though…" She tipped her head back to look up at me when I didn't finish right away, which is what I wanted her to do. I needed her to look at me for this. "It doesn't matter where we go, I'm going to be right there with you."

She nodded and I dipped my head to kiss her. She met me half-way, standing on her toes. Our lips touched and fire raced through me, breathing tired muscles back to life. I held her close, but carefully, my hands gentle against her waist, curving around to her back as her hands slid over the swell of my arms, over the caps of my shoulders to twine around my neck.

It was one of those movie-perfect kisses that made women sigh and men wish they could be that guy on the screen, and damn, did it ever feel good to be her man. To be the one to hold her, to be here for her, and to love her… because without a doubt, I did.

Out of the ashes… I thought to myself, because that was definitely what we were. A couple born out of the ashes of bitter circumstance, and while those circumstances weren't over yet, we had this. We could take on anything as long as we had each other. I needed her to know that. I needed her to believe me.

A gentle clearing of a throat, and we broke apart, though not guiltily. Not in the slightest. There wasn't room for anything negative between us.

"Damn, that was hot," Driller said, and Everleigh blushed and hid her face against my chest.

"The natives restless?" I asked, and he nodded.

"Fuck 'em," I said. "They can wait."

"What can't wait is you guys packing your shit up. We've gotta go first thing."

"You get a call?" I asked, and he looked at me like I was dumb.

"Ain't *none* of us getting a call out here, you know that! Which is why we need to go first thing."

"Where the hell you even got us going?" I demanded. I didn't like not being a part of the plan, but I trusted Driller with my life, and there wasn't anything about to change about that.

"Youngblood and Chrissy's," he said.

I rolled my eyes.

"You serious?"

"You rather park it in yet another shitty hotel?" he inquired patiently.

Everleigh answered that one for us both, shaking her head violently.

Driller laughed and said, "That's what I thought."

She turned her face up to mine and sighed, the heartbreak turning to resignation.

"Guess we need to get this place sorted," I murmured, and she looked back longingly at the cabin. She reluctantly nodded, and led the way.

Driller put an arm around her shoulders and she smiled at him. I could tell they'd had a little bonding time before this misadventure, being cooped up in a hotel room for long hours. Still, she didn't look at him the same way she looked at me. When she looked at me, there was something – I don't know – a little extra.

I was glad my girl and my best friend got along, and were the circumstances different, I might have even been brave enough to ask if she'd be willing to let us share her. I'd shared with my best friend before, and there wasn't anything like it. I don't know, maybe it was because I loved him too, and it was the closest we could comfortably get in that regard without completely crossing boundaries – fuck. It wasn't like I was in love with him, just… It was hot sharing a woman with him and was something we did every once in a while, and felt amazing and all that jazz.

I shoved it out of my mind and we climbed the stairs, Driller holding Ev's hand while I had my hands lightly on her hips, a great view of her ass as we ascended. Everleigh paused, just before going inside the back door and took a deep breath. I fitted myself to her back and pecked a quick kiss on the cap of her exposed shoulder and she shuddered slightly before stepping over the threshold, back in with the boys she didn't know.

"We good?" Skids asked, eyeing my girl.

"We're good," I affirmed and he nodded.

Driller sighed and tipped his head back, freezing as he caught sight of the loft.

"Damn, you guys have been busy," he remarked and Everleigh smiled.

"Actually," I said, "most of it has been Everleigh's doing."

"Yeah?"

"Yup."

Everleigh tried to hide behind her hair but I wouldn't let her, gathering it up and laying it over one shoulder.

"Well," Driller said, and looked to my woman, "where would you like us to begin? We can't leave that bed out on the porch like that."

She smiled and it was brittle, but she made a motion with her hands that we should sit and she stepped around me and back out the door.

"I think she's going to pack," I said, and Driller bowed and shook his head.

"Where's your shit?" he asked.

"I guess that's my cue that I should pack, too."

"You get busy," Skids said. "Yale and I are going to avail ourselves of this chess set you got sittin' here."

I nodded. "Everleigh found that up in the loft a couple days ago. She wants to learn, but I'm afraid I suck at it."

I saw her pop up over her bed outside the window at her name, and Skids chuckled, "I'd be happy to teach her. I think she'd be good at it."

I smiled and said, "She's good at everything," casting a look her way. She blushed and ducked back down.

We got to packing so we could clear out the next morning. Everleigh came in with folded piles of her clothing and placed them on the unoccupied end of the table, looking over at me a little helplessly.

"Bag full?" I asked.

She nodded and I smiled.

"How is your bag too full?" Driller asked.

"Found some things at the local thrift store right up her alley," I said looking over at him.

Golden rolled his eyes and said with a smile, "Leave it to a woman. In protective custody and still manages to clothes shop."

Everleigh was warming up to their presence, because she gave Golden the finger.

He laughed and shook his head, putting down my book he'd been thumbing through, back on the night stand.

"I'm a military guy. I can pack with the best of them. Can I see if I can help?" he asked.

She raised an eyebrow and eyed him cynically and finally nodded. He went over to her and asked, "Where's the bag?"

She went back out to her bed and brought it in, and set it beside the clothes she couldn't get into it. He unzipped it and looked in, and said, "Here's part of the trouble, you've folded things you can roll. Here, let me show you."

"Gah! Dammit!"

Everleigh jumped but Yale wasn't even looking at her, but rather at the board. Skids sat back with a shit-eating grin. Yale scowled and let his dark eyes rove over the pieces. Everleigh picked one up, a pawn, and cocked her head. Yale looked up and she set it down and pointed to herself.

"What? Do I think you're a pawn?" he asked. She nodded somberly. He scowled and looked angry. "No, and I deeply apologize if I've given you that impression."

Skids took her hand and she jumped and looked him in the eye.

"The pawn might be small, but it can be a mighty piece in the right hands. Come here and let me show you…"

I smiled to myself as he stopped their game, had Everleigh pull up a chair, and had Yale reset the board.

Golden didn't complain, just worked at repacking her bag, only stopping them to ask if she'd kept out what she'd wanted to wear to bed and what she wanted to wear tomorrow.

A sort of truce fell over the cabin and Driller and I focused on bringing in her bed, the apple crate shelves, and just generally deconstructing her area out on the porch to take it up to the loft.

"I'm sleeping with you guys," he said, straightening from fitting the bottom sheet to her bed.

"Motherfucker, this is a full."

"Don't care, she's gonna be the ham in a man-sammich tonight, because I'll be fucked if I'm cozying up to Skids or Golden. Junior down there is gonna fit his ass on the couch just fine."

"Fuck you!" Yale called up. Everleigh was fixated on the wooden chess board, not really hearing us, but rather listening to Skid's low voice as he explained something or other.

I sighed.

"Babe!" I called down, and she peered up at me curiously. "You good with squeezing between me and Driller tonight?"

Her keen green eyes flicked from me to my best friend and searched his face. He smiled down at her and tried to look harmless, which was a joke, and less like the perv he usually was, which was even more laughable. Although, I have to say, for a perv, he was still a bigger gentleman than me; respectful of boundaries, super-big on consent. I mean, I was too, but he was next-level about it.

She smiled faintly and nodded, and he raised a knee and jerked his elbow back and was like, "Ungh! Yeah, baby!"

"Guess it's you and me, G."

"Stay on your own side of the fuckin' bed, old man, or I'm totally handing you over to Lys when we get back."

Skids rolled his eyes and said, "Because Lys is totally someone I need to be afraid of."

"You've never pissed her off."

"Which I am sure you have with fair regularity," Yale said with a smirk.

Golden smirked back and said, "She's fuckin' sexy when she's angry."

Everleigh smiled and yet still managed to roll her eyes. I came down the loft stairs and said, "Babe, you might want to make sure it's set up to your liking up here."

She looked up and nodded, standing reluctantly from the chess board.

"Doesn't have to be right now, I ain't done showing you this yet." Skids smiled at her and she gave a smile back that was bordering on her impish self, and I felt a knot of tension ease in my chest. She sank back down in her seat and turned her eyes back to the board.

Driller and I exchanged a look and his eyebrows went up, questioning. I nodded and he nodded too, getting my meaning from my expression alone.

Patience. It would come up, I was sure, but now was definitely not the time, with how overwhelmed and stressed the fuck out we all were.

"It's starting to get dark in here, where's the lights?" Yale asked.

Everleigh stood up and went and got the lantern from the kitchen and he blinked at her.

"You're joking."

She smiled brightly and shook her head.

Skids chuckled. "I can see why you love this place."

She beamed at him as she lit the lantern with a strike-anywhere match and I went down to light up some of her candles along the porch rail outside. Driller got the hurricane lamps we'd brought up to the loft, and pretty soon, the cabin was a warm, cozy glow.

21

*E*verleigh…

At about the fourth yawn, Skids declared that our chess lessons were over for the night. I pouted, absorbed in his teachings and with a sigh, lovingly put away the hand-carved pieces in their velvet-lined little drawers on either side of the raised board.

It was a beautiful piece that I'd found packed away in an old suitcase with a busted lock in the loft. The suitcase had been trash, but this treasure had to be kept.

I picked up my nightgown, a find from the local thrift store, all peach satin and ivory lace, and probably straight out of the 1970's with that vintage feel. It fit like a dream and made me feel beautiful.

I slipped into the bathroom and changed into it, and when I came out, the men were all in various stages of getting ready for bed, themselves. I crept up to the loft, Yale staring at me with those dark eyes that felt like they could burn a hole right through me if only they weren't so cold.

I paused at the top of the narrow stairs and rested a hand on the rail that ran the length of the loft. I was going to miss the soft golden lamplight and the old wood worn to a satin finish. I was going to miss the quiet, the rushing sound of the river through the porch screen, and the lazy chirp of insects. Narcos stared at me from the edge of the bed and a sorrow passed briefly between us. I could tell he mourned the loss of our time together, too, the end of the peace and the solace this special place brought to us amidst the chaos, and the magic of it that brought us together despite, what seemed from the outside, absolute insurmountable odds.

I would treasure the scars on my hands, I decided. It was a momentary pain that had been unbelievably worth it, if only for the way he looked at me now.

"Come to bed, babe," he murmured softly, and Driller, who'd been hauling his shirt off over his head, completed the action.

With a crooked grin and a wink, he said, "Ladies first."

I went to Narcos, who backed his way across the bed and turned on his side, putting his back against the metal bars of the daybed's surround. I slid across the crisp sheet and cuddled up to him, fitting my head on his shoulder, beneath his chin. His arm drifted across my shoulder, holding me to him as his partner and friend slid onto the bed behind me. I closed my eyes and swallowed hard, stiffening with uncertainty.

"You're all good, bright-eyes," Driller whispered in my ear, and he laid an arm gently over my waist, his hand resting on Narcos like they'd done this before. It struck me that they probably had, but something about this felt like, at least to me, that it held more weight.

I closed my eyes and relaxed slowly into the front of my lover's body while his best friend pressed a light kiss to the back of my shoulder, his hand smoothing lightly over the satin of my gown, over the swell of my hip, to lightly squeeze my thigh with reassurance.

"Ain't no place safer than between the two of us with three brothers to go through downstairs," Driller murmured, his breath stirring my hair.

I realized he was right and I reached back and rested a hand on his jeans-clad leg. He chuckled lightly and settled and before long, was breathing deep and even. I listened to that deep and even breath, felt the rise and fall of his chest against my back, and listened to the steady tick of my lover's heart beneath my other ear.

It was a rhythm and cadence that was hard to resist and before long, I was sound asleep myself and honestly, had never felt safer or more protected – more cherished – in my life.

THE NEXT MORNING, I was woken by the weight of my hair being swept aside and the soft press of lips to the back of my shoulder, making tracks to the back of my neck. I sighed out happily, and those silky soft lips pressed a kiss behind my ear. A girl could get used to waking up like this.

"Good morning, bright-eyes."

I shivered and opened my eyes to Narcos smiling down on me, though it hadn't been his voice in my ear.

Driller's hand smoothed over my hip and halfway to my knee, much like it had the night before and I shivered again. He chuckled, his lips still behind my ear and with the sound, the warmth of his breath against my skin and gently stirring my hair, I felt my eyes widen and a gasp escape my lips.

Narcos' smile became a pleased grin. I honestly didn't know what to make of that, but at the same time, I was drowning in guilt over how aroused I had become. Driller got up slowly and backed off the bed, standing and giving a stretch. I backed away from Narcos to get up, but he grabbed me gently around the waist and dipped his head.

I turned my face up to his and felt relief flood my veins as he kissed me gently.

I could definitely get used to waking up like this.

"Don't you kinky fuckers make this any more complicated for me than it already is," Yale called from downstairs and I froze.

"You're one to talk!" Driller called back, caustically.

I looked at Narcos curiously and he pressed a finger to his lips in the classic shushing motion and winked one of his smiling green eyes at me. I relaxed and trusted that he would tell me later.

"Fuck this noise," Golden groaned. "I want my bed and my woman. You're all fuckin' knees and elbows, old man."

"Not like I was going to snuggle your dumb ass," Skids grumbled, and I stuffed a hand against my mouth to stifle a giggle.

Narcos cracked a grin and I lost it, I couldn't help it. The giggle escaped.

"What's so funny?" Skids demanded and Driller rolled his eyes. "No laughter before coffee."

"No *nothing* before coffee," Golden called out and I could hear the eye roll in his voice.

"I'll make some coffee, then," I murmured, only loud enough for Driller and Narcos to hear.

"Huh," Driller said, as I stood and stretched myself. "I guess I'm one of the chosen ones."

I blushed and smiled what Narcos called my 'Mona Lisa smile' and padded down the stairs to the kitchen.

Coffee was made, the dragons were slain, and everyone was much happier for it. Although how on earth they drank their coffee black, I would never know. We didn't have any milk left, so it was tea with honey for me.

I held up the jar and waggled it back and forth at Narcos.

"We got about an hour before we have to hit the road?" he asked.

"What for?" Skids wanted to know, and Yale echoed the inquiry with his expression.

"Everleigh to run an errand."

Yale shook his head and I twisted my lips into disappointment. It would have been nice to get a little more before we left. The hive was huge and I wanted to try my completed beekeeper's hat, which rested on top of my leather bag.

"What did you want to do?" Skids asked. Then he smiled; "You tell us *yourself*, we'll make the time."

I scowled at his blatant attempt at bribery, and with them all staring at me intently, drew a breath. My throat squeezed tight and all I managed to get out was a short, strangled noise.

"Easy now, take your time. Rome wasn't built in a day, but the builders had to start somewhere, with at least one brick. Come on now, you can lay that brick." Skid's voice was gentle, encouraging, and I looked to Narcos, helpless.

"Just you and me, babe. Talk to me," he said quietly.

I opened my mouth, drew a deep breath, and stammered out, "I'd like to get more honey."

I blushed furiously at the light smattering of applause and Skids said, "Narcos, what do you got around here for breakfast?"

Narcos came to me and kissed my forehead, "You did good, baby. You did real good. Go quick."

I rushed through getting dressed, grabbed my basket with its kitchen knife and jars, and bolted out the back door, hat in hand, before any of them could change their minds.

I made quick work of my special errand, and said goodbye to my bees, the woods, the river, and the sense of peace it had brought me. I didn't take too much honey, just a few jelly jars to hopefully last me until I could come back. One of them, I planned to give our hostess, wherever we were going.

When I slipped back in the back door of the cabin, I was greeted by some rather thoughtful looks. I blushed and set the jars on the table, and gave a little shrug.

"Now, that's impressive," Yale stated and I had to smile.

"Definitely a unique skill," Skids agreed.

"I'm impressed," Golden said and I got the impression that he didn't impress all that easily. He let out a gusty sigh and said, "Now can we please go home? I miss my woman."

"Whipped," Yale said dryly, and Golden raised an eyebrow.

"Like you don't miss Aly," he accused.

"Oh, for sure," Yale said and I could tell he just barely bit back saying more, but the sinister, dirty grin he shot in Golden's direction coupled with the hints dropped the night before led me to believe that if whips were involved, Yale was the one wielding them. It made my mouth a little dry just thinking about it and I wondered if I would ever meet the woman he was with and what she was like.

Meek. I thought to myself. *She would have to be. Meek and subservient.*

I shoved my judgments about a woman I didn't know to the back of my mind and helped with loading things out the front door and down the long walk to the motorcycles. The old truck was pulled into the garage, the cabin closed up tightly.

Skids came out with the chessboard and put it into one of his saddle-bags. When I stared at him, he chuckled and told me, "Don't look at me in that tone of voice. Lessons ain't over, yet. Gonna need some-thing to keep teaching you on."

It made me smile and nod in appreciation as he made sure that the board was secured and safe.

Narcos ended up bungee-cording my leather bag down tight behind my seat, and I held out my beekeeper's hat with a worried frown. He asked, "Anybody got any ideas on how to get this back with us without killing it?"

"Should fit sideways in one of my bags. Give it here." Narcos handed it over to Driller, who worked for several moments, kneeling by the side of his bike. He stood up triumphantly and said, "We're good to go."

It was a long ride with a few stops along the way. I expected to go over the bay bridge and into the city, but we turned off the freeway just before it and wound up in a very nice neighborhood of houses in various sizes, some older and some newly built.

The garage door on one of the houses started to trundle up at the sound of the approaching bikes, and without hesitation Narcos pulled past the pickup parked on the street, up the driveway, and into the garage, stopping beside another motorcycle parked to one side. I jumped off and worked at the chinstrap of my helmet, weary from the long ride. The garage door began to shut even as the rest of our entourage heeled down their kickstands outside.

"You made it," a voice called, and I jumped slightly.

"Sure did. Everleigh, Youngblood. Youngblood, this is Everleigh."

"Nice to meet you, Everleigh." The man nodded politely, sandy hair over a fair face with a slightly Latin cast to his features. His steely blue eyes roved over my face even as mine roved his. He smiled, flashing dimples, and I nodded politely in return.

"Ev, baby," Narcos murmured and I jumped slightly and turned back to him. He held out my leather bag, which he'd unstrapped as Youngblood and I took one another's measure. I took it, and Youngblood held open the door leading from inside of the garage to inside his house. I scurried past him nervously as Narcos caught up and followed me through.

I was half-met by the rest of the men coming through the front door, which was held by a woman with long, straight, dark hair and equally dark eyes. She was lovely, and reminded me of a young Monica Bellucci.

She shut the door behind them and turned, smiling, and introduced herself. "Hi, I'm Chrissy." I raised a hand and gave her a feeble wave. She was beautiful, compared to me, and my insecurities raged.

"That's Everleigh," Driller said with a shrug. "She needs to get better at talking."

I scowled at him and he raised his eyebrows. "*Tell* me when I'm lying, bright-eyes." I scowled harder and he gave me a tight-lipped smile. "That's what I thought."

I gave him the finger without thinking, and immediately blushed a bright crimson. Chrissy just laughed.

"Looks like she's got you pegged," she said.

"I'm an asshole," he agreed, then pointed to a round patch on his cut. "Got the merit badge to prove it." I blinked and moved a little closer and, sure enough, the patch was of the letter 'A' with wings behind it in the middle, and 'Asshole' curved at the top and 'Merit Badge' curving up from the bottom.

I closed my eyes and shook my head faintly while the rest of the guys laughed softly. Chrissy rolled her eyes behind Driller when I opened mine and smiled.

"You're probably exhausted," she said and I shrugged faintly. The ride was long, but I was used to long rides. It wasn't so bad; I loved to ride and it was probably the last time I would get to for a while.

"Come on, I'll show you up to the guest room and the guest bath." I nodded and glanced at Narcos who gave me an encouraging smile and nod of his head.

I hefted my bag of clothes and followed Chrissy upstairs and down the hall. She touched a door and said, "Bathroom is here, and the guest room…" She trailed up the hall two more doors and touched a door in the opposite wall to the bathroom and turned, "is right here." She twisted the knob, shoving it in. It stuck slightly in the frame and she grimaced.

"I keep telling Tony he needs to fix that. One of his brothers stayed with us and got angry. He slammed it so hard it hasn't been quite right since."

I waved it off. Truthfully, I liked that it stuck. It would give me a split second longer to react if things went wrong.

She smiled at me and said, "You really don't say much do you?" I shook my head and her smile grew. It was warm and inviting, and I thought to myself, I could easily like Chrissy.

"Well, that's all right. Would you like me to leave you to it for now?" I nodded and she gave a slight nod in return, before she startled a bit and said, "Oh! I almost forgot, towels and washcloths are here in the hall closet."

She ducked back out into the hall and I left my bag on the bed and stood in the room's doorway. She opened a narrow door in the hall and revealed shelves of towels and washcloths and neatly-organized spare bathroom products like bars of soap, hand soap for the sink, and others, like Q-tips, cotton balls, and first-aid stuff.

I nodded and admired the organization of it all.

I liked to be organized, which had been easier said than done, living with a bunch of drunk-off-their-asses and drugged-out-of-their-minds bikers. It was nice being in a home without holes in the walls or graffiti done in Sharpie, where it didn't stink of weed and there weren't beer stains – or worse – in the carpets, and nicotine didn't practically drip from the ceilings.

It was bright in Tony and Chrissy's home, too. The curtains were gauzy for privacy, the thicker drapes open to let the light in. *Much* better than having a big Harley-Davidson faux-fur blanket tacked over the windows, which had aluminum foil in them.

I felt like I had been living in a cave, and it was nice to be somewhere full of light and air.

I pressed my lips together and wanted to say 'thank you', wanted to say 'it was beautiful here and someday I wished I had a home like it', but the words wouldn't come. Chrissy sensed I wanted to say something, like people often did, and waited me out patiently, but I finally shook my head.

"Just relax, our castle is your castle for now. No pressure to be social; everything at your own pace."

I nodded, grateful, and she gave a little wave and drifted back down the hall, disappearing down the stairs.

I waited a heartbeat or two and raided her towel closet for a pair of dark towels I didn't think my hair would accidentally dye, or if it did, it at least wouldn't show. I went and got a dress out of my bag and winced at how rolling it had wrinkled it, but beggars couldn't be choosers and I was grateful for Golden's packing help.

I opened the closet in the bedroom and breathed a sigh of relief at the empty hangers along the rod. I plucked one down for the dress and brought it into the bathroom with me. I figured a hot shower would be really nice and the steam might help release some of the wrinkles.

It wasn't long before I had some company. I heard the door open and peeked around the curtain, relieved when I saw Narcos. He set about stripping down and I went back to washing the grit from the road out of my hair. He stepped in the tub and buried his hands in my long, long hair and stepped close to me. I immediately relaxed, smiling faintly while the hot water sluiced through my locks.

"You're so fuckin' beautiful to me it hurts sometimes," he said, in a rough whisper that was barely audible above the shower spray. I opened my eyes and his smile, a match for my own, was something else, as his earthy green eyes traveled over my face. I put my arms around him and cuddled close, and he sighed in contentment.

"I want you," I murmured and he chuckled and nodded.

"Right back at'cha, babe."

"Mm, should probably settle in and maybe wait until it's just you and me, huh?" I asked softly.

He nodded, but bent and kissed me anyways. It was like heaven, but I ached for more, for a deeper touch that only he seemed to be able to give me. When he loved my body, I swore it was like he touched me soul-deep, a connection so fine and otherworldly, I could suddenly believe that soulmates was a thing.

He gathered me close and we rested, standing beneath the hot shower spray, washing one another clean, holding each other, kissing, touching; drinking the water from one another's skins. I don't know how long we showered together, but it was enough for the water to grow tepid. We got out and started all over again, running towels over each other, exploring every inch between us through the rough, absorbent material.

"You're killing me, babe. With every look from those jewel-bright eyes, I lose another little piece of myself to you." He kissed me softly and whispered against my lips, "And I don't regret it."

I shuddered and would have given anything for him to take me. Hard, soft, I didn't care as long as he was inside me, against me, moving over me, but alas, it wasn't to be. A knock fell on the other side of the bathroom door and Tony called out gently, "Food's ready."

I hid my face against Narcos' chest as we both laughed softly, like a pair of teens caught necking on the front porch, caught by the girl's father… a rite of passage I'd never experienced, and I thanked my lucky stars for that. My father likely would have beaten my ass six ways to Sunday.

"Come on, let's get dressed and get some food in us," he said softly, smoothing my hair back from my face. I stared up into his, memorizing his smile, the light in his eyes as he looked at me and I felt like I was falling, except I never wanted to stop.

"I… I love you," I whispered, scared how he might react. I didn't have to worry. His arms went around me and he held me tightly to his hard body as if I had just given him a gift that was too perfect.

"I love you, too, babe," he murmured into my hair, then he drew back, pressing his forehead to mine. "I'm gonna take care of you," he whispered. "It'll take a little time, but I promise, you're gonna be happy again."

I smiled and whispered back, "I'm always happy when I'm with you," and it was true. He let me be me and loved me anyway. and that was so very precious.

"We shouldn't keep them waiting," he whispered. "You're gonna have to be quiet tonight, I have every intention of making love to you once we're alone."

I nodded, "I want that."

"I love that you want it."

I smiled and shook my head lightly, "Not it, *you*."

He chuckled and we broke apart, dressing quickly. I whipped my hair into a tight bun at the nape of my neck and secured it with a hair elastic as he opened the bathroom door for me. I padded barefoot down the hall with him close at my back in a fresh pair of jeans and a tee. He swung his motorcycle cut on, sliding his arms through the holes for them and tugging it in front to settle it onto his frame.

I let him go ahead of me when we reached the top of the stairs, trailing along just behind him, fingers linked. I stared at the colors of his true patch, at the knight's piece picked out in indigo thread on the large, gray shield and thought to myself, *Indeed, these colors suit him so much better.*

His protective nature captivated me, the safety I felt in his arms, the concern and love with which he touched me… it was everything I had dared to dream of for myself but that I'd never thought possible. I kept waiting to wake up from this beautiful but terrible dream but I wasn't sleeping. I was wide awake, for once in my life, and realizing that *this was it.* This was what I wanted and what my life could be and all I needed to do was speak the truth…

Wonderful smells hit us halfway down the stairs and I felt my stomach rumble in complaint that I hadn't really fed it since this morning. When we'd stopped for lunch, I hadn't been hungry, and so I hadn't bothered ordering. Narcos hadn't liked it, but he, grudgingly, hadn't forced the issue, either.

Youngblood stepped through the back sliding door with a platter of grilled vegetables, the steaks already on the table.

I went to the chair Narcos held out for me and sank into the seat, glad he let me scoot myself in, rather than taking out the backs of my knees trying to help.

He sat next to me; we were all gathered around one end of the long table. Chrissy held up her glass of white wine with a raised eyebrow and I smiled and gave a nod.

"Thank you," I managed, when she brought a glass back from the kitchen counter for me. She smiled big and said, "You're welcome."

Narcos smiled at me, too and squeezed my knee under the table, the small gesture bursting with pride.

Grilled steak and vegetables, fluffy dinner rolls, and fresh green salad greeted my eyes, which were likely bigger than my stomach, so I started small.

"Wh-where's everyone else?" I asked.

"Golden wanted to get back to Lys and his nephew, Yale wanted to get back to Aly, and Skids wanted to get back to the 10-13, his one and only love," Youngblood answered.

"Oh," I murmured, self-conscious, more than just my palms sweating. It took a force of will to keep my breath even, to not suck in air, even though it felt like my chest was being crushed as though a great fist held me, the fingers tightening, wringing the very air out of my lungs.

"What about Driller?"

"Sounded like his trap may have caught something in it," Chrissy said, taking an elegant sip from her wineglass.

"Oh, okay…" I trailed off.

Just speaking those few words in front of these two strangers had me hot and flushed, sweating and panicking in a way that made my stomach do barrel rolls. I wanted to leap from my seat and run and hide, but I forced myself to stay put, telling myself over and over that Narcos was here and he wouldn't let anything happen to me. The weight of his hand on my knee was definitely a reassuring thing.

He looked sideways at me and shot me a smile that made me want to melt, saying, "You're doing real good, babe."

"Agreed," Chrissy said.

"When do you go to trial?" Youngblood asked his wife, and Chrissy finished her bite before speaking.

"Not my case, love. It's Yale's and I'm not sure when he's taking it to trial. He's been fighting it out through a barrage of motions from the defense. My guess would be sooner rather than later."

"He have enough of a case to go to trial with?" he asked.

"For what? The drugs or the murder?"

I shifted uncomfortably in my seat and stared at the last few bites on my plate. I didn't like thinking about that: listening to King and his men laugh over killing that man, imitating him as he'd begged for them not to shoot him. I forced one more bite, then stood with my plate and moved to the kitchen. The conversation at the table ceased and all three sets of eyes followed me.

"You don't have to do that," Chrissy said kindly, when I started to rinse my plate and work my way through the rest of the dishes. I shook my head and continued to do them, rinsing them at the sink and loading the dishwasher. I needed to be up and doing something.

"I think a change of subject is in order," Youngblood said.

"Pretty much the only subject with you, Mr. Homicide Detective," Narcos said and I looked back.

Youngblood was nodding, but his steely blue eyes were fixed on me, solemn and apologetic.

I finished up in the kitchen, and finished my wine, and by the time I was through, I just wanted to go lay down. My tiredness had caught up with me.

"I'm going to go lay down," I forced out and the conversation, once again ceased. I wanted to run screaming into the night, when, once again, all eyes were turned on me. I hated that and I was desperately afraid of what it would be like with a courtroom full of people, the rest of the gang, the Knights of Crescentia, in the gallery, glaring, mocking, and threatening.

"Okay, babe. Be right up," Narcos said, worry tingeing his voice.

I nodded a bit too quickly and made my escape to a murmured "Good night" from Chrissy.

Once inside the guest room, I leaned heavily inside the closed door and felt a little better, imagining, for the moment, that I could somehow magically shut this door and shut out all that was happening. I swallowed hard. I felt like entirely too much was riding on my shoulders and that scared me. I mean, what if the jury didn't believe me? What if King didn't go away?

I knew too much.

Narcos had betrayed them.

They wouldn't stop. Not until we were both dead, and I didn't want to die.

I stared at the back of my hand where it was pressed to the bedroom door, at the slight slash of pink scar marring the back of it, where the nail had come through. I closed my eyes and tried not to think about the look in Narcos' eyes, the pain there, as he'd driven the nail through my palm.

A part of me had always known something about his look hadn't been right that night… that he hadn't wanted to, but that he couldn't give up. I couldn't give up, either. No matter how frightening, no matter how much I just wanted to find a quiet corner of some wilderness and carve out a solitary life for myself, I knew I wouldn't be able to survive that way, either. As introverted as I was, I was also prone to a terrible loneliness. I needed people around me; I knew that about myself.

I slipped the dress off over my head and hung it in the closet, setting my bag on the floor inside. I found a nightgown and stepped into it, shrugging into the straps just as a light double tap fell on the bedroom door. I turned and it opened, Narcos slipping inside with me and shutting it firmly behind him.

"You okay, babe?"

I went to him and held myself to him tightly. He put his arms around me and smoothed those big hands up and down my arms, warming my skin. The house had central air and it was quite a bit cooler than what I had grown used to at the cabin.

"Let me get ready for bed," he murmured, and held up the blankets for me to scoot under. I got into bed and his eyes met mine, his expression grave as he searched my face. I tipped my head in curiosity and he drew in a shaky breath, as if trying to decide if he should say anything or not.

He shook his head and dropped his eyes as he pulled his shirt over his head and discarded it on a nearby chair. He went for his belt and my gaze followed his every movement, sliding over every smooth, chiseled inch of him as I marveled. This big, beautiful man not only loved me, wanted me, and promised to protect me, he meant it with every fiber of his being and that wowed me like nothing else, left me sitting in awe any time I really allowed myself to take the time to think about it.

He stripped down to his boxers and got into bed beside me, his blunt fingertips trailing in a ghostly touch down my cheek.

"I'd give anything to heal you of your pained blue silence, babe. Give anything to just take the fear and anxiety away."

I smiled, no words needed, and grasped his bearded cheeks between my palms and kissed him full-on, pouring all of my love, my pride in him, and the joy that he brought me into the kiss, along with all the passion I held.

22

*N*arcos…

She kissed me, and it was like she'd opened the damn floodgates. I suddenly couldn't keep my damn hands off of her, my fingertips sliding the straps of her nightgown off of her shoulders so my lips had a path to follow across her lovely skin that was free of obstruction. The breathy moan that escaped from her lips as she tipped her head back and to the side to give me better access left me throbbing painfully in my shorts. I was about to lose my damn mind when she stood up and let the satin drift down her body to puddle at her feet.

I didn't hesitate, I bucked my hips up off the bed and shoved my boxers down. She whisked them off the rest of the way and put a knee to the bed, flinging her other leg over mine, her hands against my tattooed chest pressing me back into the sheets, her palms warm, her flesh like silk against my skin as she shimmied up my body and put her sex directly over mine.

She didn't hesitate, her jewel-bright eyes locking onto mine as she lifted my throbbing cock off of my stomach and pressed it at her entrance. She was as slick with want and need as I was desperate to be inside her as she sank slowly over the top of me. Her eyes fluttered shut, her head tipped back, her long, long hair tickling the tops of my thighs and over my knees as I got a world-class view of her perfect tits above me.

I cupped one in the palm of my hand, pinching the peach-colored nipple between the side of my hand and my thumb, gradually increasing the pressure until she cried out gently and her hips began to move. I massaged her breast, my other hand on the perfect swell of her hip, encouraging her to ride me, and ride me she did.

She wasn't rough, she wasn't too fast or too slow. She kept an even, steady rocking of her hips, a seductive motion that fucking did amazing things, my cock sliding in and out of her hot wet cunt while at the same time rocking back and forth in the deepest part of her. It was sensual and erotic, almost too much for my mind to keep up with, so I didn't try. I lay back and let her take me for a ride, watching her writhe over the top of me, watching her lose herself completely.

Her inhibitions were stripped away, her shyness, her silence, her worry, and her fear all crumbling to dust as she looked down on me through hooded eyes. Her lips parted slightly, her breath coming in ragged and uneven pants as she took her pleasure and gave me the best experience of my life, bar none. She was magic. An earthly beauty that shouldn't be able to exist, possessing the grace of water tumbling over stone, and full of life, her trust and her heart growing with the tiniest bit of care.

She was magnificent, and wild, and somehow she let me be a part of it. She let me be the one to hold her, to taste her, and to love her.

"Slow down just a little, babe. You're going to make me come," I warned, my voice tight as I fought to keep this feeling going forever. She gave me that Mona Lisa smile edged with sex and a little bit of love and my damn heart swelled so big, I thought I was about to crack it in two.

"Good," she whispered. "I want to make you feel good."

"Shit, Everleigh, you do. You make me feel incredible."

She smiled and it held a surreal light, like sunlight through the green leaves of summer and the last vestiges of my control just shredded. I gripped her hips with both of my hands, my fingers digging into her pale flesh, and pulled her down over the top of me one last time even as my hips bucked off the bed. The crash of our bodies meeting set something loose in her because she cried out, her body arching, her pussy clenching my cock in a grip so tight I didn't even know it was possible before she bowed over my body and shuddered with her release.

I felt myself pump cum-shot after cum-shot deep into her body, awash in this euphoric tingling sensation even as I cursed my own ass out silently for not being able to hold back. I loved coming in unison like this. In fact, I couldn't ever remember pulling it off with any other woman, but it didn't mean I was ready. Far from it. I wanted to stay inside her forever.

We were lucky she was on that birth control shot every three months or whatever, because if I had my way, we'd be doing this a lot more, now that we didn't have anything else to do.

She slid off to one side of me, cuddling into my side, her inner thigh pressed over me as she wrapped herself around me, snug into my side. I turned just enough to smooth some of her hair from her face and to stare into her eyes.

"I wasn't ready for that to be over," I said, between breaths.

"You act like you'll never have me again," she murmured in a silvery whisper, a smile playing on her lips.

"I'd have you forever if I could." I kissed the tip of her nose and tucked her hair behind her ear.

Her eyes widened and she swallowed hard.

"Really?" she asked, breathlessly.

"Really."

"A-are you asking me to marry you?" she asked, and her voice held a little thrill of panic to it.

Too fast, too intense. Slow it down, man.

"Maybe someday, but not today. Not any time soon, really. Not until things are resolved and you're back on solid ground."

"I don't think I've ever been on solid ground, honestly," she said and her body relaxed again, her relief palpable. I was just glad she was receptive to the idea that one day she might just be the girl I would marry. I didn't want to be like, *Oh, for sure, it's gonna happen,* because it really was too soon for shit like that, but I was catching a vibe from her like no other. We just meshed. I'd only ever experienced that with one other person, and that was Driller.

Again the thought of sharing her with him crossed my mind. My cock started to stir and I was taken a bit by surprise at the fast turn-around. I decided to try and explore with her a little.

"Have you ever really gotten to do what *you* want to do?" I asked.

She cocked her head and considered me for a moment.

"How do you mean?" she asked.

"Like, I know you took off from that town at the first opportunity, but the nomad's life doesn't really seem to be your thing. You put down roots so fast at the cabin and I honestly think that's the first time I've gotten to see you thrive. It was beautiful... but it was also sad in a way."

She dropped her eyes and listened to me, hearing me out, but didn't say anything. I waited, and finally tipped her chin lightly with a finger. She looked up at me and I asked, "What do you dream about, babe?"

"I don't," she said carefully, defensively.

"Bullshit. We haven't lied to each other once since I came clean about being a cop, let's not start now. You can tell me you don't want to tell me, if you want, but no deception. Okay?"

She met my eyes and curiosity shone in hers, curiosity, and gratitude, I think.

"I've always been fairly… flexible with my wants and needs," she said and I raised an eyebrow.

"Wants, sure… needs are a different story."

She scraped her bottom lip between her teeth and huffed out a breath. We always did a lot better when it came to talking about the past and things that once were when it came to her. The future was new territory.

"Let's talk about something a little bit easier," I ventured, and she looked grateful for the out. She nodded a little too quickly and I smiled. "Let's talk about sex."

She smiled, a beautiful grin that she tried to cover by burying her face in my chest. I laughed and she said, muffled, "What is wrong with me that sex is an easier topic to embrace?"

"There's nothing wrong with you, babe. You're just beautifully compli-cated, like one of those images made up of hundreds of thousand smaller images. Sometimes you get so immersed in the little pictures, you don't even realize they all mesh together and form one big picture."

"What do you want to know?" she asked softly, and I smiled.

"What's your ultimate fantasy? One that you've never asked for, but always wanted to try."

She swallowed hard and really thought about it, finally giving a shrug. "I don't know. I've pretty much done it all…"

"A threesome?" I ventured.

She nodded.

"With two men?"

"Oh, *no*. Always another woman."

"Ever wanted to try with two men?"

"You like to share?" she asked.

"With Driller, on occasion, but only him. Never been comfortable with anyone else."

I could see her think about it, *really* think about it, and it seemed like she liked the idea. She asked me, "You don't get jealous?"

"Of him?" I shook my head. "No."

"I mean, he's attractive."

I smiled and asked her, "You develop a little bit of a crush while in the hotel with him?"

She blushed furiously and I laughed. She slapped me lightly on the chest and cried, "Quit it! Don't laugh… but if we're being honest, yes. I thought about it."

"About what?" I asked.

"About what it would be like, you know, if he kissed me." She covered her face with her hands and made a sound that told me she was horribly embarrassed to be admitting any of this. I pulled her hands away from her face and pressed them to my body with one hand. The other, I used to caress her face.

"Nothing to be embarrassed about, babe. Attraction is a natural thing."

"Are you attracted to men?" she asked and I frowned and thought about it. Finally, I shook my head.

"No. Are you attracted to women?" I asked.

She sighed and laid her head on my shoulder.

"No, but…"

"But, what?"

"I guess it depends on the woman," she said. "I mean, out of all of the ones I hooked up with for King, I was never really attracted to any, but there was this one girl that was just like… *wow*."

I nodded. "I guess that's kind of what it's like when it comes to Driller. I can't really picture myself making out with him or like, sucking his dick, but with a woman between us – *damn*. It's the most erotic fucking thing."

"You'd really be okay with me being with him in front of you?" she asked. "Like, not jealous at all?"

"Yeah, is it something you'd want? Both of us kissing you, inside of you, touching you?" I dropped my voice to a slightly seductive whisper and at the suggestiveness of it, her eyes dilated and she tried and failed to suppress an involuntary shudder. I chuckled and said, "Well, that answers that."

"Shut up!" she cried, but she was laughing, and I was, too.

I rolled over on top of her, between her thighs and caged her with my body. I dipped my head, bringing my lips to hers, my cock hanging thick and engorged between us.

I put my lips beside her ear and pitched my voice low, quiet, and murmured softly, "My hands on your body, his lips on your skin. Close your eyes for me, babe, and just imagine it for me."

She closed her eyes, her arms going around my shoulders, cradling me close to her sweet, sexy, body. I whispered scenarios, my cock getting hard to the point of pain as her breathing became steady, even, and deep with passion. She writhed a little against me as I placed strategic kisses against her erogenous zones while I took her through everything I wanted to happen between me, her, and my best friend, and she seemed really into it.

When I slipped inside her, she was impossibly wet. Hot and slick with arousal, her desire for everything I'd suggested was clear to me. I kissed her, and made love to her slowly, taking my time with her, driving her a little mad with pleasure, taking her to that place beyond words where she sank into that river of euphoria and just floated along with me.

I smiled when we finished and she fell almost immediately asleep in my arms. I held her close and dared to dream about a future with her, hardly knowing where to begin. My apartment was small, and totally sucked. It was fine for me, but she needed air, and grass, and green growing things – something she wasn't going to get in a twelve-story walk-up in the heart of Indigo City.

I figured if I was about to start a new life, I might as well go all-in. I mean, go big or go home, right? That was hysterical, because in just a few short weeks, she'd become home for me, the only home I ever longed for. I realized I wasn't as rogue or badass as I thought I was after a year undercover. I was just all about finding some stability, for me, for her, for the both of us.

I stared at the ceiling, Everleigh sleeping peacefully against me and wondered what was around here. There were a lot of older homes in this area with enough yard that I thought Everleigh would be satisfied. It was also close enough to the city that commuting wouldn't be too much of a pain in the ass. At least not for me, on the bike.

I let myself dream while wide awake for a time, until her deep and even breathing lulled me into following her into a sleep of my own. I had a loose idea, almost a plan, forming, but unfortunately, our lives were officially on hold pending this fucking trial...

23

*E*verleigh…

I felt exposed, even though we'd practiced in an empty court-room countless times, even though there were a bare minimum of people in here. The gallery having been cleared, the only people left were the lawyers, King, as the defendant, the judge, the jury, and essential court staff.

So many people, and they were all looking at me.

The judge hadn't allowed Narcos to stay, and I hadn't pleaded, figuring it would only make things worse than they already were. Yale had asked his questions, and though I'd broken out in a cold sweat, I had managed to answer every one of them.

Now King's lawyer was getting up, and the cold pit of fear in my stomach felt lethally poisonous. I swallowed hard as he gave me an oily smile and came entirely too close to me for comfort.

"Objection!" Yale stood up, dark eyes stormy.

"I haven't even asked a question yet!" King's lawyer spread his hands as he laughed in disbelief.

"You didn't have to," Yale scowled.

"You'll address your comments to the court, if you please, Prosecutor."

"Of course. My apologies, Your Honor, but given Ms. Tate's already stated anxiety disorder – "

I tuned out the bickering, my heart in my throat as King's lawyer shifted his weight, bringing himself that much closer to me. I was determined that I wouldn't lose it, that I wouldn't clam up, that I would answer his questions the same as I had answered Yale's, no matter what he did. King stared me down, a wholly evil look in his eyes. The same evil on his face as when he'd ordered Narcos to nail me to that tree… which we'd gone over already.

"Ms. Tate?" I snapped back to the present and tore my gaze from King to his lawyer who had moved away from me and closer to the jury.

"Yes, I'm s-s-sorry, did I miss a question?"

"I asked you, have you ever been in a sexually-inappropriate relationship with Detective Rutledge?"

Sexual, yes. Inappropriate? No. Not by my standards. I didn't really care about anyone else's. I opened my mouth to answer but was shouted down by Yale with another objection.

They argued back and forth and the judge denied Yale this time, demanding I answer the question.

I swallowed hard and said into the microphone, "No."

"But you and Detective Rutledge have had sex?"

"Y-y-yes, but I don't see how that has anything to do with – "

"You don't have to, and I'm asking the questions. You just have to answer what I ask, not add your own commentary."

"Your Honor!" Yale cried, standing for a third time.

"Dial it back, Mr. Heath," the judge said, displeased.

"When did you and Detective Rutledge first start having sex?"

I shivered and didn't want to answer, but I did, and he smirked.

"So how are we to believe that you haven't been coached? Told to lie about my client and his activities?"

I was mad, very mad. I'd been called a lot of things in my life, stupid, a whore, a cunt, and a bitch, to name a few, but I had *never* been called a liar.

I sat up straighter and answered his questions as best I could, but he was lobbing them almost faster than I could answer them. I was getting overwhelmed, my panic rising, tears falling; the jury looked angry – disgusted – and things were coiling tight, spiraling out of control and just as I thought for sure I would burst completely into wild sobbing –

–That was it.

King's lawyer looked at me with disdain and said, "I have no more questions for this witness."

I held my breath, and looked at Yale whose face was made of stone.

"Redirect, Your Honor?" he said, and the judge, an old man with rectangle specs and only a fringe of white hair around his bald head, nodded, his jowls wobbling.

"Ms. Tate," Yale started, coming around the desk.

"Yes?"

"Are you lying about any of this, and I do remind you, you're under oath."

I swallowed hard, tears slipping free of my bottom lashes and tracking through the careful makeup that Chrissy had helped me apply that morning.

"No, I'm not lying. I'm scared, but I wouldn't lie. He bragged about killing that man in front of me, laughed with Grave Bass and Joker about it, and then threatened if I said anything to anyone he would kill me."

"Thank you, Ms. Tate. I have no more questions for this witness."

"Mr. Heath?" the judge asked.

"No more questions," King's lawyer said smoothly.

"Very well, Ms. Tate, you may go."

I couldn't get out of there fast enough. I didn't even look where I was going; the bailiff escorted me, my head down, my vision blurring with tears. He gripped my elbow gently and I walked stiffly, grateful when he switched sides to put himself between me and King and his lawyer's table. Yale reached out subtly and brushed the back of my hand with his fingertips, but I didn't think it was in sympathy, but rather empathy.

He really wasn't so bad, just focused and passionate about his work. He had tunnel vision; he really was trying to do everything in his power to put King and his men away for as long as possible.

The bailiff opened the little swinging waist-high door and let me through, but he had to stay behind. I tried not to stumble as I whisked my way up the aisle between the empty gallery benches to the big, double wooden doors that led to the hallway, and freedom, beyond.

I spilled out into the cavernous marble hallway and right into the waiting arms of Narcos, Driller standing nearby. I burst into tears and he held me close, Driller stepping in behind me to shield me should the door reopen, his hand going to my shoulder and giving it a reassuring squeeze, lending me strength I just didn't have anymore.

"I've got you, babe," Narcos whispered into my hair as he held me tight. His voice was resigned and I felt so awful, knowing that he was likely in a lot of trouble because of me – because of us. We knew, but we had decided to tell the truth should it come up. I just really wished it hadn't, but knew that it would once King got that nasty smile of his and leaned in to whisper to his equally-nasty lawyer.

It was my fault. I'd given us away when Narcos had stood with the rest of the gallery to leave. I'd looked at him, and I knew my eyes held a pleading that he not go, and King had read me like a book.

I hated him. I hated myself even more, for being so expressive, for adapting to not having a voice. For being so damn dysfunctional.

"C'mon, Bright Eyes, let's get the fuck out of here," Driller crooned in my ear from behind me and the two men sandwiched me between them and marched me across the shining marble floor. I didn't raise my head, I didn't come out from behind my hair. I let myself be weak, let them shield me as questions were asked, comments were made, and we waded through the crowd waiting to be let back into the courtroom.

They kept me safe. The courthouse was already secure, but Narcos and Driller kept me safe between them, protected me from reaching hands and prying eyes. All I had to endure were sneers and snide comments that were thinly-veiled threats from the Knights of Crescentia they couldn't jail, and who were here for King. I didn't listen. I didn't care. I just wanted to be anywhere but here, and Narcos and Driller were getting me out.

They rushed me into the elevator that took us down to the lobby. It was freer here, less crowded than the hall, the soaring ceiling of the court-house lobby making it so I felt like I could breathe again.

We waited for the elevator to the garage and two men flanked us. The doors opened and Narcos and Driller rushed us inside.

Driller turned and barred the men's path and said, "You can get the next one."

"We ain't doin' shit, little piggy," Rebel's familiar voice sneered, and I cringed into Narcos' side.

"That's right," Narcos said. "You ain't."

The doors slid shut and Driller swore softly and punched several garage level buttons. I looked up at Narcos, frightened.

"We're all good, babe. These dumb fucks don't know who they're dealing with."

"Right," Driller agreed. "Here we go." The doors opened on the second floor of the garage and they hustled me out.

"I thought we parked on –"

"Hush now, Bright Eyes. It's all part of the master plan," Driller declared and dragged open the door to the garage stairwell.

We hustled the rest of the way to the SUV we'd arrived in and got in. Driller got us out of there, whisking past the stairwell door as it burst open, on one of the floors Driller had set the elevator to stop at. I sucked in a sharp breath, but we were around the bend in the garage and away before they could do much more than curse at us.

I huddled miserably into Narcos' side and closed my eyes, wondering *What next?*

I thought we would go back to Youngblood and Chrissy's house, but instead, we went almost halfway across the city and dipped off the street and down into another garage. I tried not to be scared. I trusted Narcos with my life, and he trusted Driller, which was enough for me. That wasn't precisely right; I trusted Driller, too. He'd ever been kind to me, and had always been patient… I just didn't see as much of him as I did Narcos, now. He just couldn't be around.

Driller pulled into a space and shut off the engine, turning around in the driver's seat, his leather jacket, minus his cut, creaking against the leather of the seat.

"I think it's high time we all took a break from this bullshit," he declared.

I peered at him from behind a fall of my hair and Narcos chuckled, the vibration through his chest a soothing thing as it thrummed through my body where I was pressed against him.

"Pizza and beer?" he asked.

"You fuckin' know it," Driller grinned.

"What movies you got in mind?" he asked.

"Something mind-blowingly awesome," he answered and popped the driver's side door. He swung his keyring around his index fingers, the metal jangling as he caught the keys in the palm of his hand.

"What are we doing?" I asked Narcos, softly.

"Pizza, beer, movies, and if you're up for it and things go that way, maybe making your fantasies come true."

I blinked at him, at a loss for words, jumping when the rear passenger door opened. Driller held out a hand to me and said, "We're all good. We're at my place."

I reached out and placed my hand in his and he helped me out of the back seat in true, gentleman-like fashion. Narcos slid across the seat and got out right behind me, staying close, and I loved him for it.

We traipsed across the smooth cement garage to the bank of elevators and Driller punched the button. He grinned at me and winked saying, "I like pushing all kinds of buttons."

I blushed furiously at the double entendre, and he laughed and laughed, Narcos joining in. I didn't quite make it to full-on laughter, but the two of them definitely put a smile on my face.

We rode the elevator up to the third floor and walked down a long, long, hallway. The walls were brick, the carpet a deep green. Art had been hung, and narrow tables of rich dark wood holding decorative ferns in copper pots were set against the walls between sets of apartment doors, which were painted a glossy green with brass numbers set above the spy holes.

He stopped at '3C' and selected the key for the deadbolt. He swiftly unlocked it and the doorknob, Narcos at my back, hands kneading my shoulders carefully. Driller swung the door wide and made an 'after you' motion, smiling gently.

"Ladies first, baby. Shoes, though, if you please."

I smiled and nodded, stepping through the door and slipping the elegant, light brown boho leather flats off my feet. I set them aside on the tile entryway, the tiles made to look like wood and cool beneath my feet. I stepped onto the dark carpet, a charcoal gray so dark as to be almost black, and moved into the living room so that the men could follow me in.

Driller secured the door and turned to me, Narcos at my side, slipping off his nice courtroom shoes.

"Make yourself at home, Bright Eyes," he said with a wink, and I nodded, taking myself further into the living room. There was a couch, a big one, the kind that had the long lounge chair on one end and the rest overstuffed and fluffy, in a light gray. It had one of those matching big square footstools in front of the regular couch seats and looked ungodly comfortable. I drifted that way. There was a tall, black four-person dining table with four tall chairs just beyond the living room and past that, the kitchen.

"Bathroom is the door right there on the left, at the end of the kitchen," he said. I nodded and set my clutch purse on the dining room table and took off my chiffon and lace kimono-like jacket and hung it on the back of one of the chairs. I wore one of the beautiful, long, tan country lace dresses that Narcos had bought me in the little town's second-hand store and had felt pretty confident as I looked in the mirror that morning.

I was feeling a lot less confident, my nerves working overtime as I went around the couch to take a seat.

"You got anything of mine here, man? These pants are too damn tight. Makin' my balls itch."

Driller laughed and shook his head as he went around into the kitchen and got into the fridge.

"You know where my closet is, might find some basketball shorts to fit your big ass."

Narcos chuckled and said, "I'm not gonna love you anymore, you keep calling me fat."

"Now, did I say you were fat, Sunshine? No, I did not."

"Whatever, fucker. You implied it."

I giggled as Narcos disappeared into the bedroom and disappeared into what had to be a walk-in closet.

"Beer?" Driller asked me.

I nodded and pressed my lips together, wondering what was supposed to happen next, unsure if they really meant to watch movies or… The hiss and clack of bottle tops coming off killed my train of thought. He came around the kitchen island with one in each hand and held one out to me. I took it, grateful, and sipped at the cold, hoppy brew. Crisp and refreshing, it went down smooth, but I was hungry now, and pizza sounded fabulous to go along with it.

"Hang tight, I'm gonna order us up some food."

He pulled his cell out of his back pocket and set his beer down next to my purse to shrug out of his jacket and hang it on one of the chairs near my little sleeved wrap thing. He tapped out things on the screen and I took the time to look over the rest of the apartment.

There were no windows. We were on the inside of the building, so there was no light, no life moving by outside… I felt strangely okay about that, though. Safer, more secure for the time being. Like the outside world had been truly shut out and I couldn't be in any better of a safe place if I wanted to be. It was… cozy.

The entertainment center was big, the television easily one of those sixty-five-inch flat screens. It had all the bells and whistles around it. Speakers, game systems, Blu-ray player, and a full cable box setup. The man apparently liked his cinema because flanking it were shelves and shelves of movies and television series. I drifted over to those shelves and perused the selection he had, finding that his tastes mostly ran towards action and horror, but there was a surprising amount of drama mixed in, too.

Narcos reappeared from the bathroom door and I turned, raising my eyebrows and taking another drink of my beer as he looked over at Driller and asked, "This mine?" and held up a third beer from the kitchen counter.

"Yeah, yeah, man…" Driller said, barely looking up from his phone. "Pizza's ordered, too."

"Sweet, what're we watching, babe?" he asked and I shrugged my shoulders.

"You like scary movies or shows?" Driller asked and I shook my head.

Narcos went over to the end of the couch that was a lounge and carefully dropped himself onto it, putting his legs up with a gusty, satisfied sigh before taking a swig out of his beer. I stared at him and he winked at me.

"Would you watch one with us?" Driller practically begged, and I nodded.

"As long as you don't make fun of me when I don't look," I said quietly.

He grinned and said, "Deal."

I went around and curled up on the couch beside Narcos and he lifted his arms so I could tuck myself into his side.

"All right, let's see…" Driller dropped onto the couch on my other side and I smiled and took another drink of my beer.

He and Narcos argued over what to watch for the entire time it took for the pizza to arrive. Their banter back and forth left me laughing so hard, a couple of times I nearly had beer come out of my nose. I learned very quickly not to drink if I thought they were going to say something ornery.

We ate on the couch, using paper plates, the box of pizza open on the footrest, which was easily the size of a coffee table. They finally settled on a television series about a small town, a fog or mist rolling in, holding all sorts of terrifying and horrific creatures – the true terror of it actually lie within the townsfolk, and how they came apart under the pressure. It was incredibly sad and multilayered, and was difficult to watch in places. Uncomfortable not because of the imagery, but because I had lived firsthand with that kind of apathy, that distrust and negativity.

I jumped slightly when a hand smoothed along the top of my foot and up my shin. Driller made eye contact with me, and leaned in. He moved the skirt of my dress aside and pressed a light kiss just below my knee. I stared at him staring at me, and forgot to breathe at the intensity of the look in his eyes.

I jumped slightly again, when a soft press of lips met the skin where my neck sloped down into my shoulder.

Narcos' arm slid off the back of the couch and held me, firmly but gently, across my chest, above my breasts.

Still, my gaze was fixed on Driller, on those eyes of his, so stark and vivid below his thick, dark brown hair, so dark as to be almost black. His eyes, I had thought at first, were an unremarkable brown, but lit with the fire of desire, they'd turned to a molten caramel, and with every kiss he placed on my skin the heat from his gaze melted my resolve to match those eyes.

"What do you say, Bright Eyes? Ready for some dessert?"

"Depends on what you have in mind," I whispered.

He smoothed his hands against my legs, brushing my long skirt out of his way as he carefully lowered his face. I wasn't wearing any panties, a sort of personal 'Fuck you' to the legal system that had consistently fucked with my friends who were good people and rarely performed the way it was intended to when it really counted. At least, for me anyway.

He smiled when he dropped his gaze to the apex of my thighs and Narcos growled in my ear, "Just relax, babe, and keep those ankles high."

I barely had time to register what he'd said and Driller's mouth was on me, his shoulders nudging my thighs further apart, his hands draping my legs over his shoulders as he lapped at my pussy.

I gasped, and Narcos' hand was at my throat, tipping my head back, his mouth on mine, his tongue slipping past my lips to stroke against my own. I let out a decadent moan into his mouth and felt his lips curl slightly against my own as he kissed me deeply. His best friend and partner slipped a finger inside of me and it was all I could do to keep from writhing.

Narcos slipped a hand down the top of my dress and palmed one of my breasts, his mouth relentless against mine as Driller teased my clit with his own velvet-soft tongue. My hips jerked involuntarily at first contact with my most sensitive place and he chuckled against my body.

"Just relax, Bright Eyes. We've got you," he whispered against my sex, and it was the hottest thing…

I moaned into Narcos' mouth, his hand gripping my breast firmly, kneading it just right. Driller added a second finger to the first inside me and worked and teased at the roof of my vagina, seeking out that spot. He was so close to finding it, and I tore my mouth away from Narcos' and whispered, "Hotter, yeah, warmer… no, no, colder! Back the other – " I hissed and let my head fall back and Driller took the cue and released a beautiful torment upon me. He stroked my spot from within and teased my clit with his tongue.

Narcos resumed kissing me and I was pinned like a butterfly between them, my hips rising and falling off the couch of their own volition,

Driller pinning them down with one arm as he teased me, pleased me, and made me his bitch. All the while, my lover encouraged me with his mouth against mine, his hand against my breast, to take my pleasure – that there would be so much more.

I wasn't in any sort of hurry about experiencing both of these men. I wanted to take my time, savor them both, savor every moment, and let them love my body. I needed it. I needed to let go and just let someone take care of me for a change… I was so weary of drifting between dangers, hoping not to get caught up, slinking low to the ground, trying to go unnoticed. I wanted to be seen and I reveled in their full attention. Their lips on my skin, their hands on my body, safe in their arms – it was pure magic and I went from feeling like I was just barely surviving to absolutely thriving under their care.

Driller took such care with lips and tongue against my most intimate parts while Narcos ravished my mouth, exploring every bit of it. I writhed between them as they held me in a loving and tender embrace, taking me to heights I'd never been, letting me go and watching me soar.

I arched, my body drawn up off the couch as if by some great, invisible hand as lighting flashed through my nerves, flitting down every fiber and through every muscle. I twitched, my core tightening, on the very brink, and with one final firm swipe of his tongue, Driller sent me hurtling across the sky. I was falling, falling, falling, without going anywhere at all because Narcos held me fast, until my eyes could focus again and my breath, though coming in strong pants, became a little less ragged.

"That's my girl," Narcos murmured proudly, smiling down into my face where he held me across his lap.

"God, I have to get inside her, bro…"

Driller sounded in awe and I ached for a deeper touch. I looked up at Narcos who looked down at me, smiling; no trace of jealousy in his eyes or on his face.

"That's up to her, man," he said and I nodded faintly, still dazed from my orgasm, yet wanting and needing more. Narcos' smile widened and he nodded softly in return.

"Is that a yes, Bright Eyes?" Driller asked.

It took me a couple of tries, but finally my voice kicked in and I said, "Yes."

24

arcos…

We took her to the bedroom. She was wobbly, walking between us, her orgasm by my best friend leaving her rattled in all the best ways. Now the three of us were nude; she was on her knees in front of me on the bed, looking unsure while Driller rolled on a condom behind her.

I kissed her, her hair soft in my hands where I held it away from her face, cradling her head in my hands. Her lips, moving against mine, were yielding and pure silk, her mouth opening to the light flick of my tongue against her bottom lip like a flower, her body melting against mine in perfect love and perfect trust.

She jumped slightly when Driller touched her hips, drawing her back to make her ready for him. She met my gaze, her eyes troubled, worried, and I smiled at her, smoothing a thumb along her jaw and poured into my expression just how much I wanted this, how much I adored her, how much I loved my best friend. Her eyes warmed and she kissed my chest. I closed my eyes and relished the feel of her lips on my skin as she trailed kisses down, down, and lower still. I sucked in a hard breath when her slight gasp as Driller slipped into her brushed heat over the head of my cock.

She took me into her mouth and groaned, and I echoed the sentiment as her voice vibrated through my cock, sending pleasing waves of tingling sensation through me. Driller started slow and easy, making love to my girl with even, measured thrusts, gauging what was good for her and what could be better and with each thrust, she took me a little bit deeper into her mouth, her hot velvet tongue rubbing along my frenulum. I grasped her hair gently, holding it back from her face, the silky strands tangling around my fingers, warm against my hands.

I closed my eyes and concentrated purely on the sensation of Everleigh's soft mouth working my dick, straining to both not come and to let her do her thing, to just keep my hands in her hair and not try to control her head, not thrust myself deeper into her throat. It could be hot, but I wasn't willing to do that to her without talking about it first, especially given how many douchebags she'd been hooked up with before me who weren't too concerned about her consent when it came to those kinds of things.

Driller picked up his pace but kept it easy, faster but not harder. She arched lower to the bed, taking me deeper, easing into a rhythm to match his, the head of my cock nudging the back of her throat, to the point that when she swallowed, it did some really fucking spectacular things around the head. I moaned, letting out a breathy "Yeah, babe…" breathing some words of encouragement, the struggle fuckin' real to hold myself together, to keep myself from going. I wasn't ready yet. I wanted this to last for-fucking-ever, even knowing this was just the appetizer and wanting the full course meal.

"Oh, god, yeah," Driller said and I knew that tone. I knew it meant Everleigh was tightening up around his cock, that she was close, that she was going to come again with my best friend inside her, and *that* made my heart lift, its pace quicken, and a surge of desire spread out through my body, carried like quicksilver through my veins, making my nerves start to sparkle and glow.

"Yeah, yeah, yeah, Bright Eyes. Just like that. Just like that, baby. Take your pleasure," he encouraged and Everleigh took me deep into her throat, moaned around my dick, and gripped the sheets to either side of my hips as hers jerked back to meet Driller's oncoming thrust.

It was so beautiful, so pure, and she was so lost in the moment. I felt my cock pulse and I rode that razor's edge but didn't quite go over. I wasn't ready to lose myself, not yet. I wanted in that tight, pink pussy of hers. I wanted deep inside her and for my best friend to get down and dirty with us both.

"She good?" I asked, gathering her hair back from her face. He slipped out of her and she climbed my body hungrily, her mouth going for mine, her beautiful green eyes glazed with pleasure, but the fire lit in her soul matching the burn going on in my own.

"Oh, yeah," Driller declared.

"More than good," she murmured, and straddled my hips, her mouth coming down on mine where I sat up against the headboard.

She lowered herself onto me and it felt like coming home, the way I eased into her tight, sopping pussy. Her body was hot and inviting, soft and supple in all the right places, her breasts crushing against my chest, her back arching like an offering. Driller moved up the bed to kiss her shoulder, down her back, showering her with the adoration she deserved.

I moved steadily inside her and her breath fanned hot against my shoulder as she started to fly, drunk or high, off our love, off the chemicals her body released during sex. I held her to me and her hips jerked slightly as Driller rose up behind her. She groaned and moved her hips back and I smiled. He grinned at me over her back and kept teasing her body with his fingers, working her up to taking him.

I brought her mouth to mine, and thrust up into her as she knelt above me. She kissed me and I asked her quietly if what we were doing was all right.

"More," she whispered, an echo of the first time we'd kissed, the first time we'd fallen into each other's arms and had completely allowed ourselves to drown in the other. I loved it, and made eye contact with Driller and gave him a slight nod. He threw chin back, and worked at my girl's body, driving her wild.

After a little bit, he pressed his cock to her asshole and pressed his way slowly into her body. He penetrated her slowly, deliberately, easing her and us into it, and I closed my eyes and relished the sensation of my best friend's cock slowly sliding against my own through the thin veil of my woman's body.

It was the best, most erotic sensation on the planet and one I didn't think I would ever get enough of. I also didn't think I could do this with any other dude. Driller and I were just that next level kind of tight.

"Oh, fuck," he said and sucked in a breath between his teeth, going still. I moved and he hissed, throwing back his head crying, "Aw, yeah!"

I loved it. I couldn't get enough of either of them. We may not have been adventurous enough to pitch or catch for one another, or to suck each other's dicks, but this? This was fantastic, this was the closest we would ever get, and I was cool with that. He was cool with that, and whatever woman we had between us usually never complained.

This? This was different, though. This filled me with so much fucking love... for him, for Everleigh especially, even for myself, knowing how lucky, how blessed I was to be in this position, that I swear my heart grew several sizes in my chest and got full to the point of bursting.

I was sweating, on that razor's edge, flying high and drunk on their love; the both of us, Driller and I, working ourselves in and out of Everleigh, see-sawing back and forth with easy, deep, and even strokes, only stopping when he felt like he needed more lube so he wouldn't hurt my woman, right now, *our* girl...

"Oh, god!" Everleigh gasped. "Oh, yes!"

I felt her tighten up as much as she could, and pulled back just enough to look her in the eyes, which were heavy-lidded with love and lust. She bit her bottom lip in this seductive way that was even more erotic because she had no idea just how beautiful, sultry, and sexy she was, and with a final thrust, her body stiffened, coiling tight, and she dropped her forehead to my shoulder, hiding her face in the crook of my neck as her body lost all control.

I met my partner's eyes over my baby's back and the love, lust, and erotic pleasure in their depths echoed mine and I don't think either one of us could hold off with how Everleigh's body convulsed and tempted our own orgasms out of us. I watched Driller stiffen, his eyes close, and I let myself fall, all of us hurtling back to earth from the seventh heaven we'd found ourselves in, crashing into the fluffy cloud of my partner's king-sized bed and laying in a profoundly satisfied tangle of limbs.

"THAT WAS... DIFFERENT..." Driller said sometime later, when we'd managed to clean ourselves and Everleigh up and were laying in a sated, sleepy cuddle-pile, snug in his bed.

"How do you mean?" I asked softly, raising up to check on Everleigh, who had turned in her sleep and was fetched up against Driller's chest, her face angelic, peaceful in a way I'd never seen before, as she slept.

"She's 'the one', isn't she?" he asked softly, and I stared into his eyes from several inches away across the pillows.

"Yeah, man. I think so," I murmured carefully, not entirely sure what he was driving at or what kind of reaction the news was going to draw out of him. I waited on pins and needles the few seconds it took for his thoughtful face to render a verdict. He made up his mind and a slow, sexy smile graced his lips.

"I'm happy for you, man."

"Yeah?" I asked, both relieved and a little surprised.

"Yeah. She's something else and you deserve that, all of that. You deserve the selfless loving, the beauty; the grace. Just, everything. It's not gone unnoticed by me, bro, that she's just as beautiful on the inside as she is on the outside. You deserve that. You deserve all of it, and so does she."

He held up a hand over her sleeping form and I raised mine up. We clasped hands and lowered them gently, resting them over her prone and sleeping form between us. I kissed the back of her shoulder where I spooned her and she shifted slightly in her sleep, pressing the curve of her ass into my dick. I closed my eyes and settled, my best friend's words moving me to tears.

For the first time in a long fucking time, I felt whole in a way I don't think there are words to explain…

25

___

*E*verleigh…

    I sighed, and even though I was awake, I wasn't ready to open my eyes. I cuddled into the man holding me close and was rewarded with a masculine chuckle.

One that *didn't* belong to Narcos.

A bit of nervous shyness reared its head. Even though it was utterly ridiculous after what we'd done the afternoon and night before, it was still there. Irrational? Stupendously so, but then again, if anxiety made sense, it would probably be much easier to work through and control.

I opened my eyes to warm, smiling brown ones and a gentle, "Good morning, Bright Eyes…"

It took me a couple tries, but I finally croaked out "Good morning."

He chuckled deeply and kissed my forehead. I closed my eyes, a tingling sensation sweeping over me, but only a pale imitation of what I felt when Narcos did it.

Driller hummed, a satisfied sound, as he cuddled me, and said, "Not to worry about a thing, baby. He's just in the kitchen making us breakfast."

"Oh," I said.

He chuckled again and said, "Love that he trusted me to take good care of you while he cooked. Mind if I love on you some more?"

"Um, I don't know," I said, wondering why it wasn't Driller who cooked.

He must have read the slight dismay on my face, because he said, "Trust me, Bright Eyes. You want food with flavor, then your man's the one who needs to cook. I'm crap at it."

"I'm sorry," I murmured, flushing.

"Don't be, nothing happens that you don't want to." He kissed my lips gently and I felt my body respond, even if my mind was being hell over shy about it.

"Mm." He sounded as if he were savoring the taste of my lips, and butterflies took wing in my stomach. "Hey, Narcos!" he called out and I jumped.

"Yeah, what?" Narcos called out from the kitchen.

"Can I fuck your girl again?"

Narcos appeared in the doorway and shrugged one tattooed shoulder. "If she wants you to, and if I can watch."

I laughed nervously, and Narcos pushed off the edge of the doorway and came over. He sat down on the edge of the bed and put a hand on my hip.

"I have no problem with you and Driller getting it on, babe."

"Why?" I asked softly, a bit taken aback, thinking this was only supposed to be a one-time thing.

"Because I trust him and you implicitly, and I know he'll treat you right," he said and leaned forward to kiss me. He leaned back and said, "Plus, watching you with my best friend gets me all kinds of hot."

I laughed a little and read the truth in his eyes, but still, though I felt attracted to Driller, though I even felt a spark of love, it was nothing compared to the inferno I held in my heart and soul for Narcos.

Narcos smiled at me, leaned in for another kiss and whispered against my mouth, "I love you, have some fun while I finish breakfast. It's cool."

He got up and went out and I laid back down against the bed. I turned my attention back to Driller, whose eyebrows went up. I giggled and he grinned.

"Is that a yes?" he asked.

I cocked my head, letting my eyes rove over his face, and said, "Kiss me."

"Yes, ma'am," he returned, a hint of amusement in his voice as he lowered his face to mine to follow through. His mouth was kind against mine, his touch light and easy, like he expected rejection and was totally willing to back off at the slightest sense of unease from me, which made things surprisingly easy.

Our kiss intensified, and my desire to just feel good intensified with it, to capture just some of the magic of the night before to trap it in my heart like a butterfly in a jar. He tore his mouth from mine as things heated to a slow simmer between us and asked, "Can I?"

"Yes," I whispered, and he immediately went for a condom on the bedside table. He rolled it on in the blink of an eye and got between my legs, easing his way carefully inside of me.

I let my head fall back and cried out slightly, freezing and laughing when Narcos called out from the kitchen, "Yeeeah! Make it good, buddy!"

"Shut the fuck up, homeboy! I'm gonna lose my concentration!"

I stuffed my hands against my mouth to stifle my giggles, which swiftly turned to a gasp as he eased his way into me further. He was longer than Narcos by an inch or two but didn't have quite as much girth; I was grateful for that last night, let me tell you.

I'd never been penetrated by two men at once. I'd been scared, but it'd been something undeniably amazing, and I secretly wanted to try it again sometime in the future. I just didn't know if I would be brave enough to ask for it.

Driller lay himself atop me and smoothed some of my hair away from my face before he began to move.

I closed my eyes, just giving myself over to the feel of his body sliding along mine, inside me. The way he humped me was a bit awkward, with his body on top of mine like it was – almost an awkward-teenager type of thing, but I couldn't deny there was something about it that did very nice things from the inside. Like 'Oh, my god' nice things. That golden blush of pleasure unfurled from down low and began to peak in record time.

I gasped as my pussy throbbed around him, almost a preview of coming attractions and I heard from the doorway, "Oh, now that's nice. Whatever you're doing, keep doing it, man. Fuck, that's hot."

"I've got you," Driller whispered in my ear and I melted a little into the mattress of his bed, and turned my head. Narcos stood, his arms crossed, a pleased smile playing along his lips and my pulse jumped. The desire in his eyes, the shine of pride, love, lust, and all things good… Oh, my god, it was sensual.

Heat unfurled like wings in my core but it was my heart that took flight. I lost myself in the sensation and let myself go, as much to enjoy myself as to put on one fabulous show for the man I loved, because clearly, he really was enjoying every second of this as much as I was.

BREAKFAST WAS BAKED oatmeal with cinnamon and bananas. The rest of the day was spent lazily making love and watching television in a big cuddle-pile on the overstuffed couch. It was comfortable, and I felt as if I had found my bliss.

Still, as much as I loved to be between them, I really wished I could just have some time alone with Narcos. Like, truly alone. Like 'back at the cabin' alone… Alas, while the trial continued, that was not to be.

After two days with Driller, we moved again, this time to a hotel that was not the hotel that I had stayed in before. No, this one was much cheaper, though clean, and wasn't so much a hotel as a motel. An Indigo City police cruiser stayed parked right outside our door.

Narcos wouldn't admit to it, but I had to believe another, darker threat loomed. At least, it felt like it, because one of his other club brothers, Poe, stayed in the bed next to ours. Although there was definitely nothing sexual happening there. He was a sweet guy, a patrol officer with the Indigo City police, but he was just a club brother and friend. Nothing more.

The next night, Poe was replaced by Golden, who was at least slightly more familiar to me. I still hated it, though. I didn't feel comfortable talking. I loved that we could cuddle and didn't have to refrain from it, but I hated that it felt as if we were being babysat. I just wanted to get on with my life, already, but we couldn't do anything until we knew where we stood, and we wouldn't know that without a verdict.

It was the third night that Yale arrived, looking haggard, and with a bottle of whiskey. I didn't like the looks of the conversation to come. My hackles went up, my red flags raised, and it only got worse when he insisted we all have a drink before talking about anything.

I sipped from my plastic hotel cup, the alcohol smooth, yet the flavor with a bite that I found unpleasant. Yale eyed me from across the little motel room's table and finally drew a breath and said, "Have you thought about what you're going to do if the verdict comes back 'Not Guilty?'" he asked.

I shook my head. I didn't even really want to think about the possibility, but the worry in his eyes said there was a distinct one. My stomach churned with nerves as he sat forward.

"Do you know what Witness Protection is?" he asked.

I nodded carefully and glanced at Narcos, whose expression had shut down completely at the mention of it. I wasn't stupid. I knew what that look meant and I shook my head.

No. It wasn't something I would do. I wouldn't, I *couldn't* leave him behind… but I would have to, wouldn't I?

"Babe…" he said gently, and sucked in a breath.

"No," I said simply, and the finality of my tone made Yale make a face.

"It would be your funeral if he's let go," he said.

"So don't let him go."

He gave a dark snort and said, "Doesn't work like that, Everleigh."

"I don't care," I said, and turned to Narcos. "I'm not leaving you."

"Babe," he started and I shook my head, stubbornly.

"I won't," I said.

Yale sighed and downed the rest of what was in his cup and poured himself a little more.

"You might not have much choice. The jury went to deliberations two days ago."

"Shit," Narcos said.

"Why are they taking so long?" I asked.

"Who knows?" Yale said. "At least they didn't come back right away…"

I frowned. "Why's that?"

"Right away usually means an acquittal," he said plainly.

"So that means the fact they're taking a long time is a good thing, right?"

He shook his head. "A day, sure, maybe. But two? The longer it drags out, the dicier it gets."

I sat back in my seat and let the mantle of my misery settle upon my shoulders.

"Whatever happens, you're going to be okay," Narcos said and I got mad at him. I glared at him and he silenced himself, closing his mouth against whatever he was going to say next.

"Do you have to be here?" I asked Yale.

"No, I don't. I really don't," he said, and stood up with a sigh. "Keep the bottle," he said and eyed Narcos. "I think you're going to need it."

Narcos rolled his eyes at him and Yale went to the door. He paused on the way out and looked at me before saying, "Don't make any rash decisions, Everleigh. You really need to think things through. The offer is a once in a lifetime deal when it comes to wit-sec."

I simply stared at him, and he nodded and slipped out the door, shutting it firmly behind him. I turned to Narcos, acid on my tongue, but the words I wanted to use died before they could finish climbing out of the dark part of my soul.

His eyes were so full of pain, so full of misery, I couldn't speak when he said, "Don't think for a minute I *want* to let you go, babe. I just want you to be safe."

"Then come with me," I said desperately, and he shook his head sadly.

"It doesn't work that way. I can't. You'd have to go alone. They'd give you a new identity, a new social, and you'd disappear completely."

"Why?" I hated how much I sounded like I was whining. I couldn't stop the tears that stung the backs of my eyes from welling at the very thought of having to leave him. I so desperately wanted to put down roots to make a life, but only one with him in it. I loved him. I loved him so completely in such a short amount of time it was terrifying, but I couldn't deny how real it was. After all, any love that could be born in such a crucible, under such pressure, and out of such circumstances… it could survive anything, couldn't it?

Anything but witness protection… I thought to myself.

He took my hands in his as I sniffed and looked away. I turned my eyes to the ceiling, to the old air conditioning unit spewing frigid air, to the coffee maker, the worn carpet, just anything but those somber green eyes that were fixed on my face as if he were memorizing every curve, every line, every part of my being like he would never see me again.

"This is bullshit," I said, and let my tears go.

"Yeah," he agreed. "But babe, if it comes down to a life with you out there somewhere alive, but without you in it – or a life without you in it because you're dead, you know which one I'm going to choose."

He pulled me into his arms and I wept against his shoulder.

"Don't think like that, please… they could convict," I said.

"The danger wouldn't necessarily be over even if they do."

"I don't care!"

"I don't want that kind of life for you, Everleigh. One where you're always looking over your shoulder – "

I interrupted him.

"Which is just going to be my life anyways, witness protection or with you. I would much rather it be with you than out there all alone," I said. "At least, with you, I know I'm safe."

His hand went to the back of my head, his fingers burying themselves in my hair as he massaged my scalp, his other arm around my back, holding me tightly to his chest. We clung to each other in the shabby hotel room.

"Can we just pretend all of this doesn't exist?" I whispered. "I mean, we can't do anything until we know, right?"

"Yeah," he agreed, but the defeat was still in his voice.

"I love you," I whispered, and he held me even tighter still.

"I love you, too, babe. I only want the best for you."

"I know," I whispered, and clung to him back.

"We're going to have to revisit this once the decision is made."

"I know."

I pulled back and suddenly didn't care if the officer outside heard us, or about anything except being as close to him as possible. Especially if it was going to be our last time. I didn't want to think about that at all. I didn't want to think about Witness Protection or juries. I wanted to talk about a future life together. I wanted to talk about where we wanted to live and what kind of job I should get. I wanted to talk about favorite foods and what I should cook for him when he's had a bad day. I wanted to talk about gardening and bee-keeping, about his favorite things to do when he wasn't working other than fishing.

I wanted to talk about movie nights with Driller and long rides on the weekends. I wanted to exist in a time and a place where King couldn't touch me and the rest of the Knights of Crescentia wouldn't dare.

I wanted everything that I knew I couldn't have because the universe just seemed to loathe me that damn much and seemed to be incapable of giving me anything but heartache and pain.

"Don't let me go," I begged as he moved inside me, and I watched the echo of my agony reflect back to me through his eyes mere inches from my own.

"Not tonight," he promised.

"Not ever," I begged.

"Only if it's truly what's best for you, babe. I wouldn't do anything to hurt you."

Liar, my mind whispered, because letting me go would surely kill me.

26

*N*arcos…

She'd finally fallen asleep. It was the wee hours of the morning, that quiet time when the whole world was sleeping and the city was at its quietest. I managed to slip out from under her without waking, sitting up on the edge of the bed with a tired sigh.

I couldn't stop thinking about Yale's visit. About a life without her in it, knowing she was out there somewhere, wondering if she was happy, wondering if she'd found love again with someone else, wondering if he was treating her well, if she was staring at the same stars, the same moon in the sky, from could be hundreds, could be thousands, of miles away. And wondering if she would know she still held my heart in her scarred hands; that it was beating in those hands of hers out of my chest from so far away… because I swear to fucking God, that's how it would be for me.

I slipped outside, taking my burner cell with me, and punched in the only number I had memorized.

Driller picked up on the second ring, his voice rough with sleep as he demanded gruffly "What's wrong?"

I sighed and told him, "Nothing and everything."

There was a moment of silence on the other end and a creak or two as he sat up. He let out a long sigh as he tried to clear his head and finally said, "Talk to me."

I told him everything. He was the one person I never held anything back from because he didn't judge. It was the same with me, for him.

He let out a breath and said, "It's not like you to borrow trouble before it happens. Usually you got your shit together better than this."

"I love her, man. Like, I've never felt this way about any other woman and I never thought it would happen to me, but here I am and I'm so twisted up in knots over her on the inside, I just..." My words failed me and I leaned hard against the wall outside our motel room's door. I said weakly, "Help me out."

He cleared his throat and said, "First off, we ain't even got a verdict. Second off, you love her so much, you listen to what she has to say about it?"

"She doesn't want to go," I said.

He sounded frank when he said, "Then she doesn't go, bro. We protect her."

"Just like that?" I demanded.

"Yeah," he said. "Just like that." He paused and let it sink in. "You ain't alone on this, man. I know how undercover works; you're out there solo, on your own, handling what comes, as it comes, by your-self. It's different when feelings and other people get involved, am I right?"

"Yeah." I nodded, even though he couldn't see it.

"Right. Well, you're not out there anymore. You're back, and we're here. Me, Youngblood, Golden, Poe, Skids, the rest of the club – even the hose boys. We've got your back. She's your woman. You guys are a matched pair – never thought I'd see the day, but it's true, and what's yours to protect is the club's to protect. You ain't on your own anymore."

"Yeah, but Yale says – "

"Yale can suck it. He's doing what lawyers do, which is his fuckin' job. We do what *we* do – which is?"

"Boots on the ground, kicking ass, and taking names to let the lawyers sort it out later."

"Fuckin' right, man."

I breathed out, some of the crushing weight lifting off my chest.

"Thanks, bro."

"Not a problem," he said. "You know I've got you."

"Yeah, that's why I called, genius."

He chuckled on the other end of the line, and we both sighed.

"You thought about the future any?" he asked.

"Yeah, I was thinking about buying a house. Something just outside the city, maybe around Youngblood's neighborhood. Something small, with a yard so she can do her one-with-nature hippy boho shit and be happy."

"Sounds fuckin' awesome," he said.

"Driller, man, this is the woman I'm gonna marry," I said.

"I know that," he said simply and I had to smile. He was always a step ahead of me realizing shit like that. He also always kept it to himself, let me figure it out on my own, just backing me up until I had the epiphany. We were close to the same age, but he was always like the older, wiser one.

"Any luck getting the rat to take the cheese?" I asked.

He sighed and it sounded half-defeated.

"Not yet. Watch your ass, man."

"Always do."

I gave some side-eye to the patrolman in his cruiser, who was watching me but still managing to mind his own business at the same time.

"All right, man. You good?" Driller asked.

"Yeah, I'm good," I affirmed.

"Good, get your ass back in there and snuggle your future wife," he ordered.

"Sir, yes sir," I said sardonically.

"You're one lucky son of a bitch."

"I know it, and hey, I share."

"I know that's right. Makes me one lucky son of a bitch, too."

"What's mine is yours, buddy."

"Back at 'cha."

"Night, bro."

"G'night."

We ended the call and I stood and stared up at the lit buildings of my city for a while, wishing I could pick out more than one or two stars out of the sky, but, light pollution, you know?

I felt better after my conversation with Driller, I had pretty much already known what he was going to say, but sometimes I just needed to hear it anyway. You know? I wasn't worried about me, so much. I was worried about Everleigh, and that was something far more nerve-wracking. I was reckless as fuck when it came to *me*, but I wasn't about to have the same kind of blasé attitude where she was concerned. She deserved way better treatment than how I treated my own dumb ass, and the way she looked at me, the way she looked *to* me, I needed to take fewer chances. Do better by myself, for myself, if only for her peace of mind.

The motel room door opened and I turned. Everleigh was wrapped in her shawl, the one with the big pink roses on it, looking up at me sleepily through a tangle of her auburn hair.

"Hey," I murmured. "You all right?"

"I'm fine, but I woke up and you weren't in bed."

I raised my arm and she padded out barefoot, looking so small and beautiful with her hunched shoulders in her thin nightgown and that beautiful fringed shawl. She looked like an angel or a pixie, something mythical, fantastical. She tucked herself into my side and looked up at me with those jewel-bright eyes, curiosity on her face and I felt nothing but gratitude to my brother Driller for having just set my ass straight.

"What are you doing out here?" she asked softly.

"Callin' Driller," I said, and rubbed her arm up and down through the thin shawl, even though it was warm as fuck out here and there was no way she could be cold.

"What for?" she asked.

"Advice."

"About what?"

"You, WITSEC, the shit Yale had to say."

"I'm not leaving you," she said resolutely, and I smiled.

"You don't have to," I said.

"I don't?"

"Nope."

She raised her eyebrows and stared at me until I gave in and let out a gusty sigh and took her into my arms more completely. A motorcycle revved and we both stiffened, our heads turning in the direction of the street. It had to be a block or more over and the sound faded as the rider ranged out into the city, but it wasn't until the sound disappeared completely that either of us relaxed.

"We're gonna be doing that, probably, the rest of our lives together," I said, a little sadly.

"A small price to pay," she murmured.

"You really want this?" I asked, and she put her hand on my chest, her long hair tickling the backs of my hands as she looked into my eyes and I held her close.

"I want *you* and if this is the price I have to pay? Well, it's a small price in my book. You make me happy, and I don't think I've ever really been happy before…"

God, that was fucking heartbreaking.

"…and now that I have it, now that I have you, I'm not about to let go so easily."

I smiled and huffed a slight laugh, impressed with her, proud of her. I lowered my forehead to hers and said, "Okay, then, we're doing this."

"Hell, yeah, we are."

I smiled and said, "Let's go back inside."

"In a little bit," she whispered quietly. "This is so nice, just standing out here, with you."

I held her tight and she rested her head on my shoulder.

"I love you," she murmured.

"I love you, too," I whispered and she heaved such a satisfied, such a complete sigh it was like the whole universe just snapped into place. A clarity came over me, and I just prayed for the best, that the universe would finally cut this woman a fucking break, because she needed one.

IT WAS AROUND ELEVEN O'CLOCK the next morning when the burner rang. When I answered, it was Driller with barely-suppressed excitement in his voice. He blurted it out before I could even say 'What's up?'

"Guilty."

"You're shitting me?" I felt it like a bolt of lightning from the sky, the electric feelings from the top of my head, tingling down my face, all the way down and out through my toes.

"Nope, guilty on all fuckin' counts."

"Everleigh!" I called and she came out of the bathroom.

"What?" she asked, alarmed.

"You did it, baby. Guilty on all counts."

"You're joking," she demanded, stunned.

I heard Driller laugh on the phone and he said, "About a lot of things, but not this one."

I relayed what he said, but Everleigh didn't laugh, she just sank to the foot of the neatly-made bed we weren't using and folded her hands in her lap. She stared out at nothing, her mind turning so fast all she could really do was stare blankly as her emotions caught up with her and her eyes began to brim with tears.

"I gotta go," I told Driller.

"Yeah, I'll be by later."

"K, thanks."

I ended the call and tossed the phone carelessly on the unkempt bed she and I had occupied just a little bit ago, trying and failing to sleep, talking in hushed tones most of the night about life, about what she wanted, about what I wanted, and about how to possibly get there when all this shit was over.

I knelt in front of my girl and pushed her hair out of her face while she reeled from the news. Relief, fear, hope, anxiety, disbelief, all chased through her eyes, across her fair features one after the other, round and round, and I waited, my hands cradling her face, just waiting for her to land.

"Is it over?" she asked, a tear dripping from the end of her nose.

I shook my head and told her the truth. "No, but this part of it is. We've cleared the first hurdle."

She met my eyes with hers and a determination, a commitment passed between us. I nodded and whispered, "We're gonna see this through. Together."

She nodded and lunged forward, capturing my mouth with hers and it was the sweetest fucking kiss, so full of hope, so full of promise, so full of everything that there should be between lovers and partners.

"Make love to me," she whispered, and there wasn't a question mark anywhere in there.

"You got it, babe," I growled back, and I fell into her arms, put my body on her, her thighs parting, her legs wrapping around my hips, and I knew what heaven was. I knew that no matter where we were, no matter what we faced, we were each other's home.

27

*E*verleigh…

I clung to him, our mouths tangling, my hands in his hair, holding it back from his eyes even as he held mine back from mine. I wrapped my legs around his hips as he lay atop me, caging me with his strong, tattooed arms, his mouth hot against mine, his cock straining against his jeans, pressed firmly to the soaked, thin cotton of my panties where my skirt rode up.

His hands traveled down my body, over my stretched cotton tank, hitching up my skirt even higher, as my hands smoothed over the heated skin of his back. He groaned into my mouth when I skirted my fingertips along his waistband around front, finding his button already undone, my impatient fingers scrambling to lower his zipper.

He was trying to draw my panties down over my hips and I kept trying to raise them off the bed, but his body kept me pinned. We were being counterproductive in our passion and finally I muttered against his kiss, "Just tear them."

He laughed darkly, the humor ending in a heated growl as he gripped the hip of my panties between both fists to either side of the seam and *pulled*.

He did likewise with the opposite side and dragged the ruined cotton out from between my legs even as I delved my hand into the front of his pants and gripped him with a firm hand, stroking him between us gently, needing, dying for a deeper touch.

"Make love to me," I begged in a sensual whisper and he shoved his pants down around his thighs to free himself, pushed my skirt up out of his way once again, and gave me exactly what I wanted.

He slid into me, balls-deep on the first thrust and I cried out, arching over the bedspread, thrusting my tits at him in offering. He pulled my tank top down, freeing one, and immediately covered the nipple with his mouth, bending nearly double to do it.

The feel of his mouth on me, his cock buried deep inside of me, was electric. A low hum of pleasure swept through my body as he worked my nipple with lips, teeth, and tongue. His hips acted in counterpoint, thrusting as much as he could the way we were positioned, which was to say just enough to go deeper. It was just enough to send my pussy throbbing around him as the pressure built, the pleasure of his touch filling me like a cup, the liquid quicksilver of sensation rising impossibly fast, so impossibly quick that there was no avoiding being overfilled.

I gripped him, tensing my pelvic floor muscles around him, and he relinquished my nipple, arching up with a sound so animalistic it made me smile in a feral glee as we pushed each other, pulled each other along that razor's edge of pleasure so fine it was almost painful.

"Harder," I begged, "higher!"

He knew what I meant as we pushed each other closer and closer, higher and higher, towards the satisfaction we both desired, we both craved.

"Oh, God, Everleigh…" he moaned and my name, on his lips, in that way, was sweeter than any music, was more beautiful to me than any sound I'd ever heard before.

"Oh my god, *yes...*" I gasped, and spread my legs wider for him. He hooked an arm beneath my knee and laid one of my legs along his shoulder, folding me practically in half, eliciting a deep moan from me as he drove himself just that much deeper inside me, turning his head, laying a kiss, a soft bite, along the side of my calf.

"Come for me, babe, let me hear you," he murmured and I moaned, the sound disappearing into a breathy sigh as he eased his thumb between us, putting an even pressure against my clit, slicking it through my wetness and drawing torturous circles over it.

I gasped, I whined, I bucked against him to no avail, as he brought me closer and closer to that ultimate goal of orgasm. I tightened up on him harder and he hissed out between gritted teeth, his thrusting becoming more difficult as he found it harder to draw back. He shoved forward, balls-deep and I crashed against the mattress, my breath rushing out of me in a deep cry, softening the sound as I lost all control of my finer motor skills and simply shuddered beneath the weight of him, pinning me down.

God, I loved him.

I let myself drown in the warm river of glow he'd immersed me in and just drifted, holding him to me as he lay atop me. Both of us drifted together, even though in reality, we were still in the cheap motel room, lying on top of the bedspread of the bed we hadn't been using. Well, until now.

"You slay me in all the best ways," he whispered into my ear when our breathing allowed it.

"Mmm." I didn't have words, just hummed in satisfaction to let him know I'd heard him and cuddled him close to me.

He sighed and chuckled and it was the happiest sound I think I'd ever heard any man make, and it pleased me to no end that it had been made because of me.

∽

WE WENT to King's sentencing. Both of us sat behind the prosecution's desk, front row, our fingers locked, our palms pressed together.

I swallowed hard and stared at King's profile as he stood up and received his sentence, and breathed a silent sigh of relief when it was 'Life'. Granted, there was a possibility of parole, but not for at least twenty years. He looked pissed, leaned in to listen to his attorney whisper something in his ear, then turned and cast the most sinister look in my direction.

Narcos' hand tightened around mine, but I gave King nothing except my best blank look. I was terrified, but I wasn't about to give him the satisfaction of knowing that.

We stood, went through the motions of the court, and King and his cohorts were led out of the courtroom. I instantly felt a tension I hadn't realized I'd been carrying ease out of my shoulders. Yale turned and gave us a simple nod, his eyes shrouded with an unreadable look in them, his jaw tightly clenched.

We left the courtroom, Narcos hanging onto my hand and letting me out of the bench and into the aisle ahead of him, Driller right behind him.

When we reached the hall, I turned to them both and asked, "Now what?"

"You're a dead bitch!" Rebel grated, as he stepped out the courtroom behind us.

"Did you hear him threaten her?" Driller asked, amused.

"I surely did," Narcos said.

I watched silent, tongue-tied, as Narcos and Driller bantered back and forth, running circles around Rebel, who was trying to claim freedom of speech and hide behind the constitution. They were buying time, waiting for more of the Knights of Crescentia to make it to the door.

I stepped aside, relinquishing my hold on Narcos' hand when Driller stepped in to put Rebel up against the wall. Yale squeezed out of the doorway and stepped in front of me, putting a hand behind himself, and against me, to both keep track of me and to keep me from interfering as one of the Knights of Crescentia swung on Narcos.

I yipped and jumped when the brawl started, but it was all part of the plan. My presence here today was designed to provoke them, and it worked like a charm. Yale pressed me back, standing with a superior and smug look as bailiffs stepped in and more Indigo City police arrived to break up the fight.

In the end, Narcos boasted a split lip, Driller a bruised cheek and both of them displayed the biggest shit-eating grins. I smiled and Narcos held out a hand, the knuckles scraped and bleeding, and I took it gently.

"Go on, get out of here," Driller said good-naturedly with a wink. "I got this. Meet you at the 10-13 in a few hours."

Narcos nodded. "Appreciate it," he said, and Driller laughed.

"I think you've earned a break."

We followed Yale down back hallways to the service elevators where he punched the 'Down' button.

"That went better than I expected," he said, raising his eyebrows.

"Totally," Narcos agreed.

"But, do you think it will work?" I asked softly.

"Without King's brains, yeah. One of them will give up the cop feeding the club information. All these fuckers will be tied up for at least the next few months.”

Yale chimed in. “For assault, assaulting an officer, threatening a witness, resisting arrest, and whatever else I can come up with. And I can get pretty creative. It’s bought you time. Not sure how much, but you can at least breathe and get settled however you’d like.”

“Thank you,” I murmured, grateful.

He nodded, “You’re sure you can’t be talked into –“

“No,” I said quickly, and Narcos and I exchanged a look. He spoke for us both when he said, “Whatever happens, we’ll meet it head-on. The both of us.”

“Together,” I said softly.

The elevator chimed and the doors slid open.

Yale shook his head, a smile on his face as he stepped out.

“Go on, get out of here. I’ll see you later at the 10-13.”

“Thanks, man,” Narcos nodded.

When the doors slid shut, we looked at each other and burst into a fit of giggles and shared grins.

“I can’t wait to take you home,” he said.

“I can’t wait to see where you live,” I responded.

He shook his head and said, “It’s a shitty, cheap-ass studio, babe. I don’t want you getting used to it. I want to buy us a house.”

I blinked at him in surprise.

“You’re serious.”

“As a heart attack. I want a fresh start, a new beginning for the both of us.”

He touched my cheek and gently tweaked his thumb against it in the barest whisper of a touch and I blushed like I was brand new. He smiled, and just before we could kiss, the elevator jolted to a stop.

I had this horrifying image of the doors opening and something awful being on the other side, simply because it was my luck and I was just so happy right now. Surely the universe needed to send a gunman, or an accident, or something our way to ruin it.

The doors opened without incident and I breathed a subtle sigh of relief and followed him out into the garage.

Nothing happened. Nothing happened to us on the way to wherever he was taking me, either. I dared to let hope peek out from behind the typical rainclouds of my general melancholy and attempted to curb my negative thinking.

I held myself tightly to his back as we turned into an alley in the heart of the city's old town and hopped off when he went to back it into a line of others against the building.

"How far do we have to go?" I asked and he smiled and got off his bike.

"We're here, just right around the corner."

He took my hand, and we went into the bar-and-grill just around the alleyway's corner to a round of applause and rowdy cheers and whistling. I laughed and tucked myself against Narcos' chest, beneath one of his massive arms, as the rest of his true club, the Indigo Knights stepped forward to meet us.

It was overwhelming, but fantastic, positive, glowing, and wonderful at the same time.

28

*N*arcos…

"Hey, man. She looks like she's doing awesome," I leaned back against the bar and looked over. Driller stepped up next to me, Yale breaking off from him and going straight for his Aly Cat.

I cast my eyes in the direction of Everleigh, sitting among the rest of the club's women. She was smiling, genuinely smiling, but she wasn't talking, just listening, finding her own way, nodding along while the other ladies chatted.

"Yeah, she's doing great," I said.

"Taking her to your place tonight?" he asked.

"Yep."

"Cool, cool."

I tore my eyes off my girl and gave my friend some side-eye while I swigged my beer.

"Spill it," I ordered, and Driller bowed his head and laughed a little.

"Nothing, man. I'm happy for you, that's all."

"Buuut..." I lead off.

"No 'But', it's just – "

I laughed, "Motherfucker, 'It's just' is the same exact thing as a 'But.'"

He laughed too, and said, "It is not!"

"Okay, whatever, it's just what, then?"

"It's just things are changing," he said with a shrug, and I handed him my beer. He took a drink and handed it back.

"The more things change," I said, looking back at Everleigh who smiled at me from across the room, the warm glow of happiness in her eyes. I found myself smiling, too, when I finished, "The more they stay the same."

I looked back at Driller, who was searching my face, his expression too solemn for my liking. I took a swig of my beer and passed it back to him, and waved him off when he took a drink and tried to hand it back. He needed it a fuck of a lot more than I did, and I could always get another.

He nodded slowly, and I watched him work out my meaning for himself. He finally sighed and still looked unhappy.

"Move in with us," I said. "When I get us a house. Be our roomie."

"What?" he demanded, and nearly choked on another swig of beer.

"You heard me. Let's all start out together. I don't want or need you thinking anything stupid, like I'm going anywhere on you. It's always been you and me; that shit isn't changing."

"Shouldn't you check with the little missus before making unilateral decisions like that?"

I looked back to Everleigh and sighed. "You know, bro... she's so generous, so kind, I don't honestly think she'd have a problem with it. I know it'd make me feel a fuck of a lot better."

"How so?"

"Well, for one, if we're on opposite work schedules, it means she'll be home with someone I know I can trust to protect her, rather than by herself."

"True dat," he agreed.

"You'd save money, we'd save money, and really, things only have to change up if you managed to get yourself a woman…"

He snorted, "That's the last thing I need."

"Eventually," I said and he nodded.

"Eventually, but right now, I think I'm cool with one new normal at a fuckin' time."

"So you'll think about it?" I asked.

"As long as Bright Eyes is cool with it, or it's what she wants, then yeah. Yeah, I'd do it."

"You just want unfettered access to some hot pussy," Oz declared, knowing how we rolled. I laughed, and Driller finally *did* have beer come out his nose.

"She says 'No' I don't touch," he said.

I smiled, "Only reason I'd see her saying 'No' is if I weren't home and she starts second-guessing herself, or me. She fuckin' loves you, dude."

"Maybe," he said, "But nothing like the way she loves *you*."

"That's why she's *my* girl and not our girl. You never know where life's gonna take you, though."

Driller snorted and Oz shook his head, "You two fuckers are just too weird for me with the sharing shit." He walked away and Driller and I traded a look and practically rolled our eyes at the same time.

"Doesn't know what he's missing," Driller declared.

"Doesn't have a homie that he's tight with like we are," I said.

"Kind of sad for him when you put it that way."

"Right?"

"Tell you what," he said. "I'm game if she's game, but I need to hear it from her."

"That's fair enough, bro. You coming back with us tonight?"

"Nah, your first night having your woman in your bed; that should just be you two."

I snorted.

"I ain't slept in my own bed for so long, it probably isn't even comfortable to me anymore." I looked at Driller, who gave me a look in return, and I immediately went on the defensive. "What?" I demanded. "I can't even remember what it feels like, it's been so long!"

He started cracking up and I rolled my eyes. Like seriously, he started laughing so hard he couldn't even speak, wheezing out between gales of it, "You stupid."

The laughter was infectious and before long, I found myself laughing too, even though what we were laughing about was so fucking stupid.

"You guys are fuckin' ridiculous, man," Oz declared, shaking his head. "Y'all ain't even that drunk."

"Leave them alone, sensual chocolate," Pasquale came to the rescue from over by Everleigh, who'd been delighted to see him again. "It's probably stress and a whole lot of tired." He cocked a hand against his narrow waist and arched one overdone eyebrow at Oz as if daring him to challenge him on it. Oz was too busy laughing himself, shaking his head, because unlike us, he *was* that drunk, which was rare for him.

Everleigh drifted over and wrapped her arms around me, resting her chin on my chest and turning those luminous eyes up to me.

"Hello, beautiful," Driller said as I opened my mouth to say essentially the same thing.

She smiled and said softly, "Hey, how are my handsome men?" I barely heard her over the din of the bar, but couldn't help but smile when I made out her words.

"We're good," I said. "How are you feeling?"

"Overwhelmed, but I'm good too."

"You ready to get out of here?" I asked.

"You guys ready to take me?" she asked, and Driller and I exchanged a look.

I winked at him and smiled down at her and said, "Sure are, babe. There's something we want to ask you about…"

She smiled a thousand-watt smile and nodded, "Then let's go."

I WAS nervous about letting Everleigh into my apartment. I mean, it really was a piece of shit and I was kind of a minimalist. I didn't have a whole lot of personal shit. There wasn't any point, when I didn't spend any real time here.

I let her come in only *after* I swept the place and made sure there wasn't anyone lurking, still on high alert. I was pretty sure it was just going to be ingrained habit, and considering our accomplishments, it was likely to be a good thing. You know what I mean?

I left her in the care of Driller while I did my quick sweep and when I came back to the front door, my best friend was pouring on the charm, keeping my girl relaxed, and flirting like the pro at it he was.

"Okay you two, get in the apartment," I declared, and Everleigh burst into a fit of giggles at the face Driller made. He escorted my girl past me, his hands on her shoulders and I shut the door behind them and secured it.

Everleigh stood at the foot of the bed and did a slow, three-hundred-and-sixty-degree turn to take the place in.

"I can see why you want a house," she said softly, and Driller and I exchanged a look. She picked up on it right away and froze, cocking her head to one side and asking, "What?"

"Actually, we wanted to talk to you about that," I said.

"Oh?"

I nodded slowly and went to her, resting my hands on her waist, pulling her close, smoothing my hands under her little jean jacket, over her dress, and feeling up her lithe body underneath it. Driller moved in to stand behind her and took her jacket from her, tossing it carelessly onto the foot of my bed. He smoothed his hands over her back, along her shoulders, digging his thumbs ever-so-slightly in between them.

I smiled as Everleigh groaned in pleasure, her eyes slipping shut. I smiled at Driller, who winked at me and put his lips next to her ear.

"How would you like this whenever you want it?" he murmured low and rough, teasing.

"Mmm," she hummed out happily with the notion as he placed his lips on the cap of her shoulder in a light butterfly kiss.

"I would know you were safe." I said, pitching my voice low, "even when I couldn't be home."

She opened her eyes and looked up at me through her lashes, her pupils already dilating with desire as Driller deepened his attentions, kissing the erogenous zone on the side of her neck. I let my hands wander over the smooth cotton and rough embroidery of her little tank-dress and she let out a little breathy sound that immediately had my dick stirring behind the fly of my jeans.

"I'd have my own room, separate from yours, so no pressure."

"Have a bad dream and I'm not there, you can go crawl in with Driller," I murmured, kissing her softly.

"It'd lessen the financial load on y'all and on me," he murmured, cupping her breasts through the front of her dress.

"You don't have to seduce me into thinking this is a good idea, you know," she whispered, and we both laughed while I captured her mouth and Driller unzipped her dress to kiss down her back.

Loving her between us had become so damn easy, and she'd gotten better at trusting and feeling us both out. I was sure with time and clear communication, this would work for the three of us well. I was glad that she seemed open to the idea of the three of us living together, and admittedly, it took a load off my heart, knowing that she would be good if I had to be away.

She fell so naturally into our arms, fit so beautifully between us, it made my heart heavy with joy, made it ache and hurt so good with happiness, the peace it brought me a soothing, calming balm to my soul.

Even without a roof over our heads, the future was bright, held happiness and hope, and for Everleigh, it had been a long time coming.

A *long* time coming.

29

$\mathcal{E}$verleigh…

I straightened with the frame for the hive I was working on in my hands. Chrissy had spoken to Golden's girlfriend, Lys, about me and Lys had used several of her connections through her florist business to find me a beekeeping job. It was in the city, too, at the university-run conservatory in Hilltop Park. The big, old, glass building was full of growing plants from all over the world that needed pollination, and they needed an experienced beekeeper for their six hives.

Lys had managed to get me an interview, which really consisted of me proving I had the necessary skills and that I knew what I was doing, which I had, three weeks ago.

Things were far from perfect. Narcos was on suspension for his relationship with me, and could potentially be fired. Driller was also facing disciplinary action for his conduct surrounding his refusal to tell his higher-ups where we were at at any given time throughout the whole debacle.

As it turns out, his hunch was correct on that. The Knights of Crescentia had gladly given up their contact inside the Indigo City police department. It had actually turned out to be a small group of somebodies, all of them in Narcotics. One of them was Driller and Narcos' very own Captain.

They were still trying to decide what to do with Narcos, considering it was the same Captain that had put him on disciplinary suspension without pay to begin with. Narcos was working with the police officer's union to mitigate the damage, but the whole thing was one big, giant mess.

The only positive it afforded any of us was that he had the time off he needed to go house-hunting.

His lease had come up on his apartment, and we had moved everything temporarily, to his storage unit and were staying in Driller's slightly larger apartment for the time being. I found it to be stifling, though, with the apartment's lack of windows and light, though I wouldn't admit it to either one of my lovers. Still, Narcos knew, and he also knew that if it hadn't been for this job, with its green growing things and my ability to be outdoors flitting from greenhouse to greenhouse, I probably would have gone completely batshit insane by now.

The sound of a motorcycle pulling through the park caused such a confusing mix of apprehension and excitement in me that my stomach lurched, yet I maintained my focus on what I was doing, lest I injure any of the bees I'd been charged with caring for. When it was safe to do so, I straightened and looked around.

"Everything okay, Evy?" Professor Donnell, an older, thin man with round spectacles who reminded me of Captain Picard from the Star Trek series, eyed me from behind his beekeeper's mask. He wore the full suit while I just kept to my self-made beekeeper's hat. I lifted the thin veil of gauzy material back over the brim of the straw hat I'd affixed it to with my careful stitching and smiled precariously, nodding.

He didn't know anything about where I'd come from, and I preferred it that way. I felt the knot of apprehension loosen in my chest when

Driller popped up over the slight grassy hill that separated the area we kept the beehives in from the park's driveway back to the greenhouses where we did the growing, which were much different from the big greenhouse where we kept the plants on display.

"Oh, dear," Professor Donnell said, following my gaze. The sappy smile slid off my face and I waved Driller off. He stopped a ways away while the Professor explained.

"Please do be patient with us, I'd hate for you to get stung!" he called out to him.

"Thanks for the warning," Driller called back, and then hung back while the Professor and I finished up reassembling the hive from our check.

When our work was done, a matter of twenty minutes or so, I forged across the grass, my full skirt brushing along the perfectly-mowed top of it and went to Driller, giving him a hug.

"You knew I was coming, right?" he asked.

"Of course I did, I just wanted to finish what I was doing and help out as long as possible."

He smiled warmly and kissed the top of my head, giving me an extra squeeze.

"You all good, Doc?" he asked. "If so, we got a house to go look at!"

The professor pushed his glasses up on his nose, the fringe of his hair sweat-soaked and sticking up at odd angles from his scalp and I was glad I skipped the hot, heavy, beekeeping suits in favor of my cooler, lighter ensemble.

"Oh, yes, our work is finished. You two have fun!" he called.

I rolled my eyes slightly.

House hunting was proving to be difficult. We just hadn't found anything that suited us yet. It wasn't like we were being overly picky, it was just that we knew what we wanted and the right place with the right feel at the right price hadn't come along yet. It was like the things we wanted were at each point of a triangle and everything we had looked at so far only had two.

Driller walked with me to one of the greenhouses, where I kept my things, an arm around my shoulders as he asked about my day. I answered his questions, relaxed and comfortable with the close contact. I felt a little sad that while I was growing to love him a great deal, I just didn't find myself *in love* with him the way I was with Narcos. While it bothered me a great deal sometimes, it didn't seem to faze Driller in the slightest, which was something I was eternally grateful for. In fact, he was so laid back and easygoing about it, I almost wondered if he were really human and not some sort of angel, sometimes.

"You doing okay?" he asked, leaning against the inside of the doorframe as I hung my beekeeper's hat on an exposed nail.

I smiled and nodded, "Of course, why?"

"You looked, I dunno, almost sad there for a second."

I sighed, then spoke my mind, something both Narcos and Driller had been encouraging me to do more of.

"Sometimes I worry about you," I murmured. "I feel, I don't know… guilty."

He smiled and it was a good smile, before he pushed off where he rested his shoulder and came to me. He paused in front of me and caressed my face lightly with the back of his knuckles.

"You love me, don't you?" he asked.

I nodded, "I do…" I trailed off, trying to figure out how to tell him in a way that wasn't quite so brutally honest, but he winked at me, and I think he knew in his own way.

"That makes me feel pretty good, Bright Eyes."

"Yeah?" I asked, and I knew it held an edge of melancholy.

"Considering how in love you are with my best friend, the fact you've got any room for me left in that big ol' heart of yours… I'll gladly count that among my blessings," he murmured.

I smiled and bowed my head and said carefully, "Someday you're going to make some woman very happy, the way Narcos makes me happy."

He tipped my chin lightly with his fingertips and his eyes were serious when they met mine.

"I can't tell you how happy I am for the both of you, baby. What you two built in the face of all that fucking bullshit? Well it's a goddamn miracle and it couldn't happen to two better people. I'm grateful that you two make room for me in the face of it all."

I smiled, happy tears threatening, and hugged him tight. He laughed and hugged me back, saying "Right, can we drop the heavy emo shit for now and get going? Your man is waiting for us."

I laughed and nodded stepping back and said, "Sure."

"Oh," he said, and I turned from taking up my purse, my eyebrows going up. "In case you were wondering, I love you, too, girl."

I smiled and laughed lightly and he reached out; I stepped past him and he put a hand on my back, a comforting, gentlemanly gesture and let me lead us out the doorway.

The ride to wherever this new house was was freeing. The wind therapy blew away some of the cobwebs and cares. We went over the bay bridge, which was always one of my most favorite rides to embark on. Nothing but water stretching out wide, and the road rushing beneath the bike's tires, the wind washing over me, my fears and doubts left to drown in the bay.

Driller was a little more of an adventurous rider than Narcos, gunning the engine, going faster than my beloved, less concerned when I wrapped my legs around him and threw my arms wide, tipping my face into the sun. The laughter he sent flying behind him hit me full-on in my soul and I felt as bright on the inside as the summer afternoon sun shining down on my face.

The salty air whipped past us, and I put my arms back around Driller, cuddling against his back, the Indigo Knights colors rough against my cheek but in an undeniably comforting way.

When I'd first hooked up with the Steel Wraiths, Sledge had told me everything about how an MC was supposed to operate, about the principles they held dear, about brotherhood, about family, about how it was supposed to be you and your brothers standing against all comers, protecting what was yours and living life on your own terms.

It had sounded beautiful, and freeing, and I had wanted to believe that it could really be that way, but I quickly realized that the outlaw life? It was simply trading one 'man' for another. Instead of government ruling over them all, putting them in shackles, in chains, they had worn chains of their own making, shackled themselves to a life with no roots, dooming themselves to a life of constant running, constant kowtowing to men stronger than themselves.

They'd turned themselves into animals, fighting for scraps from the president's table, stabbing each other in the back, cutting each other's throats to rise in the ranks, shitting on anyone lower than themselves in the hierarchy just to make themselves feel better.

It wasn't even a bastardized version of what it was supposed to be, but all of them were so focused on themselves they couldn't see how their chosen leaders kept their boots on their necks, kept them down in the ranks while they laughed at the gladiatorial show the members put on while they feasted.

Of course, I had been just as blind in my own way. Buying into the bullshit, going from bad to worse myself.

It wasn't until Narcos and the Indigo Knights that I realized that a club could really operate the way they were initially intended to, and that when they did, it was beautiful. The members were each happy and healthy, the women bonded to them glowing with pride, healthy, loved... There was such love among the Indigo Knights and it was so beautiful it made me ache with sadness that it had taken me so long to see what could be, what should be...

We wound through a neighborhood of newer, cookie-cutter houses, down closer to the water where the houses became older craftsman cottages and bungalows. I perked up when the houses became different, older, cuter. The yards were maintained and well-tended, fenced neatly.

I spotted Narcos' bike parked against the curb in front of an adorable little cottage and the realtor, Georgia, standing beside her champagne-colored Lexus in the driveway in front of the little added garage.

Narcos gave a wave as Driller guided his bike smoothly up to the curb and I jumped off into my beloved's arms first thing, my heart swelling with love to so full I thought it would burst.

"Hey, babe. How was your day?" he whispered into my ear, his warm breath stirring my hair, tickling my neck.

I smiled and just held onto him for an extended moment before answering, "Fine."

"Yeah? That's good to hear."

"Looks good," Driller called, the bike's chugging ceasing. Georgia picked her way down the sloping drive in her heels and came towards us, smiling.

"I like that it needs work," I whispered.

"Yeah, me, too," Narcos murmured as we looked at the dilapidated paint job on the outside of the house.

"It *just* came on the market. We didn't have time to pretty it up at all, but it's exactly what you've said you're looking for," Georgia said.

"Let's have a look," Narcos declared, and tucking me between himself and Driller, we all followed Georgia up the drive and onto the little front porch.

She unlocked the door and shoved it in, and I think I immediately fell a little in love.

"Oh, my god… the floors are original wood," I breathed. They had all of the character a century or more could bring to them.

We went through the whole house, room by room, and talked about what could be rather than what was. There was a lot of work that would need to be done before we could even move in, but I wanted it. I wanted it *so* badly.

"Could you give us a minute?" Driller asked and Georgia smiled her perfectly-painted lips, patted her perfectly-coifed brunette hair and with a nod, turned and clipped sharply to the front door across the hardwood, in her heels that matched her Lexus outside.

"She already knows she's sold it," I said softly.

"Yeeeah," Narcos drew out the word, and Driller finished his thought.

"She just doesn't know for how much, yet."

I snorted and fought not to laugh.

"It's so beautiful, you guys, and I grew up in a house like this, although in much worse shape."

"Yeah? I didn't know that," Driller said.

"Mm, mine had a spiral metal staircase and the attic was converted into a whole other room," I said.

"That's an idea," Narcos said.

"You thinking what I'm thinking?" Driller asked.

"Our office up there, keep work out of sight out of mind?"

"It would let us keep the third bedroom down here as a guest room," I said.

They looked at each other and nodded.

"Did you see the shed out back?" Narcos asked, and we drifted to the back door. The deck would need to be replaced, but I wasn't really a fan of decks. I preferred paved patios that were more one with the garden, but sure enough, there was a newer shed out there on the edge of the back yard.

"Could make it into one of those she-shed things for you, Bright Eyes. Only fair if we take over the attic," Driller said.

"I could keep my own hive back here," I said softly. "There's room and there are gardens all through the neighborhood."

"I think we're all agreed," Narcos said, beaming and I bit my bottom lip and grinned.

"Think we can get it all done by the time my lease is up?" Driller asked.

Narcos and I both nodded and laughed.

"With the rest of the club as backup, hell, yeah," Narcos said.

"Fuck, man, we're totally buying a house," Driller said, and rubbed a hand over his hair.

"Well, we are," Narcos said and Driller gave him a flat look. I left them to argue while I looked around on my own, drifting out the door and into the fenced back yard that was desperately in need of a new fence, but that would come along with everything else.

"I could put down roots here," I said and turned back to the guys, and Narcos smiled at me, love and pride radiating off of him like heat shimmering off the sidewalk out front.

"Baby, you already have."

He was right. I could already feel a growing attachment to the place, and I looked up into the summer's blue sky and sighed.

"We all agreed, then?" Driller asked.

"Let's do it," Narcos said, and I don't think I could smile any bigger.

"Let's hope our offer is the one that's accepted," I said and we went back into the house hand in hand, and out to deal with Georgia.

30

*N*arcos…

It was raining outside. The disciplinary hearing room had windows, sitting on the ninth floor of city hall. I stood in front of the panel with my union rep at my side and waited to hear them out, see what I would be facing. I was nervous, but not too bad. I think Everleigh was dealing with enough anxiety for the both of us. She was sitting behind us in the gallery with Driller, wringing her hands, her bottom lip worried between her teeth.

"It is our decision that you be moved out of Narcotics to the Robbery division," the spokesman said. "A disciplinary letter regarding this matter will be placed in your permanent jacket. Your suspension has already been served."

I was okay with that, all of it, but my union rep went to work, did his job and got at least half of my pay from that suspension returned. All in all, it wasn't much of a punishment. I expected the letter in my jacket, and I'd *wanted* to go to Robbery, so I was chalking this up as a win.

Out in the hall, Everleigh burrowed into the front of my body and hid her face. I knew her tears were tears of relief, but when one of the panel members came out into the hall and saw us, sympathy crushed his expression and I couldn't resist playing it for what it was worth.

"It's not your fault, babe," I murmured, and hugged her tight.

"Young lady, I assure you, as bad as it sounds, Detective Rutledge was let off comparatively light, considering what could have happened."

Everleigh nodded against my dress blues and I said, "He's right, and thank you, sir."

"My pleasure. Try not to think about it," he said and trailed up the hall away from us.

Driller grinned and shook his head saying under his breath, "He bought that hook, line, and sinker."

"Yeah, well, hopefully he'll remember it when it's your turn," I muttered.

"True that," Driller commented. He was in deeper shit, technically being my superior officer and being willfully insubordinate. We'd see sometime next week, or the week after, what was going to happen to him. His union rep was still duking it out for him.

"Let's go home," Everleigh moaned and pulled back to wipe at her face. Driller shook out a handkerchief from his pocket and handed it to her.

"Which one?" he asked.

"*Home*," Everleigh repeated with emphasis.

"Gotta change first," Driller said.

"Yep, let's go."

We went back to Driller's apartment first and changed into comfortable clothes we didn't care about. We'd been making mad progress on the house with the club's help, and if we were lucky, it would be ready to move into by midsummer.

The bedrooms were finished except for paint, and the bathrooms were under construction, along with the kitchen, but right now, our focus was dry walling the attic and laying a floor up there.

"You ready?" she asked quietly and I could tell she had a renewed vigor where getting the house worked on was concerned.

I captured her gaze with mine and smiled teasing her gently when I asked, "What's your hurry?"

Her expression, to my surprise, sobered and she went very still. She cocked her head and said, "I feel like we just cleared yet another hurdle and the finish line feels like its *right there*, you know?"

Driller paused behind her and straightened up, pulling on his jeans the rest of the way. He cocked his head and said, "Talk to us, Bright Eyes…"

"I guess I'm excited," she said. "I just never realized how much excitement and anxiety had in common."

I chuckled and went to her, drawing her into my arms and said, "Are you telling me you just can't wait to start our lives together?" I asked.

She nodded and said emphatically, "*Yes.*"

Driller laughed outright and said, "Baby, the house being done or not, you're here. Your life together has already started."

She stopped and it was like she was having some difficulty processing that. She said reluctantly, "I know…" but I could tell she wasn't quite convinced. Like the front of her brain, logically, knew that it was true, but the back of her brain, her emotions, hadn't quite caught up to the notion.

"We'll get there," I promised, and she smiled up at me.

"I know, I just guess that being there, working on it with you guys, it's my favorite place to be, you know?"

I nodded slowly and said, "Yeah, it's *ours*, not *his*, or *mine*, or *yours*."

"Exactly."

Driller nodded slowly and came up behind her and pressed a kiss to the back of her neck. She closed her eyes and trembled and he murmured low in her ear, "I can't wait until we can do this in your house… for real, you know?"

"*Our* house," she whispered, and turned in my arms to face my best friend. She kissed him gently and I went rock hard.

He drew back and searched her face and said, "You start us down that road, we won't make it to the house today."

"Fair enough," she declared, but she had a hard time keeping her hands to herself despite it and I could tell, she was in the mood and wanted us both. I couldn't wait until we could get moved in either, and every day we spent there working on it, got me closer to my goal, too. The one where I made Everleigh my wife.

With the rain, we piled into the truck I'd bought off a local guy for the purpose of making the renovations on our place easier. That, and when those renovations were done, Everleigh was going to need a vehicle to commute with, one capable of hauling materials for her beehives and whatever else she got into.

It wasn't a very big truck, and she was snug between us for the trip across the bridge, not that she ever complained about that. She left her hand on top of my thigh as I drove and curled her other in Driller's.

We arrived safely, the house just as we left it, and went inside. The majority of it was plastic and drywall dust, drop cloths and emptiness. Right now, it was just a house, but hopefully, soon it would be a home.

The bedrooms were done and carpeted in case we needed to move in before everything was totally completed. One of the bathrooms was close to finished, the sink and the toilet functional.

The kitchen had a sink, and the floors and tile backsplash and the walls were done, but it was still waiting for appliances, counters, and cabinetry.

We still had decisions to make before we put in the spiral staircase to get up to the attic. Namely, whether we were going to open up the floor and make it run from basement to attic. We were definitely putting the washer and dryer down in the basement, maybe an extra freezer and pantry space, too. Like I said, decisions. The biggest job for now was finishing the drywall and the flooring up in the attic, and for now, a simple A-frame ladder took care of getting up into and out of the space.

I went up first, and Driller stabilized the ladder for Everleigh. I reached down and helped her through the hatch, even though I didn't really need to. She had it on her own, it was just nice to have any excuse to put my hands on her. Driller grinned and raised his eyebrows behind her back and I gave him a knowing smirk.

We got to work; the sheetrock was pretty much up, and the joints between the sheets mudded or whatever. We were in the land of never-ending sanding. The plywood sheets laid down for temporary flooring were covered in fine dust.

We put on our masks and eye protection and each grabbed our sandpaper tools and got to work. We were almost finished with this part, and while Driller and I sanded, Everleigh ran the shop-vac to mitigate the dust falling.

We had the windows open up here to help, too, while we worked and I was hoping we'd finish up the sanding today and be ready to prime next time. It was just another hurdle, albeit much smaller, for us to clear in building our new home.

I threw chin at Driller when the vacuum quit, and he pulled off his mask and said, "Hey, Bright Eyes."

When Everleigh turned to him, I dropped to one knee behind her, slipping my fingers into my jeans pocket and plucking out the classy engagement ring Driller had helped me scour antique shops for, over the last couple of weeks.

When he was sure I was set, my best friend asked her, "Can you hand me that pack of sandpaper?" He pointed behind her and she turned, freezing, her hand falling on her breast as if to put her heart back in her chest when she saw me.

Her cat-green eyes widened and her face went slack with surprise as I held up the ring and said, "Everleigh Tate, would you please do me the honor of becoming Everleigh Rutledge, and make this house a home with me?"

The question hung between us, her voice frozen in her throat, tears springing to her eyes and making them luminous, even as they spilled in muddy tracks down her cheeks.

"Are you serious?" she asked, in barely a whisper, her voice filled to the brim with disbelief, which broke my heart just a little. I mean, how could she *not* know how much I wanted her?

"I've never been more serious in my life, babe. I want it to be you and me forever. I love you, and I want to show it to the whole damn world."

She pressed her hands to her chest and crumbled. Dropping to her knees and throwing her arms around my neck, she said *"Yes!"* with such a desperate wanting I felt like my own heart was about to explode.

"Fuck, yes!" Driller cried and cheered as I held my woman tight in my arms, her lips finding mine, the kiss between us sealing our fate, our stars crossing in the sky, and they could have become their own constellation.

"I love you, babe," I whispered, smoothing a hand through her dust coated hair.

"I love you forever," she whispered back, and I held her tight and looked up at my best friend, whose own eyes were glassy and starting to brim.

"This counts as one of the best moments of my life, and I ain't even in this," he declared and I felt such a wholeness, such a completeness in that moment, you just don't even know.

EPILOGUE

*E*verleigh...

We'd made it through the winter, the house was finished and ready to move in, and today? Well, today was the day for at least Narcos' and my things to arrive.

I waited at the house eagerly for them to arrive with the rest of the club. They'd taken my little truck, which I was still scared and hesitant to drive anywhere but between here and work, leaving their bikes parked in the garage. Youngblood was supposed to meet them at the storage place with *his* truck, and the rest of the club and their women were dividing and conquering.

I was expecting them here any minute. By myself. For the first time. Without one of either of the guys. I was nervous and overwhelmed already, and they hadn't even gotten here yet! I bounced lightly on the balls of my feet when I spotted a car coming down the lane. It was a dark SUV, Chrissy behind the wheel, Lillian, Backdraft's girl, in the passenger seat, Pasquale and Aly shoving each other in the back seat to look out the windshield, waving at me exuberantly from between Chrissy and Lil.

I smiled, despite my fizzing nerves, but I had nothing to worry about. Still, the flurry of activity, conversation, and unpacking that ensued as soon as the guys arrived with the trucks was almost more than I could take! I hadn't realized just how introverted I was, even among people that cared, that treated each other and myself very well, and when the crowd thinned and people began to go home, I was relieved.

Narcos and Driller remained, the ruins of pizza boxes and beer cans littering our kitchen. It was stocked with the things from Narcos' kitchen, which was a damn site more than what Driller had in his. He hadn't been lying when he'd said he was a terrible cook. One of the first nights he'd fixed something at his apartment for us, it'd been some ungodly concoction of boxed mac-and-cheese along with canned chili. I'd asked what it was and he'd answered me, "I don't know, but it's hot, it's brown, and there's a lot of it."

Narcos and I made sure to cook as often as possible after that, which I fear was somewhat enabling, and I had to admit, when Driller 'cooked', he rarely did – rather he spared us by ordering out, like now.

"You doin' okay, babe?" Narcos asked me, and I smiled, spinning my engagement ring gently on my ring finger with my thumb, a nervous habit or tic that I'd developed.

"A little overwhelmed," I admitted.

"Then that's my cue I should probably go," Driller said, wiping his mouth with a stray napkin and tossing it down.

"I think we'll head out with you," Golden declared.

Lys smiled warmly, and before I could open my mouth to protest, she said, "We still have to pick up Manolo from his grandmother's, so please, don't feel like you're chasing us out. You're not. I'll check for those bulbs when I get home and make sure to get them to you if I still have them. I swear I do, though."

I genuinely smiled. Out of all of the Old Ladies of the Indigo Knights, I do believe I liked Lys the most. She was low-key, like me, and we had so much in common when it came to our love of green and growing things.

I went around and hugged her, and Golden, too. They let themselves out, and Driller swung on his jacket and cut.

"You aren't staying?" I asked, and he smiled and came to me, kissing me gently before shaking his head.

"There'll be plenty of nights, Bright Eyes. There's only one first. It should be reserved for you two."

"I both love you and hurt for you that you think that way," I whispered and he grinned and winked.

"No bad days," he said and tweaked my nose. "Seriously. There's this blonde chick I've been meaning to bang, and I'm going to check and see if she's hanging at the 10-13."

I rolled my eyes. I never let on that it bothered me when he talked of other conquests. I knew they didn't mean anything, but out of sight out of mind, you know? Besides, it wasn't his issue, it was mine and I needed to deal with it myself, decide why it was I felt the way I did about it. Then, if it was something to talk about, then I would talk, but not until I understood why, myself.

"Okay," I said, and Narcos came around the kitchen island and clasped hands with Driller, pulling him in for a tight hug.

"See you tomorrow, man."

"Yeah, yeah! You two christen the new place. Do me proud, 'k?"

"You got it," Narcos said, laughing.

I smiled and hugged Driller one last time and murmured, "Please, ride safe."

"Anything for you, baby."

He went out and suddenly, it was just me and Narcos. I felt my shoulders drop and my mask slip and he was suddenly there, holding me tight.

"You look so tired, babe," he said with a sigh.

"I am, but it's the good kind of tired."

"Yeah?"

"Very much so."

"Too tired to..."

I looked up at him with a slight smile and said softly, "Take me to bed and find out."

His answering grin made my heart swell and his mouth slowly descended to mine. I wrapped my arms around him and he bent, just enough, his hands sliding down my body. I gave a little leap and wrapped my legs around him, his hands going to the outsides of my thighs, hitching me up higher, his cock swelling beneath his jeans and pressing against me.

He marched us through the house, to the bedroom we'd set up his queen-sized bed in and he set me on the edge. I immediately worked his belt tongue loose with trembling fingers, my desire making me jittery, my mouth watering at the mere thought of having him in it.

I freed him from his clothing and stroked him twice with my hand before taking him into my mouth and almost all the way to the back of my throat in one stroke. He let out an explosion of breath, his head going back, his hands going to his hips as he fought to hold still and I smiled around his dick in my mouth.

I loved bringing reactions like that out of him, I loved when he stood and shook and shuddered, fighting himself to hold still while I worked him across my tongue.

I made love to him with my mouth while he pulled his shirt off over his head and toed off his boots. I helped with his pants, getting them down far enough for him to take over by stepping on them. It was a strange sort of feeling, this strong and beautiful man, allowing himself to be stripped and vulnerable while I was still clothed.

He watched me work him, his breaths coming in the deep and even cadence of a man being satisfied completely, an erotic sensuality to the sound. He gathered my hair, while I worked my skirt up my legs, spreading my knees apart so he could step between them, step closer, so I could take him deeper into my mouth.

He lifted my blouse and I pulled him free from my mouth, sucking him off, just long enough for him to pull the blouse over my head and discard it.

I grew wet, my inner thighs growing slick with my need. I'd skipped panties today, and I was glad I did. It was one less obstacle to getting my needs met as our passion slowly heated, creeping towards critical mass. His fingers worked the hooks at the back of my bra, the tips skimming up my back, along my shoulders, sweeping my bra straps down my arms, the garment ending up in my lap before tumbling to the floor at my bare feet.

"Fuck, babe, you suck me so good," he whispered, and I felt myself smile in pleasure. I liked that I pleased him. The fact that I pleased him so well left me all aglow with accomplishment, a tingling sensation starting in my breast, flitting out along my nerves, concentrating at my nipples and deep within my sex.

He swept his fingertips in a ghost-like touch over my skin, over my back, along my arms, to my hands at his hips, back again, tracing my collarbones before he buried them lavishly in my hair, holding it back so he could watch me. I rolled my eyes up to meet his and he closed them, nearly undone.

He pulled on my hair gently, and I drew back off of him as he whispered, "My turn."

He stood me up and pushed my gypsy skirt off of my hips. He told me to get on the bed, to lie on my stomach, and I did, trusting him, knowing that whatever he had planned he was bound to make it feel good. He always did.

He kissed my shoulder, my back, over and over, each placement of his lips different from the rest, along my spine, one ass cheek, the other, the crease where my ass met the back of my thigh, lower; behind my knee… each touch of his lips warm, like silk, my body heat rising, my desire with it until I squirmed beneath him and practically begged for him to enter me, be inside me, join with me, and be one with me.

He put his hands to my lower ass, pried me apart and stabbed his tongue into my pussy, teasing my opening with light little flicks of his tongue until my moans trembled and took on a whining quality. I writhed underneath him, but he lay on my lower body, pinning me. My palms pressed flat to the coverlet, sliding along the crisp material as I fought to hold still and lost.

"Please," I begged, "Please!" and he chuckled darkly, not done playing. He slid fingers into me, teasing and groping around inside my pussy, looking for that spot he knew drove me crazy. He found it and I cried out, my hips jerking, and when he was sure he had it, that the golden pulse and glow of orgasm was well on its way to building, he replaced his fingers with his cock and move inside of me, nice and slow.

I tried to writhe, but he held me down, a prisoner at the mercy of his beautiful torture as he worked me, bringing me into a sweet sort of agony, my pussy tensing, throbbing in time with my heartbeat, as I was *so close* but missing that final piece that would give me the release I needed.

He kept me there for what felt like hours but could have been minutes. Of course, it could have been hours, too. I lost all sense of time, all sense of space as my world narrowed down to the feel of my man at my back, pressing me into his bed, the feel of his fingers between mine, clutching my hands to the bedspread, his palms pressed into the backs of my hands.

"Come on, babe. You can do it," he whispered, his breath hot in my ear, tickling my neck. "Come for me, babe, you can do it."

I let out a thin, whining wail, as I was so maddeningly close and he thrust harder, deeper, stronger and a little bit faster. It was just enough, my clit exposed as he drew back, thrust against the bedding, and when he thrust forward? A delicious, beautiful friction, and my world exploded. The stars in the sky found their way behind my eyelids as if I hurtled through space and time.

He held me tight as my pussy pulsed around him and he cried out above me. I thrust my ass up to meet his wild thrust and he bottomed out, touching places so deep inside me I didn't think they could be reached, sending me spiraling into another exquisite cacophony of cries.

I came back to the present, to myself, with the weight of my man on top of me, his lips playing across my back, across my shoulders, as he lazily kissed along my skin, both of us so drunk on our love we couldn't move much more than what we already were.

I gasped for breath, his own sending a warm wash of tingles across my back.

It was the first time for the both of us in our new house, but it would be far from our last. In each other, we'd taken root, we'd found home, and we were totally complete.

ALSO BY A.J. DOWNEY

The Sacred Hearts MC

1. Shattered & Scarred

2. Broken & Burned

3. Cracked & Crushed

3.5 Masked & Miserable (a novella)

4. Tattered & Torn

5. Fractured & Formidable

6. Damaged & Dangerous

The Virtues

1. Cutter's Hope

2. Marlin's Faith

3. Charity for Nothing

The Sacred Brotherhood

1. Brother to Brother

2. Her Brother's Keeper

3. Brother In Arms

4. Between Brothers

5. A Brother's Secret

6. A Brother At My Back

7. A Brother's Salvation

ABOUT THE AUTHOR

A.J. Downey is the internationally bestselling author of The Sacred Hearts Motorcycle Club romance series. She is a born and raised Seattle, WA Native. She finds inspiration from her surroundings, through the people she meets, and likely as a byproduct of way too much caffeine.

She has lived many places and done many things, though mostly through her own imagination…An avid reader all of her life, it's now her turn to try and give back a little, entertaining as she has been entertained.

Stalker Information:
www.ajdowney.com

www.ingramcontent.com/pod-product-compliance
Lightning Source LLC
Chambersburg PA
CBHW070608170726
48291CB00003B/745